THE
FAMILY
HOME

BOOKS BY MIRANDA SMITH

THE
FAMILY
HOME

MIRANDA SMITH

bookouture

Published by Bookouture in 2022

An imprint of Storyfire Ltd.
Carmelite House
50 Victoria Embankment
London EC4Y 0DZ

www.bookouture.com

ISBN: 978-1-80314-470-2
eBook ISBN: 978-1-80314-469-6

For Harrison

PROLOGUE

Sunday, 2:15 a.m.

When I wake up, I'm on the sofa.

My throat is dry.

My head hurts.

My back aches.

Sleep. My body and mind crave it.

The world beyond the windows is still dark, yellow squares from neighboring buildings the only light source. There are a few more hours until sunrise. I'll rest better in my own bed.

The television is on, midway through some movie I've watched a dozen times. My body shakes when I try to sit up. I'm exhausted from a busy weekend. First date with Dylan. Mabel's birthday party. Dinner with Rebecca. Memories from each event run into the next.

Maybe I just had too much to drink.

I follow the shadows of blue and gray, stumbling through the open bedroom door. *My* bedroom door. Matthew's room is locked, on the other side of the apartment.

I stop at the foot of the bed, teetering as I take off my boots and socks. The air prickles my exposed skin. I'm climbing onto the mattress when something misplaced catches my eye.

The bed isn't made as I left it. The pillows and bedding are bunched together. No, not pillows. Something else. I reach out my hand.

There's someone beneath the covers.

Matthew? My mind goes to him, the last man who shared my bed. But it can't be him.

Did Rebecca follow me inside? Fall asleep in the bedroom while I took the couch? How drunk *were* we?

No, I remember watching the car she was in drive away, remember entering the apartment alone. Fear grabs hold when I realize the person beside me could be an intruder. I leap from the foot of the bed to the wall. I flick the light switch.

Yellow light floods the room, stinging my eyes, bringing what's on the bed into focus. A person, but he or she isn't sleeping.

There's too much blood for that. It is soaking the sheets, sprayed across the headboard and walls. Splattered, like something Mabel might paint. No, no. I can't think of my daughter right now, in this moment, as I stare at a dead body on my bed. A stranger?

Please God, let it be a stranger.

I back out of the room, raising my hands to shield my face. I stop when I notice the smudges of red on my palms, in between my fingers. Streaks of blood stain my clothes. Did it get there when I climbed onto the bed? Or was it there before...

I rush into the living room, kneel beside the sofa where I'd left my phone.

But when I find it, I don't call the police.

I call Matthew.

ONE

LILLIAN

Before: Friday Night

My key enters the lock, and I step inside the apartment.

Every time I come in, the place takes my breath away. The open foyer that bleeds into a large living room, the long glass windows encased in exposed brick. Above, black ducts and pipes, a modern industrial look so different from the home we built back in Seaside Cliffs. Below, dark wooden floors, still lustrous from lack of touch. No one lived here before me.

And him.

I close my eyes, can still imagine Matthew beside me when we found the place.

"I think this could be it," he said. "We'll take it."

When the beauty wears off, reality sets in. I'm reminded why I'm here, and my stomach turns. I'm stepping into another life, one I was never meant to have.

"Wow," Dylan says, standing behind me in the doorway. "Nice place."

"Come on in." I feel like I have to say the words, offer a

formal invitation. Dylan is the first man I've invited into the apartment since the divorce.

"I've walked by this building a dozen times, but never been inside." He's still taking in the view, his gaze landing on one of the pipes. "How long have you lived here?"

"Almost a year."

"It's really beautiful."

"Thank you." I move over to the stainless-steel refrigerator, my nerves easing as a cold blast of air hits my skin. "Wine?"

"Sure."

Dylan and I met online, where I've met every potential suitor since the divorce. My other dates have led to nothing, but something about tonight feels different. Somewhere between ordering appetizers and sharing dessert, I felt something. A spark. One I haven't felt since, well, Matthew.

I never imagined that I'd be looking for love a second time around. When Matthew and I were engaged, popular breakup songs would come on the radio, and although I sang along, I also remember thinking, naively, that I'd never again listen to such ballads and relate to the singer's plight.

I've found my happy ending, I thought.

I was terribly, terribly wrong.

I inhale, tossing back a sip of wine. I have to stop thinking about the past. About what could have been. That's why I made the bold decision to invite Dylan inside for a nightcap, even if it is against the rules Matthew and I have set. And, yes, one drink is my honest intention. Of course, if the spark continues, swells into something more heated, that wouldn't be so bad. Maybe *that* is what I really need.

"So, I can't ask you about work. That would be breaking the rules?"

"That's right."

My rules for tonight's date came from my best friend, Cat. She's been single longer than me, but she actually enjoys it. Her marriage with Ted fizzled out ages before the divorce papers were signed. She's now an expert at post-divorce dating and has been pressuring me to move on with my life.

She told me the best way to get to know someone you meet online is to stay away from any topic that might lead back to trauma, i.e. why you're single, your childhood, your job. Cat may not be the best at commitment, but she knows how to have fun. And isn't that what dating after divorce is supposed to be about?

I suggested the idea to Dylan before we ordered drinks, as a way to break the ice, and he agreed to play along. His acquiescence made me like him instantly. And now I'm sitting beside this person I know very little about, yet who already feels familiar.

I know he has a daughter—six-year-old Danielle, the same age as Mabel—and I know he's allergic to cats. He's also divorced, but I didn't ask why. I know that he's from Kentucky, but have no idea what brought him to Anne Isle. He hasn't mentioned his job, but I know the scar on his chin is from a boating accident when he was twelve, and he's been nervous around the water ever since.

"Favorite vacation?" he asks, continuing the game. He sits beside me on the sofa, stretching his arm so that his hand rests on my shoulder.

"Good one," I say, handing over his wine. The first place that comes to mind is Mexico, where Matthew and I went on our honeymoon. I bypass that answer, instead choosing a vacation I took once in college. "Canada."

"Nice. I'd have to go with Costa Rica."

He continues talking, sharing details about his trip. As he speaks, I take in the full view of him. His dark hair, freshly cut near the scalp. His broad shoulders, relaxing beneath a powder-blue dress shirt. The delicate way he brings the wineglass to his lips, the dark stubble along his jaw. Dylan is very handsome, and I find myself opening up to the possibility this could turn into something more than a fling.

He rests his glass on the coffee table and stands. "Mind if I use your bathroom?"

Before I'm able to answer, he's walking toward the nearest bathroom, directly in front of us. I'd prefer he use my bathroom, which is connected to my bedroom, but he has already shut the door.

I give my body a little shake, thankful for a few seconds to compose myself. When I'm in the midst of easy conversation with Dylan, I forget how inexperienced I am. How ill-prepared. I take out my cell phone, using the camera to check that my hair is in place and my makeup hasn't smudged. My cheeks seem abnormally red, and I'm not sure if it's because of my blush, the wine, or my nerves.

Dylan returns to the living room, but his demeanor has changed. He no longer leans toward me on the sofa, but sits rigidly. He takes a sip of wine without saying anything.

"Everything okay?"

"Mmhm."

What have I done? What have I not done? The man who walked into that bathroom seemed into me, and the one who exited will barely look in my direction.

"Would you like more wine?"

"Actually it's getting late. I think I might head out."

"Is something wrong? I thought we were having a good time."

"We were." He pauses, reluctant to share what's on his mind. "You told me you've been divorced for over a year."

"I have."

"I couldn't help noticing there's a pile of men's clothing on the bathroom floor. And toiletries on the sink."

Dammit, Matthew. Even after the divorce, his clutter still finds a way of annoying me.

"Dylan, it's not—"

"Look, we barely know each other. You don't owe me any excuses, but I don't want to get involved in anything complicated."

"What I'm *owed* is a chance to explain," I insist. Being so abrasive on a first date isn't ideal, but his words are heavy with accusation. "Those clothes belong to my ex-husband, Matthew. You used *his* bathroom. If you'd given me the opportunity, I would have directed you to mine."

"What?"

"Matthew and I live here together. Well, not together. We share the same apartment. One of us stays here while the other one is back at our house with our daughter, Mabel."

Sweet, darling Mabel. She is the reason Matthew and I will do whatever it takes, no matter how unconventional, to keep the family we promised her together.

"You live with your ex. But you're not in a relationship?"

Here it is. The conversation I always dread having. Divorce and a young child are enough baggage without having my ex sleeping across the hall. It would take a special person to accept our situation without feeling jealous.

"Our split was amicable. When we decided to divorce, we thought it would be easier on Mabel to remain in the family home. What's the sense in her staying at my place one weekend, his place the next? We're still a family. Mabel has one home, one bed, one house, and two parents who love her very much."

"And that works for you?"

"It has for the past year. It sounds messy, but there's nothing romantic between the two of us anymore. Matthew has a serious girlfriend. I'm even friends with her."

He still seems hesitant. "This isn't some kind of weird group sex thing, is it?"

"Definitely not." I laugh nervously. "We have separate

bedrooms. And bathrooms. It's just like having a roommate, but we're never here at the same time."

"Well, it's an unusual arrangement, but it sounds too detailed to be a lie."

"I'm not a liar."

"I'm sensing that about you."

He moves closer. The chill he brought with him into the room has dissipated. I've told him our situation—which wasn't the plan until at least date three—and the world didn't combust. Maybe there's hope after all.

He moves closer, and I think he might kiss me. My heart starts pounding, my body hyper-aware of his touch, then I feel a strong vibration against my leg. I realize it's his phone, ringing. He looks down.

"This is the sitter," he says, pulling away.

"Go ahead."

He walks toward the windows, keeping his voice low. I take the last sip of wine, looking back toward the front door, a useless attempt to give him privacy. Our night was back on track, but I understand the never-ending responsibility that comes with being a parent all too well.

"Bad news," Dylan says as he walks past the sofa. "Danielle has a stomach bug. The sitter says she's been up and down all evening."

"Oh no."

"I need to go home."

"Of course."

I stand, following him to the door. For a brief moment, I fear this is a ruse. Maybe our night wasn't as fun as I thought it was. Maybe he's acted out this whole scenario as a way to get out of my apartment. Then again, I felt the phone ringing... right as he was leaning in to kiss me.

He stands in the doorway, before entering the hall. "I had a really nice time tonight, Lillian."

"I did, too."

"It would be nice to see you again. Maybe get to know a little more about you?"

"I'd like that." My cheeks feel warm again. "Go be a dad, and we'll talk soon."

I stand in the doorway, watching him leave. As he descends the steps, my neighbor from across the way, Mrs. Haynes, exits her apartment. Hoppy, her sandy-haired Pomeranian, is on a leash at her side.

Mrs. Haynes makes a point to stare at Dylan's back before addressing me. "Never know who I'm going to find coming out of your place."

She's the local all-seeing spinster; every neighborhood and apartment complex has one. She knows about my arrangement with Matthew, and I suspect she doesn't think much of it.

I force a smile. "Good evening, Mrs. Haynes."

I close the door, disappointed Dylan had to leave so abruptly, but still smitten with tonight as a whole. Not even Mrs. Haynes' judgmental stares can dampen my glee. After several stumbles since the divorce, I'm finally finding my footing again.

It would be nice to have a second chance at a happy ending, even if I don't deserve it.

TWO

LILLIAN

Before: Saturday Morning

Waking up inside the apartment never feels right. I think it's the quiet. It bothers me.

I remember when Mabel was a baby, those never-ending days when Matthew would be at work, and I'd be home alone with her, my ears ringing with her frequent cries and the continuous loop of children's programming. I rarely had a moment to myself. My body longing for a shower, a chance to wipe off the sweat and grime acquired after a day of parenting. I'd fantasize about eating a meal. Not scarfing it down, but actually eating it, chewing and appreciating each morsel.

I longed for quiet.

Now, my time with Mabel is never enough. As soon as I feel comfortable again, like some semblance of the family we once were remains, my time is up, and I'm back here, in this cold, silent apartment.

Today is different, though. Special. Mabel is turning six, something that brings me joy and queasiness all at once. How is it that my vibrant, beautiful baby is turning into a child?

Matthew and I struggled to get pregnant, had many months where we wondered if parenthood would ever happen. Her pure existence eclipses all the suffering of the past couple of years.

I hurriedly put on makeup and pull back my hair, eager to leave the quiet of the apartment and be near her again. When I finish getting dressed, I stare at my reflection, analyzing the fine lines that appear along my temples when I smile. I've reached the age where I'm not sure if I'm young or old. I know this much: heartache ages you. Some days, I feel far older than my thirty-eight years. Other days, I look in the mirror, expecting to find the carefree twenty-something of my youth, raven-haired and bright-eyed, moving to seaside Anne Isle to attend college.

At school, I quickly became friends with Cat, the one relationship that has stuck. I recall her infatuation with her new boyfriend, Ted, can remember her pestering me to go on a date with his roommate. Matthew. The four of us were inseparable during those years, and our paths never seemed to stray far from each other.

Matthew and Ted went into business together, and after several false starts and failures, they created Voyage, a digital chartplotter app that's now used by boaters across the globe. For lakes and oceans alike, users can perform navigational tasks in a matter of seconds from the convenience of their cell phones. Ted and Matthew started developing the app after we graduated, worked hard to perfect the technology.

It took several years before they started recruiting investors, and eventually Voyage was bought by a company specializing in electronic navigational charts, and for more money than we could have ever dreamed. Ted and Matthew are still primary shareholders, working together at company headquarters in downtown Anne Isle.

We had love and youth and success. After some false starts and failures of our own, Matthew and I had Mabel. We were all so lucky once, our lives a sort of fairy tale, except the endings fell apart. After the briefest of honeymoon periods, Ted and Cat's marriage imploded, mostly because of his wandering eye and staunch work ethic, but also because of her endless nagging and overspending. Their divorce was brutal, causing a rift so large I'm surprised Anne Isle didn't declare a day of celebration when their marriage finally ended.

Not long after, my own marriage ended, but not for the reasons you might expect.

As I drive to our house, I barely register each turn. It's all muscle memory at this point, as I cruise past the downtown storefronts and pause at the school zones leading to the Seaside Cliffs subdivision. Beyond the wrought-iron gates are manicured lawns in between rows of large houses, all new and oddly similar. Pale-gray plaster and dark-shingled roofs, some burnt orange and others harsh black.

I catch sight of our house, at the very end of the cul-de-sac, and my heart leaps, as it did the first day we moved in. It's two stories, with a large front porch, perfect for sitting and watching the sun set behind the cliffs in the evenings. The second floor has a balcony, attached to the room that was once our master bedroom. It's still my room, on the nights I stay here. Matthew has created his own sleeping space in our massive basement.

I remind myself of everything we still have. This house. Our family. It might look a little different than we intended, but it still exists.

I place my duffel bag on the bench beside our front door and ring the bell. I have keys, of course. I still live here, part of the time, and I could enter the house whenever I wanted, but I try to be respectful when Matthew is here. Boundaries is what makes our arrangement work, and if someone is going to start pushing them, it won't be me.

Matthew opens the door. He's wearing checkered pajama

bottoms, his light-brown hair is disheveled, and there's a dishrag over his shoulder.

"You have a key. Why don't you just come in?" He bends down and grabs my bag for me, pulling it inside. "Thank God you're here. Mom has been asking about decorations since I picked her up at the airport, and I don't even know where to start."

For a brief, happy moment, I'd forgotten about Jane. She lives in Florida, so I don't have to endure her often, only when she decides to fly in for special events, like this.

"I told you to wait on me."

He looks at the watch on his wrist. It's a gift I gave him on our second anniversary. He sighs in relief. "I didn't realize how early it was."

"We have plenty of time. Stop stressing."

Mabel comes into the kitchen, almost knocking me over with a hug. "Mommy!" I hold her tight, marveling at her honey skin and silky brown hair. When she looks up at me, it's my own eyes staring back.

"Are you excited about your party?"

"Dad made me clean all last night," she says, looking up at me for sympathy.

"As he should."

"Happy birthday, by the way," Matthew says.

"Thank you," Mabel and I answer in unison. She looks at me, and we share a giggle.

Mabel came two weeks before her due date, in the wee hours of my thirty-second birthday. It makes the bond between us more unique, I think. I'm happy to forfeit my own celebration to make the day all about her.

"I'm about finished in here," he says. "Mom is outside, if you want to get started decorating."

"Feel free to join us when you can," I say, turning for the door.

"Oh, and Rebecca offered to grab the cake from the bakery," he says. His tone falls slightly. "Unless you'd rather do it."

"That would be great," I say. "We need all hands on deck."

I first met Rebecca when she was Mabel's preschool teacher. Now, she's Matthew's girlfriend. They've been dating for six months. She's a few years younger than us, but not so much that it's a cliché. I'm happy Matthew has moved on since the divorce. I only wish I could do the same.

"Are you sure?" Matthew asks. Again, boundaries. We're both reluctant to push them.

"It's fine. Really. Saves me the hassle."

We're a modern family now, I think. This is us. Our new normal. Funnily enough, those phrases are all popular television shows from the past decade. Fractured families finding their way back together has become entertainment, or perhaps it's just relatable. We're not the first family to navigate a divorce, trying to keep our hearts and tempers intact. We've chosen a new life to replace the one we wrecked.

I walk out to the backyard. When we built this house, we did so with entertaining in mind. I tried to imagine all the birthday parties and holidays we'd have over the years, the celebrations for Matthew's company. Now, the only joint events we host are for Mabel, but that doesn't make the backyard any less majestic.

There's a wide covered patio stretching along the back of the house, cedar beams holding the awning in place. The center of the yard has a rectangular pool, gray sea glass bordering its outer perimeter. Beyond that, a privacy fence separates us from untamed woods. Most people would probably prefer taking in a beautiful view from their back porch in the evenings, but I didn't like the idea of Mabel being exposed. When we decided to build, I was adamant about the front of the house facing the cliffs, the backyard being enclosed. I wanted those protective barriers in place.

"Where should we start?" calls a familiar voice.

At the corner of the yard stands Jane, my former mother-in-law. She's spraying a water hose on the shrubs lining the fence.

"You don't have to do that," I say. "A landscaping company comes once a week."

"If this were my garden, I wouldn't waste the money," she says. "What's the point of having one if you aren't taking care of it yourself?"

I have to fight myself from reminding her this isn't her garden, but I bite my tongue, standing still as she wraps her arms around me in a passive-aggressive hug.

"How was your flight?" I ask, searching for an easy conversation starter.

"Quick and painless. I only wish I could stay longer," she says. "How's the apartment?"

"You should ask Matthew. He'll tell you all about it." I start sorting through decorations, trying to ignore the pious tone of her voice. "Let's get going."

My relationship with Jane didn't sour until after the divorce. Out of everyone in both our families, she took it the hardest. *In her day and age* couples found a way to work through their problems, she insisted. She's never come out and said it, but I know she wonders what could have possibly turned me away from her perfect son.

If she knew, she'd never look at either one of us the same.

THREE

LILLIAN

Before: Saturday Afternoon

The party starts at two o'clock. Fifteen minutes later, the pool is full of children, Mabel is sailing on a donut float in the middle of the water. The smile on her face makes all the effort from this morning worth it.

"Want me to take over lifeguard duty?" Matthew asks, joining me at the side of the pool. "You can greet the guests as they arrive."

"I'm fine here."

As much as Mabel and I love swimming, the water makes me nervous. I'd rather Matthew mingle with parents so I can keep watch. I'm friendly with most of our guests, but he's better at making small talk.

Anne Isle is a close-knit community, mostly rich, fiercely pretentious. The wealthier residents usually grew up here, like Ted, although he's financed purely by the success of the company. Most middle-class residents settle here because Anne Isle University is only forty-five minutes south. That's what brought Matthew and me here, and the success of Voyage allowed us to stay.

Once you get past the veneer, you realize everyone in the Seaside Cliffs neighborhood has a connection to someone else, most links superficial, but some stronger and sincere. Our friendships with Cat and Ted date back to college. Our neighbor, Harriet, is married to David Moore, the mayor. She owns her own dance studio and is a member of the school board at Anne Isle Elementary, where Rebecca works.

It's a tangled web, a little incestuous, mostly harmless. And still, after all these years, I'm happy to be included, at least part of the time. The rest of my days are spent at the apartment, but it could be worse. I could be like Ted, exiled permanently to the other side of town. He wasn't even invited to the party because Cat will be here.

Soon Harriet joins me. She's wearing a pair of Lululemon leggings and a "We Want Moore" shirt. David is up for re-election in November, which means every social event, even today's party, is an opportunity for her to campaign.

"Shelby has been talking about the party all morning," she says, nodding at her own daughter in the pool. She gives me two kisses on my cheeks. "Everything looks great."

"Thanks."

"You should throw parties more often. You're great at it. Whenever David makes me plan something, it feels more like work than fun."

"Oh, it's still work," I say, slipping my hands inside my pockets.

By the patio, I spy Cat walking in, carrying a violet gift bag. She is dressed in black capris, hot pink sandals and a coordinating top. Harriet and I wave her over.

"Hot as hell today," she says, pressing down the flyways around her face.

"You're more than welcome to hop in the pool with the kids," Harriet jokes.

"Please. I'm running to the salon after this. I have a date tonight." Her cheeks flush. "Someone new."

"Sounds fun."

"Ah, he's a bit younger. Not sure if it will go anywhere past the bedroom, but I'm okay with that." She pulls down her sunglasses and gives a wink. "Speaking of dates, how was yours last night?"

Harriet smacks my arm. "You had a date?"

We've had multiple iterations of this conversation in the past few months, and each has ended with me rolling my eyes, Harriet digging for details, Cat convincing me to get back on the horse. This time, when I recall last night, I smile. "It was actually very nice."

"Really?" Cat takes off her glasses to better gauge my reaction. "Tell me all about him."

"There's not much to tell, really. We decided to play the game you suggested."

"Oh good." She steeples her palms and dances her fingers. "You need some fun in your life. Did he stay the night?"

"No. I mean, I think it was headed in that direction. But he has a daughter, too, and he had to leave early. But I really liked him. I could see it going somewhere."

"It's about time you moved on," Harriet says. "It's clear Matthew has."

As she says this, I spot Rebecca on the other side of the pool. Her hair is styled just like mine, straight and parted down the middle. She's carrying a sheet cake in her hands, Matthew guiding her to the buffet table. When she catches me watching her, she smiles and nods. I wave.

"I have moved on. I just haven't found a serious relationship yet."

"Doesn't it bother you at all?" Harriet pushes. "The fact

that Matthew is already dating again? And Mabel's teacher, at that."

"Don't make it sound so salacious. Everyone knows they didn't start dating until after the divorce," Cat comes to my defense, then turns to me. "It's hard for people to understand your situation, you know. Most people couldn't handle it. I'd rather die than be around the girls Ted dates."

My eyes don't leave Rebecca. Every so often, she'll stop what she's doing to speak with our neighbors and friends. It is a bit jarring, seeing her fall into my old life so seamlessly, but that's just Harriet getting into my head.

"I want Matthew to be happy," I say. "It's better for Mabel and for me."

"Even if you want your ex to be happy, you never want them to be happier than you," Cat says. "That's the secret to divorce."

Even though Cat is a dear friend, it's difficult for her to understand my post-divorce relationship with Matthew. Her hardened take is a product of nurture, not nature. I can still remember the giddy, love-struck girl she used to be in college, the way she'd look at Ted, her gorgeous face lighting up. Most people label Cat a gold digger but I believe she would have stayed with him through almost anything, even if Voyage never made it big.

But Voyage did make it big, and with its success, Ted changed. He was as savvy as ever, but he allowed his professional triumphs to pad his already inflated ego. And then came the women. After a few years, he didn't care about hiding them from Cat—he saw infidelity as a privilege he'd earned. Each fling that didn't mean anything to him chipped away at my friend's soul. By the time she finally filed for divorce, she was out for blood, transformed into the stereotype of an ex-wife living off resentment and alimony. She mentions the cost of their attorneys at least once in every conversation.

"What do you know?" Cat's eyes are squinted, staring at someone on the other side of the pool. "She came."

"Who came?"

"Blaire Walsh," she says. "She never comes to anything anymore."

"She declined my invitation to Shelby's party last month," Harriet adds. "Can't say I was surprised. Blaire has never wanted to make friends in this town. Makes me feel sorry for the boys."

By the patio steps, stands a woman. Tall, blonde, rigid. She looks very much like a Greek statue in her gauzy maxi dress, and her life is equally tragic. Ask anyone in the neighborhood, and they'll tell you about the untimely passing of her husband, Richard.

A trio of boys come running up behind Blaire, their eyes glistening at the sight of the pool. They cannonball into the water, splashing the adults standing around the edge. Most parents would be mortified, but Blaire's face stretches into an embarrassed smile. The boys' presence is the only thing that makes her appear more than stone.

"Good for them," Cat says. "It's been two years since Richard died. They have to move on at some point."

"Would you?" There's a seriousness to my tone I don't like, so I clear my throat, manipulate my voice to make it sound more conversational. "I mean, if your husband died, wouldn't you have trouble moving on?"

"Please. I'd be happy if Ted had upped and vanished. Would've saved a fortune in lawyer's fees."

There it is, I think, swallowing a laugh.

Marriages unfold differently, stay intact like Harriet and David's, or turn people into enemies, like Cat and Ted's. Remain amicable, like Matthew's and mine. But no one wants to end up like Blaire Walsh. A widow. A reason for people to whisper and pity and proclaim *bless her heart* before going about their days.

"Hot dogs are ready!" Matthew shouts.

The kids scurry out of the pool, splashing water, and corner Matthew by the barbecue. He's holding the food platter above their heads. The entire scene makes me laugh, releasing the tension that's been building inside since this morning. When my present life and past life intersect, the collision can often be overwhelming.

"If I wasn't talking to *you*, I'd say he's a keeper," Harriet says to me, nudging me with her elbow.

"Mabel and I are very lucky."

I'm used to neighbors prying. After the divorce, people only wanted to know how I'd cope. Would I turn divorce into a financial enterprise, like Cat, losing the husband but keeping the status? Or would I fade away like the countless what's-her-names of yesteryear?

Most of our friends wondered what drove us apart in the first place. They were shocked to hear the golden couple of Seaside Cliffs was calling it quits. We offered them the typical excuses:

We drifted apart.

We became more like roommates than lovers.

Our spark burnt out.

Much of what we told people is true. What we leave out is the real reason we had to separate.

No one can know that.

"You're the happiest divorced couple I know," Harriet says. "That's for sure."

"Hell, they're happier than most married couples," Cat adds.

Matthew and I were so happy once. Grounded. In love.

I can almost pinpoint our most joyous moment together. Remember the warmth of his hand intertwined with mine, the pleasurable vibrations humming through my body when we kissed. The cool night air crystalizing around us, locking that moment in time.

And I can remember what happened later. How everything fell apart.

FOUR

MATTHEW

Before: Saturday Afternoon

Lillian and I were so happy once.

I actually proposed to her on her birthday, ten years ago. It took months of saving to afford a weekend away in the mountains—I saved even more to buy the ring. The sun was setting over the trees, orange rays shining on her skin. She was wearing a white dress, her hair falling in loose waves down her back.

I asked. She answered. We kissed. I'd never seen her look more beautiful, and it was the happiest I'd ever been in my life, until Mabel was born.

Thinking back to that moment, it's like peering into another life. Before Voyage took off. Before we built the house in Seaside Cliffs. Before we became parents.

Who would have known how much significance this day would continue to hold for the rest of our lives? And who could have known we would no longer be together? That we'd be celebrating in each other's presence, but not as the family we'd intended.

And it's all my fault.

Lillian is sitting on the patio, Mabel at her side, a dozen or so kids with towels draped over their shoulders standing around them. Lillian helps Mabel open her presents, taking careful time to thank each parent and child who brought a gift. Being at the center of attention has never been Lillian's preference, and yet she's a marvel at it.

I don't love her anymore. I practically had to force myself out of love with her. It was one of the hardest things I'd ever done. For a while, I didn't know if I'd survive our separation. Most days, I didn't want to survive it, so I turned to alcohol, eventually realizing I needed to stop thinking of my own loss and focus on what was best for her.

She needed me to let go, so she could be free from the pain I'd caused. And I like to think she's happy now. She deserves it. She was there when I needed her most, stood by me after I did what I did. Most people—

"I'm guessing my invite got lost in the mail."

Ted walks around the grill to sit in the chair closest to me. Even though it's Saturday, he's dressed in a suit, careful to carry on the company image.

"I didn't really think it was your scene."

As I say the words, I catch myself scanning the pool area for Cat. It's common knowledge the two can never be together. I didn't invite him for that reason. It's been either/or with them ever since their divorce. It would be a lot easier on them and everyone else if they'd learn to be civil, like Lillian and me.

"I come bearing gifts. Candy for the birthday girl, wine for the birthday woman."

He holds up two bags like props, and I sense he's here precisely because he knows Cat is around. He isn't the type to wait on an invitation; Ted takes what he wants from life.

"How sweet you remembered," I say, sarcastically. "Place them over there with the other gifts."

"Jane let me into the house. I haven't seen her in ages. How long is she in town?"

"Just for the weekend."

"I guess that means it's your turn at *la casa*."

Ted likes to rib me about the apartment. He'd rather die than live under the same roof as Cat, but there's a lot about our dynamic he doesn't understand. Our backgrounds are vastly different. Ted comes from money, and even though he hates to admit it, that's shielded him from the realities of life over the years.

It wasn't until Voyage made it big I realized how much work goes into maintaining a high-end lifestyle. The taxes and insurance and legal fees. Lillian and I saved on that last front because we used mediators instead of lawyers, but it still feels like we're one disaster away from losing everything.

And that's why, financially, sharing an apartment makes more sense than selling the house and taking a loss, or pouring even more money into two separate homes. More importantly, our arrangement best serves Mabel.

Ted watches as Lillian and Mabel open more presents. "Man, kicking her out on her birthday. Seems harsh."

My eyes follow his. Lillian is holding up a Queen Elsa bathing suit, the guests around her oohing and ahhing. I feel a pang of guilt. Lillian is willing to take the apartment tonight because Mom is rarely in town. She insisted the party would be enough, but I know she deserves more. She deserves to spend her birthday with her daughter, and it's my fault she can't.

"Any other reason you stopped by?" I'm annoyed that he's making me reflect.

"You know me too well." He leans closer to the grill, lowering his voice. "I was wondering if you'd talked to Lillian about our new business opportunity."

I pinch my lips together and exhale through my nose. "Unbelievable."

"Please. The offer has been on the table for weeks. I couldn't wait until Monday to find out."

"I never said I was talking to her about it now. It's her birthday, for goodness' sakes."

"Last weekend, Mabel had a soccer game. The weekend before that, the two of you were going to *Disney on Ice*. I don't remember the excuses beyond that. I just know you keep putting it off."

"And you thought you'd pressure me at my daughter's party?"

"We're partners, Matthew. I'm not trying to muscle you into anything. But at some point either you're going to have a conversation with Lillian or a conversation with me."

"I'm done talking for the day. I'd rather enjoy the party." I stab a hot dog with the tongs and bring the meat close to his face. "Care for some lunch?"

"You should be fined for serving that processed junk to a bunch of kids."

"Says the functioning alcoholic."

"Speaking of alcoholics, I think I spot my ex-wife in the corner. Should I say hello?"

"Play nice."

"Fine. I've ruffled your feathers enough for the day. I might wander back into the house, strike up a conversation with Jane. It's been a long time."

"That sounds like the safer choice."

Before walking away, he claps my shoulder and says, "We didn't get to where we are by playing it safe."

It sounds like a threat, but maybe, more simply, it's a reminder. Ted and I were strangers when we ended up roommates our freshman year at college, but we quickly gelled. Same interests, same hobbies, even if Ted was always more of a risk-taker. His streak of rebelliousness has benefited me several times. In business, he knows when to push me forward, just as I know when to pull him back.

As a husband, however, he was a mess. I didn't even blame Cat when she finally filed for divorce, and remember sweating bullets thinking she might go after the company. She didn't, and I'd like to think it's because I'd always been good to her, but it likely had more to do with Lillian's influence. Just another way Lillian has managed to save me over the years.

I tried to be the antithesis of Ted in my own marriage, and yet I ended up in the same situation. Divorced.

At some point I need to talk to Lillian about Voyage, but I'm dreading it. How many times can you break the same person's heart?

FIVE

LILLIAN

Before: Saturday Night

What a day.

My skin is sun-soaked and tingling, my cheeks stiff from smiling. Now, I sit in the dim family room, watching *Frozen* for what must be the hundredth time. Mabel rests her head on my lap, the weight of her feeling heavier tonight than usual. She's getting older, and while I'm thankful for the new memories we're creating, I'm reminded of just how much time with her I'm forced to give up.

At least I was able to be with her on her birthday. *Our* birthday. I'd rather stay the night, but Jane's only in town until Monday, and I know she wants quality time with her grandchild. It's only fair that I let them have the evening and tomorrow, then I'll move back into the house at the beginning of next week. It's these small compromises that make our arrangement work. Little gives and little takes.

Still, when I hear the front door open, my heart sinks. Matthew walks into the house, followed by Jane and Rebecca.

"Who wants pizza?" It's Jane's voice ringing through the

house, interrupting our cozy moment. Mabel leaps from the couch, skipping into the kitchen.

"I'm still stuffed from cake," I say, following her.

"I might steal a piece for later tonight," Rebecca says.

"There's plenty. Take as much as you want."

"When Matthew was younger, I'd stay up the entire night before his party baking a cake," Jane says, reaching into a cabinet to pull out paper plates. Three paper plates, to be specific. She focuses on Mabel. "Want to try some pepperoni?"

"Just cheese," she answers.

"All right. All right."

"I'm going to head out," I say, wrapping my arms around Mabel.

"Happy birthday, Mommy," she says, leaning into my embrace.

A year ago, Mabel would cry when Matthew or I left for the night. She's adjusting, which is all we really want. The joy in her voice lingers in my thoughts as I walk outside. The temperature has dropped and the sun is gone, replaced with a salty breeze.

I look back at the house. Part mine and part Matthew's. All Mabel's. Still, I worry we're not giving her enough.

"You okay?"

Rebecca is to my left, walking to her own car.

"Saying goodbye doesn't get easier," I answer, honestly. "Aren't you staying?"

"No." She makes a face. "I was given the impression Jane only wanted family around."

I smile tightly. I've had what feels like a lifetime of Jane's digs and insinuations. I'm still dealing with them even though Matthew and I are divorced.

"Say, I was about to go grab dinner," she says. "Want to join?"

"That's okay. I'm going—"

"Back to the apartment? Join me. We can turn it into a birthday celebration."

"We already had a party."

"Yeah, I didn't think the whole princess theme was your idea, but I guess I was wrong." She smiles. "Come on. We've both been dismissed here. Let's make some fun of it."

I don't dislike Rebecca. I know society says I should view her as the woman stepping into the role I once filled, but I don't feel that way. There are multiple people to blame for the end of my marriage, but she isn't one of them.

"Sure," I say. "Why not?"

There are worse ways to spend an evening.

SIX

LILLIAN

Before: Saturday Night

Rebecca is very beautiful. She has long dark hair, a creamy, sun-kissed complexion and large blue eyes. Her features mirror mine, actually—although she comes across looking more put together.

Cat usually refers to Ted's newest flings by their most damning physical feature.

Elephant Ears. Botox Barbie. A-cup Anna.

She's bitter and angry with Ted for everything he put her through during their marriage. I'm actually thankful for Rebecca's presence in Matthew's life. I read once that when a spouse dies, the happiest couples often remarry quickly—it's a testament to how much they miss that stable, supportive presence in their lives. I guess that's how I feel about Matthew moving on with Rebecca: if our relationship couldn't work, at least he's trying to recapture what we had with someone new.

"Should we order another round?" she asks.

"We probably shouldn't."

There's a small pause, and I suddenly get the feeling this night means more to her than it does to me, even if it is my birthday.

My birthday. There's no one else with whom I can celebrate. Cat is on her date, and most of my other friends, like Harriet, are at home with their families. The evening has drifted toward that gray area I've grown to hate, and going back to the apartment this early will only make it worse.

"What the hell?" I say. "Let's do it."

"Great!" Rebecca's mood lifts immediately. She places our order, then says, "I'm curious. How long did it take Jane to warm up to you?"

I laugh. "She was very standoffish when we were dating. Territorial. Our relationship didn't improve until we got engaged, and then again after Mabel came along."

"It's not just me then."

"It's definitely not you. And if it makes you feel any better, she quickly ditched all the niceties once divorce was on the table."

"Matthew and you have one of the best co-parenting relationships I've ever seen," she says. I'm sure she's had her share of awkward conferences with parents of former students. "If the two of you are so civil, you'd think she'd treat you better. Maybe I should run now."

"Don't." I take another sip of my drink. "Jane has her good qualities, too. She's never shied away from helping us with Mabel. And Matthew cares about you. I can tell."

"It can be hard sometimes, living in your shadow."

Is that how she really feels? Or does she simply believe she's supposed to feel that way? The ex-wife and new girlfriend at constant odds. Rebecca and I have never fallen into those roles. Even now, it feels like I'm out with a friend instead of Matthew's new partner.

"Matthew and I were good together, until we weren't. People like Jane will toss around all these phrases. *We threw in the towel. We gave up.* Like our divorce is a defeat. I don't look at it that way. I think the smartest thing we did was know when to change direction, before we ended up so bitter with one another it ruined the friendship we have."

I picture Cat and Ted. Once, they were a beautiful couple, and they held onto that so tightly that by the time they decided to end their marriage, they'd exhausted themselves. Now, they can barely be in the same room. I can't imagine having that much resentment toward Matthew, especially with Mabel involved.

Then I think of something else Cat said. *You want your ex to be happy, but never happier than you.* I take another sip, rinsing the words from my mind.

"You and Matthew are both good people. I think that's why it works," she says. "He's overcome a lot. I know you were a big help in getting him sober."

In the months following our divorce, Matthew relied heavily on alcohol. He blamed himself for what happened to us, and drinking was the only way he could ease his guilt.

"Even if we weren't together, I never wanted to see him like that," I say. "You were a big part of his recovery, too."

I was the one who first confronted Matthew about his drinking and insisted he reach out to David Moore. Before he was mayor, David struggled with his own addictions. He now leads an AA group in the basement of the Baptist church once a month, and I urged Matthew to go. After that conversation, Matthew still had several relapses. He'd have a few weeks of acceptance, then another bender. It wasn't until Rebecca entered his life that he made a consistent effort to change.

"Matthew isn't perfect, but at least he isn't violent, like my ex."

I shift uncomfortably in my seat.

"Violent?"

"I would have thought you already heard."

I shake my head, suddenly feeling uncomfortable. I first met Rebecca when she was Mabel's preschool teacher. She was engaged at the time. I can still remember the charming photos on her desk when I went in for a parent conference. Rebecca in a white sundress standing beside a tall, blond man with tattoos running up and down his arms. There were pictures from his proposal on the beach. From the outside looking in, it appeared she lived a charmed life.

I knew the engagement ended seeing as she's with Matthew, but I had no idea why. Before they started dating, my only connection to her was through the school. Harriet and Cat wouldn't waste time gossiping about the lives of Anne Isle Elementary teachers—they tend to treat Rebecca more like the help than a peer.

"I don't like talking to Matthew about him," Rebecca continues. "About what he did to me."

I can see the story is begging for a release.

"What happened?"

"Our relationship had always been tumultuous, but we'd been together since high school. I thought his mood swings and temper tantrums were normal. He was controlling at times, but I thought it was because he loved me so much." She rolls her eyes, trying to play off how naïve she once was, but pain etches her expression. "After we got engaged, I thought we'd fight less, but the opposite happened. When I finally got the nerve to end things, he wouldn't accept it. He attacked me."

She stops talking, and I realize I don't want to know anymore. I don't want those images in my mind, Rebecca's petite body pummeled by fists, by the man who was supposed to love her.

She clears her throat and sits up straighter. "The neighbors ended up calling the police. By the time they arrived, I had a dislocated shoulder and a broken wrist."

"That's awful, Rebecca."

"There were warning signs, and if I'd paid attention to them earlier, it never would have gotten that far," she says. "Sometimes I still think it's my fault."

"He's the one to blame, not you. It's not always easy to know what to do."

"At least I no longer had a choice about going back to him. He went to prison, which gave me the space I needed for a clean start." She laughs dryly. "They shortened his sentence for good behavior. Do you know how ridiculous that sounds? I spent two days in the hospital, but he gets released for being *such a nice guy.*"

"When does he get out?"

"Last week."

I sit up straighter. "Does Matthew know?"

"This is the first time I've said it aloud." She points to her glass. "Liquid courage."

And it makes sense now, why she's so desperate to keep the night going. She doesn't want to be alone.

"Is he allowed to contact you?"

"No. There's a restraining order in place. So much has happened since then, I'd like to think he wants to start over. And then I have days where I think I'll never fully recover from what he did."

"One person, one choice, doesn't define you." Without thinking, I reach across the table, clasping my hand over hers. "You're so much more than your worst experience."

As the words leave my lips, my drunken thoughts just a half-step behind, I wonder if I'm talking to Rebecca, or myself.

Rebecca is still, staring at the table, and for a moment, I think she might cry. She smiles instead.

"Thank you for being so nice to me."

"You've been good to the two people I care most about in this world," I say. "It's the least I can do."

This is how it should be, I think. This is the adult way to handle the dissolution of a marriage, the beginning of something new.

SEVEN

LILLIAN

Before: Early Sunday Morning

Neither of us is fit to drive. We share an Uber, stopping at my place first. As I open the car door, my head spins. I can't remember the last time I had this much to drink, or the last time I had this sort of spontaneous fun.

"Thanks for inviting me out tonight."

"It was a blast."

I think back to what Rebecca said about her ex, imagine the uneasiness she must feel about going home alone. "You know, you can crash here, if you want."

"Isn't that against the rules?"

I roll my eyes. Part of the agreement when we leased the apartment was not bringing love interests inside, a rule I broke last night with Dylan. It surprises me Matthew has stuck to the rules this long, considering how serious their relationship has become.

"I don't think Matthew would mind."

"Thanks for the offer, but I've been fantasizing about my own bed."

I understand that all too well; on the nights I'm here, I dream about my real bed, back at the house, the curtains pulled tight across the balcony window, blocking the view of the cliffs and water beyond.

"Have a good night," I say, sliding out of the car.

"Hey." She stops me. "Don't think I'm corny, but I left a little gift for you by the front door. I wanted to do something for your birthday, before I knew we'd end up having a proper night out."

"You didn't have to do that."

"I wanted to," she says, waving goodbye.

The door closes, and I watch as the dark sedan pulls out of the parking lot, merges onto the empty main road. I can't remember the last time I've been out this late. It's like stepping into a former version of myself, one that existed before Matthew and Mabel and everything else.

When I arrive at the front door, there's a small gift bag leaned against it. Inside is a candle, a box of chocolates and a bottle of Casamigos, my favorite tequila. Matthew must have helped her with the gift. The note reads: *Happy Birthday* —*Rebecca*.

She's too kind, especially to me. But I enjoy knowing someone out there is thinking of me, as I slide the key into the lock and enter the lonely apartment.

I stop at the kitchen, unable to resist one more taste. I grab a glass from the cabinet and pour a hearty serving. I sit on the couch, sampling the chocolates and sipping the tequila. I turn on the television and flip through the channels. Before I can reach for a second glass, my eyelids are heavy. I stretch out on the sofa, which only brings me closer to sleep.

Then, I'm there.

When I wake up, I'm on the sofa.

My throat is dry.

My head hurts.

My back aches.

Sleep. My body and mind crave it.

The world beyond the windows is still dark, yellow squares from neighboring buildings the only light source. There are a few more hours until sunrise. I'll rest better in my own bed...

EIGHT

MATTHEW

Now

It's too early for the alarm. Too late for a phone call.

I'm tempted to roll over, surrender to sleep, but the sound persists.

My hand slaps against the nightstand, hitting the lamp and knocking over a box of tissues before landing on my phone.

The screen's light stings my eyes when I read Lillian's name.

"Hello?"

"Oh, thank God." She's panting and, it sounds like, crying. "Matthew, something happened. I need your help."

The clock by the bed confirms it's nearing three o'clock in the morning. I sit up straighter in bed, her fear contagious.

"Where are you? Are you safe?"

"I'm at the apartment. In the breezeway." Her words and sobs band together, making it difficult to understand what she says. "There's someone in the bedroom. I can't go back in there."

"An intruder? Have you called the police?"

"I don't know!" she shouts. "I think... I think they're dead."

"Dead? Were you attacked or—"

"After I came home, I fell asleep on the sofa. Just now, I woke up. When I climbed into bed, that's when I saw the... the body."

None of this is making sense.

I ask the key question.

"Lillian, who is inside the apartment?"

"I don't know. I couldn't tell. There was too much blood."

Blood. The picture in my mind keeps getting worse and worse. Even in the dark bedroom, I find myself squinting, trying to banish the images from my brain.

"Lillian, you need to call the police."

"Okay."

There's a detached quality to her voice. Her words float. I'm not convinced anything I'm saying is registering; she's likely still in shock.

"Mom can stay with Mabel. I'll be there as soon as I can."

I'm already out of bed, sliding my feet into a pair of loafers. I'm in front of the closet, pulling out a hoodie and sweats. All the while, I'm thinking of Lillian and how scared she must be. How confused.

"I'll call them now. I didn't know what to do." She pauses, and I can hear the rumblings of another voice in the background.

"Lillian, is someone there?"

"It's Mrs. Haynes. I woke her with all the screaming."

Screaming. Normally, Mrs. Haynes is a nuisance, but it gives me comfort that Lillian won't be waiting alone.

"She can stay with you until the police arrive. Everything will be okay. I'm coming."

As the words leave my lips, I feel a wave of a déjà vu.

Memories I've locked away escape to the forefront of my mind. I'm reliving the emotions again—the shock, the disgust, the fear. But I can't think about that night now.

Because on this night, Lillian needs me.

NINE

LILLIAN

Each blink feels like the one that will wake me up. I'm in a nightmare, one with claws so deep they refuse to release. And yet, with every passing minute, it becomes more real.

First, the questions from the 911 operator, then instructions, her voice telling me where to go, what to do. Mrs. Haynes waits with me in the breezeway, saying very little, her eyes on the apartment front door like something evil might emerge.

Then the officers arrive. Clean uniforms and young faces, busting through the doors of my apartment, my limp finger pointing them in the direction of the bedroom.

Now, I'm sitting on the sofa, a blanket wrapped around my shoulders. One of the officers said it would help with the shock, but my body continues to tremble. Matthew still hasn't arrived, and I'm impatient. I need answers, and even if he can't provide them, I won't feel so alone.

There's a commotion at the front door. I stand, hoping it's him. But it's only more police officers. This time, not in uniform. An older man in a brown suit walks inside, and behind him...

"Dylan?"

The last person I expected to see. He stares back at me with the same confusion. Pulls something out of his jacket pocket.

"Detective Dylan Logan," he says. The badge gleams beneath the overhead light in the living room where we sat together drinking wine. He nods at the man in front of him. "This is Detective Ralph Spelling."

The older man is looking around the apartment, assessing the scene. That's what this is now. A crime scene, no longer my home. Spelling has yet to look at me. I don't think he heard me refer to Dylan by his first name, either.

So, Dylan is a detective. That's the job he agreed to avoid discussing. Now I know, and not because we've grown closer. Because he's here, investigating the murder of the stranger in my bed. The look on his face is hard to read, but I sense it is best to keep quiet. Right now, I'm not sure if our history works in my favor or against it.

Dylan and Spelling follow the younger officers into the bedroom. They stay in there for what feels like an eternity. There's a strangeness in the air, knowing there's a dead body on the other side of the wall. And the mood is made stranger because Dylan is investigating the death. Just last night, we almost kissed.

"You don't understand," I hear Matthew say, his voice echoing from outside. "I live here, too."

I hurry to the front door, tapping the officer blocking the entryway. "He does. This is my ex-husband."

The officer gives Matthew another once-over before allowing him inside. Matthew wraps his arms around me, and only then do I feel my anxiety begin to dwindle.

"Are you okay?"

"Just in shock. And confused," I say, aware of my tears dampening the fabric of his hoodie. "What took you so long?"

He pulls away, looking past me, at the open bedroom door.

"I had to wake Mom. And then I needed gas. It took longer than I wanted."

I wonder if all the commotion woke Mabel. Before I have the chance to ask, Dylan and Spelling come back into the living room.

"Who's this?" Dylan asks.

"I'm Matthew," he says, holding out his hand. "I live here, too. In the second bedroom."

He looks back at me, only for a second, before shaking Matthew's hand.

Spelling looks at me now, gesturing in the direction of the sofa. "Want to walk us through what happened here?"

We sit, and I pull the blanket tighter around my shoulders. "I don't know what happened," I say. "I don't even know who's in there."

"Start with earlier today," Spelling says. "Were you home alone?"

"I was gone most of the day. It was my daughter's—" I stop speaking, looking at Matthew. "*Our* daughter's birthday. We had her party at our house—"

"I'm confused about this." Spelling leans back, pointing one hand at Matthew, the other at me. "Are you two married?"

"Divorced," Matthew answers. "We split our time between the family home and this apartment. Our daughter stays at the house full-time. When one of us is there with her, the other one stays here. Hence, the separate bedrooms."

Spelling gives Dylan a skeptical look, and shrugs his shoulders. "Continue."

"I spent most of the day at our house getting ready for the party," I say.

"What time did you leave?"

"Around seven. I ended up going out for dinner and drinks with a friend."

"What's the friend's name?" Dylan asks, pulling a notepad out of his jacket pocket.

"Rebecca."

"Rebecca?" Matthew asks in surprise.

"You know her, too?" Dylan asks.

Matthew nods, without explaining.

"And what time did you return to the apartment?" Spelling asks.

"Just after midnight. I ended up falling asleep on the sofa. It was after two o'clock when I woke up and decided to move into the bedroom. That's when I found the body."

Spelling and Dylan look at each other. It's hard to decipher what their stares mean.

"Did something wake you?" Spelling asks. "A loud sound, someone at the door, a phone call?"

"No, I just woke up."

"Why didn't you just go straight into your bedroom after you returned home?"

"I don't know. Normally, I would. But we'd been drinking, and I was tired. I sat down to have a nightcap and some chocolates and I just... passed out."

"Drinking," Spelling says. "Any drugs?"

"No, definitely not."

"So, you have no way of knowing how long the victim might have been in the apartment before you arrived home?" Dylan asks.

"No. I'm just as confused as you. The only entry is the front door and the back patio, which were both locked. The only other person who has a key is Matthew, and, as I've told you, I was out most of the day."

"Did you recognize the victim when you found him?" Dylan asks.

Him. So, it's a man inside my bedroom.

"No. As soon as I saw the body, I was so scared I left the apartment."

"And you called 911?"

"Yes."

My body temperature rises a hair. Technically, I called Matthew first. I'm still not sure why. Perhaps it's because I'm used to turning to him in moments of panic, not the police. But I don't want to say anything that would make me look suspicious. Already, I'm feeling the anxiety you experience when you pass a squad car on the highway. Even though I've done nothing wrong, the pure presence of officers gives reason to worry.

"What about you?" Dylan says, looking at Matthew. "When's the last time you were at the apartment."

Matthew turns to me, then looks at the ceiling, trying to count back the days.

"Mabel's been with me at the house for the past three days. And before that, I was at my girlfriend's house... I guess it was last Friday."

Last Friday. I'm the only person who has been in the apartment in the past week. Well, me and Dylan. And the dead man in my room. My mind screams, how did he get inside, and why is he here? Then, quieter, when did Matthew start spending his days away from the house at Rebecca's place?

Dylan nods, jotting something onto the notepad. He stands. "We'd like Lillian to come to the station to answer some more questions."

There's something odd about the way he doesn't address me, instead directing the comment to the entire room.

"She's already answered your questions," Matthew says, standing. "Can't she come in the morning?"

"We'll need to collect her clothing. It's procedure. And we might have a few more questions once we finish up here," Spelling says.

"It'll be fine," I say, turning to Matthew. "Go be with Mabel. I'll be at the house as soon as I can."

"Are you sure?"

I nod, my eyes flitting from him to Dylan to Detective Spelling. Then something else catches my attention. All of our attention. We turn and stare.

The wheels on the gurney squeak as it's pushed across the room. On it, rests a zipped up bag, the stranger's body inside. A stale scent enters my nostrils, and my throat clenches, like I might be sick.

This isn't a dream. It's not even a nightmare.

This is all frighteningly, sickeningly real.

TEN

LILLIAN

I'm sitting in an interrogation room, waiting for the detectives. I've already been here for over an hour. First, filling out paperwork about the apartment and what I witnessed, then stripping my clothes, trading them for a generic pair of sweats. After posing for photographs, I was finally allowed to wash the blood from my hands, red water circling the corroded drain of the sink.

I need sleep. I'm tempted to put my head on the table and rest, but choose not to. I saw once on a news report that only guilty people sleep when they're waiting to be interrogated, and I'm not guilty. The police are speaking to me as a witness, but I can't shake the feeling that I'm in trouble. If anything, I'm a victim. A man was found in *my* apartment. A stranger. I still have no idea how he got inside, which means I won't feel safe once I return. And I don't know why he was there... could it have been to cause me harm?

I look at my phone for the time, then remember it's dead. It died shortly after I got here. Matthew sent a text to tell me Mabel was still asleep then—poof—the screen went black.

The door opens, and Spelling walks inside, followed by Dylan. They look about as exhausted as I am.

"Thanks for waiting," Dylan says.

They didn't make it sound like I had an option. "I'm very tired. I'd like to go home."

"We have some questions," Spelling says. "We've been able to piece a few things together since we last spoke."

"Do you know how the man got inside my apartment?"

There's a long pause before Spelling speaks, and I notice it's still not an answer to my question. "You said you arrived home around midnight?"

"That's right."

"And you're sure the door was locked when you arrived?"

"Yes. I remember using my key." I think I remember. I'd had so much to drink. My desperation for sleep makes my memory foggy, even now.

"When you returned home, did anything seem misplaced? Like anyone had been inside the apartment when you were gone?"

"Nothing I noticed. Rebecca had left a present outside by the front door. But inside, everything looked the same. Just as I'd left it."

"A present. For your daughter?"

"The present was for me. Yesterday was my birthday, too."

"Well, happy birthday." Spelling says this with a fake tone that makes my skin crawl. Dylan keeps staring at the notepad, as though I'm the last person he wants to see right now.

"Your neighbor waited with you," Dylan says. "Mrs. Haynes."

"Yes. My screams woke her."

"She said you were already on the phone when she approached you. Were you speaking to 911?"

This is the first question I have to really think about before I answer. I'm careful not to say anything that might contradict myself. The police could easily look at my phone records.

"No. I called Matthew first."

The way Spelling reacts, looking at Dylan, then me, convinces me he already knew I hadn't dialed 911 right away. Mrs. Haynes must have told him.

"Why would you call your ex-husband before phoning the police?"

"I was in shock." My voice is defensive, so I level out my tone. "Matthew lives there, too. I guess on some level I thought he might know something. And I was scared. I wasn't thinking straight."

"The two of you seem pretty cozy for a divorced couple," Spelling says. "You live together. You call him before you call the police. He showed up at the crime scene to make sure you were okay."

Before I respond, I look at Dylan. A memory flashes from the other night. The look on his face when he found Matthew's clothes in the bathroom. *I don't want anything complicated.* He must be wondering about my answer to this question, and not just as it pertains to the investigation.

"We don't live together." I pause, letting that point sink in. "We share an apartment. It's in our best interests financially, but more importantly, this arrangement provides a stable home environment for our daughter. Matthew and I are close because of Mabel. It's totally understandable he was the first person I called. If the situations were reversed, I suppose he'd do the same."

"What did Matthew say to you?"

"He told me to hang up and call the police." I look at the table, twiddle my thumbs. "It's very easy for that to be someone's first reaction, especially when you're around these situations for a living. I've never seen so much blood before."

The images return. My lavender comforter turned

burgundy. The freshly painted walls, streaked with blood. Just yesterday, the room was all mine. Now it has been invaded, tainted.

"Have you noticed anything strange in the past week?" Dylan asks. "People lurking outside your apartment. Anything to make you think someone might be following you."

"No. I'm telling you, nothing upsetting happened until I turned on the lights and saw the body."

"What about your car? Have you had any trouble lately? Any fender-benders?"

My car? Why are they asking about that? "No. What's that have to do with anything?"

Spelling opens the folder on the table, flipping through papers, but he doesn't take any out. "Does the name Carl Gates mean anything to you?"

"No, I don't know anyone with that name."

Spelling pulls out a photo and lays it flat. "Meet Carl. The man inside your apartment."

My body clenches, using every muscle at my disposal not to show a reaction.

I know the man in the photo.

But not as Carl.

A blazing heat starts at the back of my neck, spreading to my cheeks.

"I understand, in the midst of shock, you may not have recognized him," Dylan says. "Does he look familiar now?"

"No."

The word escapes before I can decide what to say. In a matter of seconds, my body and mind have gone on the defense, protecting me from what's to come, because this situation has just gotten much worse.

The man in the photo told me his name was Ben. We met online. On the same dating website where I met Dylan.

"He's a mechanic," Spelling says, taking the picture and

sliding it back inside the folder. "He's married with a baby on the way."

I cover my mouth to stifle a sob. "That's... that's just horrible."

It's as though the room is put on pause. Dylan staring at me. Spelling staring at me. My mind, trying to wrap itself around the situation I'm in, assess the potential damage. I've been awake too long. I've had too much to drink. I don't think I can withstand one more question.

Spelling stands. "That's all for now. Thank you for being patient with us."

He reaches out his hand to shake mine, and I wonder if he can feel the layer of sweat that's formed on my palm.

"We'll be in touch," Dylan says. "Don't go back to the apartment until we give you the okay."

"And don't leave town either," Spelling adds. "Do you have a place to stay?"

Dylan and I lock eyes, briefly. He already knows what I'm about to say. "Yes, I do."

I stand to leave, my dead phone in one hand, my keys in the other. That's when I remember.

"I don't have my car."

"I can give you a ride," Dylan says, before returning to a hushed conversation with Spelling.

When we leave the station, I allow Dylan to lead the way. I keep my head down, trying to ignore the stares of the people we pass. He instructs me to sit in the back seat of his car. I wait until we've pulled out of the parking lot before I speak.

"Your partner. Did you tell him you know me?"

Dylan's hands tighten around the wheel as he turns onto the highway leading to Seaside Cliffs.

"I'll be telling my supervisor once I get back to the station."

"Isn't it a conflict of interest or something? For you to be working on this case?"

"That'll be up to the boss." He pauses. "I don't think it will be a problem. I'm more an acquaintance than anything. It's not like we know each other."

The way he says that last sentence stays with me. We don't know each other. *I don't know you*, he's really saying. *I don't trust you.*

ELEVEN

MATTHEW

What I want more than anything is a drink. The cravings never fully go away, but I'm more tempted during uncertain moments.

I'd like a nice glass of pinot noir. A strong, clean pour of whiskey. Even a cold bottled beer would suffice. I sort through the options in my head, relishing in and resenting each possibility.

I've been sober for eight months and four days—my longest stretch since I started attending AA meetings. As much as I want to give into my temptations, I can't. Being sober is the only thing that keeps me in control, and I need that to deal with the situation we're in.

I don't understand what happened at the apartment, not even after being there, watching the police walk around the scene in their gloved boots, catching the whiff of blood which permeated the air. I don't know how a stranger could have gotten inside. I've not stayed at the apartment in over a week. Lillian was the only one who could have seen anything amiss. How could she have seen nothing? How come she can't explain how that man ended up in her bed?

No, no. I don't need to start traipsing down that path, questioning what Lillian did or didn't do. If I know one thing for sure, it's that my trust in Lillian is absolute. She's a good person. The mother to my daughter. She's been there for me when I needed her most.

I hear keys turning the lock at the front door. I stand, my nerves jittery. Lillian walks inside. She leaves her belongings on the kitchen counter, then she just stands there. I've never seen her look this exhausted. Not after giving birth. Not after Mabel's month-long stint with colic. The woman standing before me looks like an emaciated stranger.

"Are you okay?"

I walk closer, and she collapses into me. She doesn't say anything, but I can hear heaving and sniffling as she cries into my chest. I let her cry, to release all emotion before she explains what's happened. That's what she would do for me if I was falling apart.

That's what she did.

"Is everyone sleeping?" she says at last, pulling away from me and collapsing onto the sofa.

"Yes," I say, then go on, "I can't imagine how frightening it was finding a stranger like that, but you shouldn't be this upset." I watch Lillian, waiting for a reaction, but the one I'm expecting never seems to appear. "We haven't done anything wrong."

"I know that." She looks at me with bleary eyes. And something else in her stare. Fear. "But I think this could be bad. It's more complicated than I realized."

I listen as she repeats everything she told me back at the apartment. She was drunk when Rebecca dropped her off. She passed out on the sofa, before moving into the bedroom and finding the body. A stranger. That's where her story begins to change.

"I didn't realize it until they showed me a photo," she says, "but I know him. *Did* know him. We met online."

"Online?"

"A dating website."

I stand, raking my fingers through my hair. "You'd been dating the man who died in our apartment?"

"We'd been on two dates. It's not like we were in a relationship."

"How could you not recognize him?"

"All I saw was the blood and... I was in shock. After they showed me a picture back at the station, that's when it clicked."

"Did you tell the police?"

"No." Her tone is defensive. "I mean, I'd already told them he was a stranger, and I was afraid if I admitted to knowing him, it would only make the situation worse. Now I'm worried the police will uncover the truth. We exchanged messages online, called each other. Even if—"

"Even if what?"

She exhales. "He gave me a fake name. When I met him, he said his name was Ben. His real name is Carl Gates. And he's married with a baby on the way."

I spin away from her, running my fingers through my hair again, this time pulling on the ends, needing a jolt of pain to snap me out of this. "You dated this man, even though he was married, and then he ended up dead in our apartment."

"I know how it looks, but he didn't tell me about his family. He didn't even give me his real name."

Think, think. "We still don't know a cause of death. Maybe he killed himself. He could have been obsessed with you or something."

"Maybe. But like I said, our relationship was casual. I certainly didn't care that much for him, and I doubt his feelings were that intense for me."

I believe her. She seems stunned and scared, but what's happened must be a medley of horrible coincidences, certainly nothing she intended. I move closer to her, placing my hand over hers.

"I'll work on finding a lawyer. Just in case. Right now, everything looks bad. But we'll be able to figure this out."

"This isn't an unpaid parking ticket, Matthew. It's a murder investigation. And I'm already lying to the police."

"Once we have a lawyer, you can explain everything. You made a mistake."

"I can't afford to make mistakes," she says, a tremble in her voice. "The last thing we need is the police looking into my past."

"*Our* past," I remind her.

The single event that somehow tore us apart and forever linked us. But what happened at the apartment has nothing to do with that, even if the emotions feel the same. The confusion and paranoia and fear. Nothing else.

"I'm here for you, okay?" I add. "Just like you were there for me."

She nods, but refuses to look at me. Maybe she doesn't want to worry me anymore. Or maybe she's hiding something else. I blink several times, my eyes aching, when I realize light is bursting in through the windows. The sun is rising.

"Mabel will be awake in a couple of hours," I say. "You should get some rest."

She nods, standing. She leans in for another embrace, holding me a second longer than expected.

"I'm scared, Matthew."

I rub her back. "We're going to get through this."

It's not a promise, or a lie. Only a hope. Because even though I believe Lillian didn't intend for anything bad to happen last night, I can't ignore the fact that everything just became a lot more complicated.

TWELVE

LILLIAN

I didn't think I'd be able to sleep. I thought worry would keep me awake, but when I stretched out on my mattress, in the master bedroom Matthew and I once shared, my body turned off like a device that had been unplugged.

It's nearing noon when I wake, and now memories from last night are starting to emerge. Blood on the bed and the walls and the floors. The eerie quiet of the apartment. My stomach dropping when I realized I actually knew the man who died inside those walls. I wonder, will I ever have another day without thinking about him? The past has a way of haunting you. I know from experience.

Matthew knocks, then opens the door gently. "How are you?"

"Still trying to wrap my head around everything."

He nods. "It's a beautiful day. Mabel wants to swim."

Something inside my chest leaps at the thought of Mabel. If it weren't for her, I'd be tempted to stay in bed the rest of the day. "I'll be down in a bit."

I don't waste time getting ready. I throw on a pair of lounge shorts and a T-shirt, tie my hair into a low bun. All I want to do is be near my daughter. When I go downstairs, she's sitting at the dining room table enjoying the last bites of a peanut butter and jelly sandwich. Her bathing suit is already on, a towel draped around the back of the chair.

"Mommy!" She scoots her chair away from the table and comes running toward me. Her arms wrap around me, and for the first time since I found Carl's body, I feel complete.

"Daddy says you want to go swimming."

"Thirty minutes." Jane appears, collecting Mabel's plate. "That's how long you have to wait before getting in."

Mabel is still clinging to my waist, but I look down just in time to see her excitement deflate.

"Go out to the patio and put on your sunscreen. By the time it soaks in, you'll be ready."

She skips toward the door, circling back to grab her towel. "Are you swimming with me?"

"Maybe later."

My joints and muscles still ache from the interrupted sleep. I pull out a coffee pod and plop it inside the Keurig, careful to avoid Jane as she washes dishes in the sink.

"I heard you had quite a night last night."

I wonder how much Matthew has told her. Probably everything. After all, he had to wake her in the middle of the night to join me at the apartment. She must have cornered him with a dozen questions once he returned.

"Thank you for sitting with Mabel until we got back," I say, watching the liquid drip into the canister.

"It's why I'm here," she says, drying off her hands with a dishrag. "It must have been awful, seeing something like that. And how bizarre that someone was able to break into your apartment without you noticing."

I close my eyes, but that doesn't stop the images from appearing. The body. The blood. The fear of knowing I was there alone.

"If you think this could get dicey, I'd be happy to stay a while longer. My flight is in the morning, but I can easily reschedule."

Jane isn't going to let the conversation drop. And I don't want to think about things getting *dicey*. Not now.

"Flying out tomorrow sounds fine," I say, walking away, coffee mug in hand, before she can say anything else.

I step through the sliding glass doors, early afternoon sunlight kissing my skin. Mabel is still rubbing sunscreen into her shins. Matthew and Rebecca are on the opposite side of the pool, in deep conversation. I hadn't realized she was here. She stands abruptly when she sees me and walks over, her arms wide.

"I came as soon as Matthew told me what happened. Thank God you're okay," she says, embracing me. "I feel guilty for having left you."

"You couldn't have known what would happen. You were just dropping me off."

Across the pool, Matthew is watching us, and I wonder what he thinks about the two of us heading to the bar after the party. I wonder what he thinks about everything.

"Have you spoken to your landlord about what happened?" Rebecca asks me.

"Matthew is going to give them a call tomorrow."

"Maybe they have surveillance video or something. It might show how that man was able to get inside."

"I'm sure the cops are looking into it," I say, just to be polite. I already know there aren't cameras. Matthew and I asked about them when we started renting the place. The owner said so many people have their own individual security systems, it was a waste of money.

It doesn't feel like a waste now.

"Mom, can I get in the pool now?" Mabel shouts.

"Yes, honey. Go on."

"Just a bit longer," Jane says, stepping outside and sitting in the lounge chair closest to the door. "Don't want your tummy to turn."

"She's fine, Jane!" There's a harshness in my tone I'm used to suppressing, but I'm not in the mood to have Jane, or anyone, interfere with my parenting right now. Within a few minutes, Jane has wandered back inside.

"Are you sure you're okay?" Matthew asks, walking over to me.

"I'm fine. Just tired," I say, crossing my arms. "That's a myth about the swimming. Mabel will be fine."

"You seem on edge."

"Of course, I'm on edge! You know what I went through last night. The last thing I need is parenting advice from your mother."

Again, my tone is harsh. I wish I could take back the words, even if they're true. Rebecca has pulled down her sunglasses, turning her face away from me. Matthew watches Mabel in the pool, his jaw clenched.

"On second thought, I think I will get something to eat," I say. "Maybe my own tummy is turning."

I return to the kitchen, determined to make something for breakfast, even though I don't feel like eating. Routine. That's what I must stick to, or else every emotion inside me will unravel.

I reach for the eggs and a frying pan. I crack the shells, watching as the yolks sizzle. Each movement is an attempt to swat away my memories of last night, my fears for the day ahead.

A loud knock on the door startles me, and the pan topples from my hands, clacking against the ceramic tile. I stare motionless, trying to imagine who might be standing on the front steps. All I can think of is Dylan and Spelling. They've returned to take me away, and this time, they'll make sure I can't leave.

Another knock. "Lillian? Are you in there?"

It's Cat's voice, a warm, concerned tone that melts the fear I was facing. I open the door wide and wrap my arms around her, almost knocking her down.

"My goodness, I came as soon as I heard. Are you okay?"

"I'm getting through," I say. "I can't believe people already know what happened."

"All I heard was a body was found at your apartment complex. Word started to spread it was your apartment." She pulls away, giving me a protective once-over. "Thank God you're okay."

"It's not good people are already starting to gossip. What are they saying about me?"

"Don't think about any of that." She leads me over to the sofa, the same place where I'd sat with Matthew last night, filling him in on how things were becoming progressively worse. "People know better than to talk shit about you in front of me."

"It looks bad," I tell her, feeling the urge to talk this over with someone.

I tell her everything. That I barely have any memories of the night.

That Carl and I had been on two dates, although he'd told me his name was Ben.

That I have no idea how he made it into my apartment.

My fears that the police suspect me.

"Turns out the dead man, Carl, is married with a baby on the way. So now it looks like some love triangle gone wrong. At least I'm afraid that's what the police will think," I say. "When the cops showed me a picture of him, I said I didn't know him."

"Why would you do that?"

"I was afraid of what they might think and I froze," I say. "You can't tell anyone I admitted to knowing him."

"You have my word." She squeezes my hand. "But it's probably only a matter of time until the police figure it out on their own."

"I know. And I'm afraid of what will happen to me when they do."

Finding a stranger's body would be frightening enough, but realizing I knew the victim sends a shiver up my spine. I have an uneasy feeling that what happened last night wasn't by mistake or coincidence. How else would Carl get inside the apartment? Matthew and I are the only people who have keys.

I stare outside, watching as Mabel jumps into the pool, a wide smile on her face. Just yesterday, we'd been surrounded by friends and family. Could one of them have gained access to the apartment? Slipped one of our keys from its ring? No one would do that unless they had a connection to Carl, and it appears I'm the only person who knew him.

Rebecca walks to the edge of the pool, holding a towel. After the party, she'd insisted we grab dinner and drinks, which is unusual. Is it possible she was trying to keep me away from the apartment? Distract me? Beside her, stands Jane, her arms folded across her chest. She left the house after the party to get pizza with Matthew. Could she have slipped away, gone to the apartment during that time? I realize not knowing what happened has made me paranoid of everyone.

"Did you sleep with him?" Cat asks, breaking my concentration.

"Who?"

"You know," she says, lowering her voice. "The dead guy."

"No! I've not slept with anyone since the divorce. Carl and I only went on two dates. I never even brought him back to the apartment."

"So, he's not the date from Friday night?"

"No!" I didn't feel a spark with Carl or anyone else. Not until the other night with Dylan, but that ship has already sailed and sunk. "I don't think that's going to go anywhere now."

"Why?"

I exhale. "He's the detective on the case."

Her lips part, and her jaw drops. "You're kidding me."

"No. And to make matters worse, I met Dylan on the same website where I met Carl."

"What's Carl's last name?"

"Gates."

Cat chews on her bottom lip. Thinking. "Don't know him. And I know everyone in town."

"This whole situation has left me rattled. I'm used to being in control."

"Give it time. It's early stages. There has to be another explanation. Anyone who knows you knows that you're not capable of murdering someone, and the police will see that, too."

I'm thankful for Cat and her friendship, for her kind words and faith, but she doesn't know all my secrets. Would she look at me the same way if she knew the worst thing I'd ever done? Would she still be willing to defend her closest friend? The guilt I feel from having to keep that secret is a poison, and I fear what's happening is my reckoning.

"You've got a good team of people around you. Me. Matthew. The police will get to the bottom of this. You're a victim, too. I can't imagine how traumatizing it was." Cat squeezes my hand. "Tell me what you need me to do."

"Right now, I need to find out exactly who Carl is and what the hell he was doing inside my apartment."

Cat doesn't argue with me. She knows I can be impatient and stubborn. What she doesn't know is the real reason why I'm so determined to solve this mystery. I can't risk the police digging into my personal life.

There are too many secrets of my own that need to remain hidden.

THIRTEEN

LILLIAN

Monday morning, I awake to the sounds of a lively household. I listen as Jane loads her luggage down the stairwell, as Mabel gathers her belongings for school, as Matthew panics to find his keys. I can't bring myself to join them, so I remain in bed.

Once the house is silent, I sit up, my thoughts circling around the burning question that needs to be answered: Who is Carl and how did he get inside my apartment?

Comparing the smiling face I met over coffee to the wide-eyed corpse on my bed makes me sick and angry. Why was he deceiving me? There must have been a reason he gave me a different name.

He's definitely not Ben. Unlike my date with Dylan, "Ben" and I shared information about our lives right away. He said he was a financial analyst, divorced, originally from Ohio. No kids.

Either way, it wouldn't matter. Ben/Carl is a liar. *Was* a liar. Now I need to find out how much he lied about.

Carl and I only went on two dates. Last month, we met for dinner at an Italian restaurant downtown. He walked in wearing a dark suit and a genuine smile. I'd dressed up, too, but

I didn't quite feel comfortable. Dating after a divorce is hard. It's like trying on an outfit you wore more than a decade ago, the fabric not quite fitting, and the styles having changed.

Still, his smile put me at ease. His overall demeanor suggested he was nervous, which I found surprising given his good looks. As one course rolled into the next, the conversation picked up. He asked me several questions about myself, wanted to know why my first marriage had ended. It didn't come off as prying, more like interest. I appreciated the fact he wanted the night to be focused on me. By the time the tiramisu arrived at our table, I was confident nothing romantic existed between us, but the evening had given me practice for, hopefully, more dates to come. If my next date was with someone I actually connected with, I wouldn't come off as a bumbling fool.

I assumed Carl felt the same way. He told me he enjoyed the evening, but when we exited the restaurant, he didn't initiate a kiss or offer to walk me home.

I was surprised a week later when he insisted we meet again, and this filled me with another concern: dating meant not only connecting with other people, but disconnecting. In an instant, I was transported back to my high school days, the suffocating feeling of knowing you've outgrown a person. I didn't want to hurt Carl's feelings—he'd done nothing to deserve that —but I didn't want to pursue anything with him, either.

I declined his invite, blaming childcare. But he asked to meet two more times after that. Finally, I agreed to grab a quick coffee. Maybe seeing each other again in person would make him understand what I had already realized: the two of us were not a romantic match.

He met me outside my apartment, claimed his office was within walking distance. We strolled two blocks to the nearest coffee shop. We talked for twenty minutes before I worked up the nerve to tell him I wasn't yet ready to start dating. He took the news with ease. He certainly didn't act like someone who had been pining after me. *Obsessed*, as Matthew said. When we left the coffee shop, each of us walking in different directions, I assumed I'd never see him again.

My emotions are working in overdrive now—paranoia, fear, worry. I realize there's another, lesser emotion brewing. Shame. Because even though I had no idea who Ben/Carl really was, I let him into my life readily. I told him things about myself. That I worked part-time at Harriet's dance studio. That I'm divorced. We talked about Mabel.

Our conversations remained surface level, never igniting the spark I remember having with Matthew, or for that matter, Dylan, but I still let him in. I offered glimpses into my life, however brief, and now I know that person I let in was a fraud. I was duped.

Which brings me back to my original question: Who is Carl?

He isn't hard to find online. We have just enough mutual connections in Anne Isle for his face to appear after a few minutes of searching. That handsome face. That smile, the gate-keeper of his lies. Because he's not a financial analyst. He's a mechanic. And he's definitely not divorced.

Looking at Carl's profile, it's quite obvious that he's married. His wife's name is Alaina, and she looks nothing like me. Petite, bleach-blonde hair, olive skin. In every picture, she's wearing name-brand clothes and flashy jewelry. Her most recent photo shows her cradling a baby bump. This child has lost his or her father before even being born, left to a beautiful mother, who will likely run herself ragged looking after them.

Why was Carl at that restaurant or that coffee shop when he had all this? A beautiful life. Why was he in my apartment? In my bed?

I look beyond the statuses and the pictures he's posted. I

notice he has several friends, most of them women. As I scan the pictures he's been tagged in, I see pictures of him at various bars and restaurants. Huddled around other guys, posing on a rooftop. In fact, there are very few pictures of his family at all, outside of the usual dates. Christmas. Easter. Maybe he wasn't avoiding his wife for just me. Maybe Carl was the type of person who has many interests outside the home.

The top of the page is filled with condolences, the comments updating every time I hit refresh. Friends sharing pictures and memories and #prayers. Noticeably absent, is any comment from Alaina. Although, on second thought, maybe her silence isn't that strange. She's just lost her husband. If something had happened to Matthew when we were married, even now, the last place I'd want to be is on Facebook. Of course, people are different; for some, it's the first place they'd visit.

I click on Alaina's profile. As I take in more details, I notice their lifestyle seems rather glamorous, especially for a mechanic. That's a judgmental reaction. Maybe Carl owns his business, maybe he built it from the ground up. I know very little about cars, but I remember the suit he was wearing on our first date. Tailored and expensive. If he'd told me then he was a mechanic, I probably would have needed convincing. I guess that's why he lied.

One of the reasons.

My search has produced more questions than answers. Of course, that's social media for you. A platform that lets people present the type of person they want to be, not necessarily who they really are.

What if Alaina knew about Carl's philandering ways and she's responsible for his death? If she followed him to my apartment, she must already know who I am. Or, at least think she knows. Revenge over an infidelity is a motive, but it still doesn't explain how either of them made it inside my apartment.

I stare at Alaina's beautiful face.

Who are you? I wonder. Who was your husband?

I need to know who Carl and Alaina really are, and I can't find out through a computer.

I have to see it with my own eyes.

FOURTEEN

LILLIAN

The house is the same one I saw on Facebook. Large, white brick, black storm shutters. The cars, a black Lexus parked next to a silver Suburban, are the same, too. So at least these parts of Carl's life aren't a lie.

I drive by the house, then loop around the block, passing it again. After my third pass, I decide to park a block away, on the off chance someone noticed my car circling the neighborhood. I step outside.

Above, the sky is a blinding shade of blue. The air is crisp, laced with the musk of leaves burning in the distance. My nose tickles. I walk casually toward the house, hands in my back pockets, acting as though I'm on a midday stroll.

I'm a few steps away from the mailbox when the front door opens, catching me off guard. I turn my head, hoping whoever walks outside won't notice me spying. No one is calling out to me, so after a few steady breaths, I look up. There's a blonde woman standing at an open door by the minivan, balancing a tray of food in her hands.

I don't know that I recognize her at first. It's hard to tell, between the distance and the bright sun and my attempts not to stare. I wonder if I'm at the right house after all. Then she turns, and I get a full view of the woman's pregnant belly. It's Alaina.

A curse word zips through the air, just as a platter of food smashes against the concrete. Without thinking, I walk over to her, her feet surrounded by globs of banana pudding and crumbled wafers.

She curses again.

"Can I help?" The question exits my mouth faster than I can think to stop it.

Alaina looks at me now, dead-on. She's not wearing the makeup I saw in all her pictures online. Her hair is pulled away from her face, her clothes wrinkled and shins covered in splattered dessert. But it's definitely her.

Now, I wonder if she'll recognize me. That's one of the reasons I came here, even if I'm stunned to be this close to her. If she reacts, I'll know she's involved with what happened at the apartment.

She curses a third time, exhales. "No, no. Thanks for offering."

She turns, walking over to the side of the house and grabbing the watering hose. She sprays water on the concrete, until all the clumps of food have washed away into the grass. I jump back, careful not to get any sludge on my shoes.

Alaina doesn't know who I am. Even if she knew about Carl's adultery, she couldn't very well follow him to my apartment and kill him there without at least knowing what I look like. I'm walking away, smiling at this small victory, when she calls out.

"Hey! If you're still offering, you could help me with the rest."

I stop, unsure at first if she's talking to me. When I turn, she's waving me back toward the house.

"Come on. It's just a couple more trays. Might save me from making another mess."

Once near the van, I see the entire middle row is stacked high with aluminum trays.

"They're from the church," she says, as though reading my mind.

"Having some kind of party?" I hate myself for even asking, especially when I know the answer, but I'm trying to gauge her reaction.

She lets out a small, sad sound. "No. The opposite, actually. There's been a death in the family."

"I'm so sorry."

I've never been a good actress, an even worse liar. As the words leave my lips, I worry they'll sound staged, fake. It's not until I've spoken them that I realize I'm being sincere.

I'm sorry for what this woman is going through.

I'm sorry for her grief.

I didn't cause it—have no idea who did—but I'm saddened, nonetheless.

She smiles tightly, the strain of a person trying to fight off tears. "Help me?"

I don't have a choice. This woman is asking for help, struggling through all of this alone. The least I can do is literally lighten her load. But once I step inside the house, the smell of pine and bleach tickling my nose in a different way, I regret it. What am I doing? I merely wanted to get a glimpse of the real Carl's life. Now I'm walking inside his home. Having a conversation with his wife.

"Right in here is fine," she says, dropping the trays on a center island in the kitchen. The cabinets are chocolate brown with gleaming stone countertops. It's a beautiful space. And I wonder, again, if a mechanic's salary could afford this luxury.

"Thanks for the help." She holds out a hand. "I'm Alaina."

"Not a problem." I wonder whether I should give her a fake

name, take a page from her husband's book, but decide to get on my way instead.

"You live around here?"

"Tourist." I take another step toward the door. "Thought I'd take a walk outside. Enjoy the weather."

"Yeah, it's beautiful out there today. I have tons of family visiting, but I ran them out of the house. They need a little sunshine in their lives. At least I can give them a warm meal when they get back. Minus the banana pudding."

I laugh softly.

For whatever reason, maybe it's the desperation grief instills, she wants to talk, and it appears I'm the only one around.

"Who died?" I ask.

"My husband."

I grab my chest, reacting how I imagine I might if someone told me the same shocking news about Matthew. Again, I'm not faking. "That's awful. I'm so sorry."

"It's still not really hit me, you know? I keep waiting for him to come home from work." Her voice catches, and she raises a hand to cover her mouth.

I keep pushing. "What happened?"

"The police aren't sure. All I know is they found his body. They brought me downtown to identify him."

It's unclear where everything is located in the station. Interrogation rooms, jail cells, morgue. But I can't help wondering if at the same time I was being questioned by detectives in a dingy interrogation room, Alaina was only a few walls over identifying her husband's remains.

"How are you holding up?"

She shrugs. "I don't know. I'm obviously shocked, sad." She pauses, rubs her hand over her stomach. "I didn't expect to be this angry."

"Because you don't know what happened?"

"No. I'm angry at him. My husband wasn't an easy one to figure out. He did a lot of things that made me scratch my head, and after a while I just started looking the other way. But now where's that leave me? A widow. Raising a baby alone. Mourning a man I'm not sure I even knew."

It's like the static in the air has slowed, time itself coming to a halt. The world around us continues, but Alaina and I are in this kitchen, separate from that. Uncertainty imprisons us both in different ways.

She looks at me, wiping a tear from her eyes. "I'm sorry. I don't even know you. Here you are, hoping for a nice walk. Now you're stuck in some crazy lady's kitchen."

"It's fine, really. I wanted to help."

Again, I'm being genuine, so genuine that I'm irritated when my phone begins to vibrate, interrupting the moment. The name on the screen reads Matthew. I silence the call.

"The family," I say. "How are they handling it?"

"It'll take time. The rest of their lives." She pauses. "If anything, maybe this will teach us to make better choices."

"What do you mean?"

"Nothing. I shouldn't have said that. My husband wasn't always the most cautious, that's all. But that doesn't matter. He still didn't deserve..." Her words fall away and she covers her mouth with the back of her hand. "I'll get through this. One day at a time."

"I'm sure you will," I say, looking back toward the open door.

"Thanks again for your help." She smiles through tears. "Sometimes I think it's easier to talk to strangers than to those closest to you."

"I know exactly what you mean," I say, taking one more look around the house before walking outside.

I'm still unclear about who the real Carl was—even his wife

doesn't seem to know. At least she doesn't recognize me, which gives me hope she had nothing to do with Carl's death.

I wish I could provide Alaina answers to some of her questions, but I'm still searching, too. I need to solve the mysteries surrounding the death—and life—of Carl Gates.

FIFTEEN

MATTHEW

.

Every morning, I push through the clear glass doors at Voyage headquarters, and my mind revisits where the company started.

Ted and I became roommates after I moved to Anne Isle for college. We first bonded over our love of the water. Growing up in Anne Isle, Ted was learning to sail around the same time most kids were learning to ride a bike. Back in Florida, my experience came mostly from working fishing boats at the docks. When we first started sailing together, we'd pull updates from various apps and websites about alternate routes and weather conditions. Ted and I wanted to streamline that information, and our respective degrees in business management and software development assisted us along the way.

By the time we graduated, on and off discussions about starting our own business had shifted into serious discussions. We cleared out space in Ted's parents' basement, calling it our temporary workspace. Years later, we were still working out of the basement, still hunting investors, still struggling to place Voyage in the right hands. The walls were yellowed with mildew. Our desks were pieces of plywood atop old sawhorses.

Ted's mom's treadmill stood in the corner of the room, collecting dust.

On more than one late night, I worried we'd never make it out of that place. Never get our business off the ground. We kept working, brainstorming new ways to improve the app. In our later models, we even integrated the use of social media, allowing other boaters to share their favorite fishing spots and local marinas. All those years of hard work paid off when the software finally sold.

Now we have an entire building, not just a room. There are gleaming floors and glass walls. Our executive assistant, Mandy, sits behind a large oak desk Ted had specially made in Columbia. I give her a quick wave before climbing the steel staircase leading to the second floor. My office is on the left, Ted's on the right. I cut the corner, marching into Ted's office and shutting the door behind me. He's already at his desk, holding a phone to his ear. I wait for him to end the conversation.

"You're never going to believe who wants to have lunch with us tomorrow," Ted says.

I don't want to know because I won't be able to go.

"We need to talk."

"I don't like the look on your face."

"Something happened this weekend. Something bad."

Ted stands, comes around to my side of the desk, and leans back. He crosses his arms over his chest, waiting.

I tell him about what happened Saturday after the party, about meeting Lillian at the apartment before she left for the police station.

When I'm all out of words, Ted speaks.

"I'd heard a man had been murdered, but I had no idea you were wrapped up in it."

"We're not. Neither of us did anything."

"So, neither of you know how this guy ended up inside your apartment?"

"I don't know him at all. Lillian says he's an acquaintance, at best. She has no clue why he was there, let alone who killed him."

Ted walks over to the large glass window looking over the bay. The view always reminds me of when Ted and I first started sailing together because it was usually at this spot. Everything, for us, has come full circle.

"Finding a dead man inside your apartment is the last thing I expected you to tell me."

"I know." I run my fingers through my hair. "I'm still trying to wrap my head around what happened. I may need to be out of the office over the next couple of days so I can meet with a lawyer."

"*You're* meeting with a lawyer?"

"Yes."

He walks closer, settling into the leather chair beside his desk. "I don't know why you're getting entangled with this at all."

"Because... because it's Lillian. And a man was murdered inside our apartment."

"When's the last time you stayed there?"

"A week ago," I say. "I've been spending my nights away from the house with Rebecca."

"Okay, so you didn't know the victim. Lillian did. You weren't there when it happened. She was." He frowns, raising his hands. "Sounds to me like you're not involved."

"This could be bad. She needs my help."

"She's not your wife anymore, Matthew. Lillian's a strong woman. She can take care of herself."

"She's Mabel's mother," I counter. "And she's still my friend. If something bad happens to her, it will affect me and our daughter and all the other aspects of our life."

The comment lingers as Ted ponders the possible implications. Finally, he stands, returning to the far side of his desk. "Fine. Do whatever you need to do."

"I'm not asking for your permission. I'm simply telling you why I might not be available."

"Understood."

"What's with the tone?"

His posture straightens. "You're not going to like what I have to say."

"Try me."

"You're too close to this. Too close to Lillian. The two of you have made your breakup as amicable as possible, and I admire that. For Mabel's sake. But you decided to get divorced for a reason. So you could live separate lives. That's not the case if, every time Lillian has a problem, she's running back to you."

"She's not running back to me. I want to help her."

"That's part of the problem. You're too much of a nice guy. I worry she's taking advantage of that." He pauses. "She has before."

My skin flushes. Ted thinks he knows the truth about what ended our marriage, but he doesn't know the full story. I can't expect him to understand. He has never made such a suggestion about Lillian before. Why is he doing it now?

"We're still a team. We have to be. And like I said, anything that happens to her could bring me down, too."

"Only if you let it." He pauses, tries to smile. "Look, I know I'm not exactly the best person to be doling out relationship advice, but, as your friend, I think this is one battle you need to let Lillian fight on her own. Focus on yourself and your future."

"My future?" I scoff as his point becomes clear. "You're only saying that because of the offer."

In the chaos of the past two days, I'd almost forgotten about our potential business deal. Not that Ted ever goes long without mentioning it. He even brought it up at Mabel's party.

Last month, our board decided they wanted to expand Voyage, and they believe the best way to do that is to move headquarters to Florida. There are more opportunities there that would give the business and brand a fresh start. Although I'm happy with the company's growth, Ted is always searching for bigger and better. His ultimate goal is to have Voyage become the navigational product of choice for international shipping companies, and moving away from Anne Isle would give us exposure.

But it would also mean disrupting my co-parenting relationship with Lillian, which is why I was hesitant to mention the idea even before this disaster at the apartment. What would be best for the company would be the worst option for my family, and even though Lillian and I are no longer married, I haven't settled on a decision.

"I'm not using this tragedy as an excuse to abandon Lillian and move the company to Florida."

"I'm trying to look out for you."

I take another look around the room, trying to clear my mind. All of this could have been taken away two years ago if it weren't for Lillian. She stood by me when other people wouldn't have.

Shouldn't have.

"Lillian did not kill that man inside our apartment. I trust her."

"She knows you do," he says. "And she could very well be using that trust to manipulate you."

I stare at the floor, shaking my head. There's no convincing him. "Look, you know people around here better than I do. I need a criminal attorney."

"Barry Walters," he says without hesitation. "That's who I'd recommend."

Barry is a friend, and it feels strange bringing him into this, but I need someone I can trust. Someone who will understand

Lillian and I are blameless, no matter how damaging the case might appear.

"Thanks." I head for the door.

"Aren't you curious who I'm meeting for lunch?"

"Who?"

"Elliot Lyon. He wants to invest a hundred thousand dollars in the newest software," he says. "I guess I'll handle the conversation myself. Tell him you had a family emergency."

"Good," I say. "Try not to mess it up."

As I walk down the stairs, out of our posh office, back onto the streets, I fear I'm the one who is about to wreck everything.

SIXTEEN

LILLIAN

After leaving Alaina's house, I get in the car and drive straight to The Studio. On weekdays, I work there from noon until four, just in time to pick up Mabel at school. As much as I'd like to continue diving into Carl's life, I have work. Some routine might be good for me.

Harriet hired me to work at her dance studio around the time my divorce was finalized. Before that, I worked as a guidance counselor at the local high school. It wasn't a lot of money, but it was fulfilling work. For years, when Ted and Matthew were broke, still trying to get their business off the ground, I was the one paying the bills. Most people assume I left my career because Voyage made it big, but that's not why.

I quit because the fertility drugs I was taking were making me sick. We'd been trying to conceive naturally for years with no success. When the company sold, we finally had enough money to afford IVF. Before then, we'd been scraping by, the idea of dropping twenty grand on fertility treatments a pipe dream. No one knew about our struggles, not even Cat.

It was a strange time in my life, having so much to celebrate and mourn all at once. Ted and Matthew had worked hard over the years, had made so many sacrifices, and were finally being rewarded. But nothing outweighed the deep, personal loss I was coping with behind the scenes. It was another several months of sickness and nausea and hopelessness before we finally conceived Mabel. Once she was born, I wanted to savor every minute with her, and because Voyage was thriving, I could.

Now that she's in school, I don't want to return to counseling. I'd rather busy myself with school functions and being an involved parent, but I also resent the stereotype that I'm living off my ex-husband's dime. That's why I continue working at The Studio, to fill the hours and to silence the gossip.

As I'm walking inside, two men are on their way out. I'm already in the waiting room before I recognize who they are. It's Detective Spelling and Dylan, walking right past me and entering a four-door sedan.

I look back at the front desk. Harriet is there. When she sees me, her eyes drop.

"Good morning," I say, my voice artificially optimistic.

"Lillian! You're a little early." Her smile is too tight, and her voice almost sounds strangled. "I've been swamped since Mabel's party. I meant to call."

I look around the room. There's only one other person standing by the front window. She's tapping on her phone, likely sending a text. I wait for the woman to enter the locker rooms before approaching Harriet.

"Those detectives... were they here to talk to you?"

It's obvious Harriet is searching for ways to avoid looking at me, busying her hands with miscellaneous paperwork on the desk.

"Yes. They told me about what happened over the weekend. That must have been terrifying for you!"

"It was." I pause. "What did they say?"

"They were just asking questions. About you."

"I'm sure they're only trying to gather as much information

as possible," I say. "Anyway, I'm here now. Head out for lunch. I'll have the books sorted by the time you get back."

Harriet stands still and, finally, looks at me. Her eyes are watery, her cheeks flushed.

"It sounds like a pretty serious situation. I'm sure you could use some time to deal with the aftermath."

"I might need time off later in the week, but I'm perfectly capable of working today." I need to work so I can stop obsessing over Carl and Alaina.

Harriet's smile is strained. "It's just... not necessarily the best look for The Studio, having you here. Or David's campaign. It's a small town and word travels quickly. I'd already heard there had been a man murdered this weekend, I just didn't know you were involved."

"I'm not! I mean, I had nothing to do with it."

"I'm sure, I'm sure. I know you could never be responsible for something so horrible," she says. "But it happened at your apartment. People will have lots of questions, and I don't know if you need to be behind the front desk until you have a few more answers. David's re-election is right around the corner. I have to be careful with the way things... look."

It's taken me this long to put together that one of my closest friends is firing me. My mouth hangs open, but words refuse to come. I'm not sure what I can say to defend myself. What proof I can offer that I had nothing to do with Carl's death.

"Harriet, please. You have to unders—"

I stop talking when the door opens and a pair of women enter the waiting area.

"Welcome to The Studio," Harriet chimes, her smile now genuine. She looks back at me, lowering her voice. "I'm really sorry for what you're going through, Lillian. Make sure to give me a call once everything is figured out."

I pull my sunglasses over my eyes, concealing my tears, and

return the way I came. This is tearing through my life, leaving me hurt and sad and angry. Harriet's words ring inside my head.

I know you could never be responsible for something so horrible.

If she only knew the truth. I didn't kill Carl, but I have made horrible mistakes. No one would look at me the same if they knew the truth about my past.

In my back pocket, my phone begins ringing, a welcome distraction. It's Cat.

"Just checking in," she says. Sometimes I think her flair for drama has superhuman elements. "How are you?"

"Where are you?" I ask, yanking open my car door.

"Uh... my house—"

"I'll be there in ten minutes."

Right now, I need to revisit the mystery of Carl Gates, and I need the only friend I have left to help me do it.

SEVENTEEN

LILLIAN

Eleventh Street Mechanics is abandoned. At least that's how it looks.

None of the employees are here. I suspect some are back at Alaina's house, enjoying food from the church. Others might be mourning. A few are probably just happy to have the day off from work.

"What exactly are we doing?" asks Cat, her perfectly manicured nails tapping against her seat belt.

"I told you, I need to figure out who Carl really is."

After I left The Studio, I drove to Cat's house to cool off. She poured me a drink while I filled her in on my conversation with Harriet. She offered to make lunch, but I was in no mood to eat. Instead, I asked Cat to ride with me on a little spying expedition. Before her divorce, she'd take me with her as she drove around town snooping on Ted and his mistresses. This time, the stakes are much higher.

"So, why are we here?"

She looks to her left at the cars in various stages of repair. There's a small building connected to one of the mechanical workstations. My eyes land on the crooked sign, which reads CLOSED in bright red letters.

"This is where Carl works," I say, unbuckling. "I'm going to look around and see what I can find."

She swings her hand in my direction, trying to hold me in place. "Are you crazy? You can't go in there alone."

"Are you offering to come with me?"

"And go down for trespassing? I'm trying to tell you we need to get out of here."

I look across the street, wondering if this place has been searched the way the apartment was. It doesn't seem likely. Police might have come here asking questions, but maybe they haven't really looked for anything. Not yet.

Carl is a victim in this scenario, not a suspect.

But to me, something about him—about our limited interactions together—is very suspicious. I need to know who he really is, why he was really inside my apartment.

"I want you to stay in the car. Honk the horn if anyone shows up."

She grabs my arm, her grip tight. "This is crazy, Lillian. You need to let the police handle this."

"The police suspect me. Harriet fired me because they were sniffing around The Studio."

"Harriet fired you because she cares too much about what people think," she says, rolling her eyes. "That doesn't mean you can start investigating on your own. Besides, how do you even know he works here? I thought you said he was a businessman."

"That's what he told me. He also said his name was Ben. I found this place when I looked him up on Facebook using his real name," I say. I don't tell her about my visit with Alaina this morning. If she thinks checking out his auto shop is risky, she'll think I'm nuts for hunting down his wife. "He lied to me and I need to find out why."

"Are you sure about this? I mean, someone murdered this

guy. You don't know what kinds of people he dealt with. Who might be watching us this very moment."

"Which is why I need you to honk the horn if you see anything weird."

I get out of the car before she can stop me. The door isn't even shut before she starts patting the horn, startling a flock of birds in a nearby tree. I smack her arm.

"Will you stop?"

"This is stupid, Lillian. Just listen to me."

"You said you wanted to help. If I don't find anything, I'll leave."

I don't even know what I've come here for. But I doubt Carl walked into my life by chance.

She leans back in her seat, defeated. "Ten minutes. I'm taking off if you aren't back by then."

"Thank you."

I wander around the yard.

Behind the locked building are a few more cars, their rusty paint jobs signaling disuse. In one corner of the lot, nestled along the back gate, is a grungy-looking single wide trailer. I walk over to it, looking around. There aren't any signs outside, but it doesn't look like someone's home. This place must be associated with the property.

I walk to the front door, but find that the screen is locked. When I look closer, I see the ragged mesh has frayed, leaving a spot just large enough for me to fit my hand inside. I do, tilting my body lower, so that my hand can reach the lock. I hear a click, and the rickety screen creaks open. When I try the handle to the actual door, it swings back with ease.

I ready myself, a sudden wave of fear taking over and keeping me in place. Again, what have I come here to find? Maybe being here will only cause more trouble in the long run, but I can't return to my house with all the quiet and unanswered questions.

I step inside.

The place is filled with the warring scents of cigarette smoke and Pine-Sol. There's a loveseat against the far wall, a small window above it. To my left, I see an open door leading into the bathroom. Between those two landmarks is a small desk and computer. This must be the office space for Eleventh Street Mechanics, a far cry from Voyage headquarters. On the wall hangs a large calendar with various dates and indecipherable reminders. On the table are stacked leather-bound notebooks, and when I flip through them, I find notes about payments and insurance policies.

Suddenly, in my mind, Carl is alive, sitting here at this desk, thumbing his way through the books, pausing to check his computer and scroll dating sites. I look around the rest of the space, but find little. Some work jackets hanging from a rack. A small refrigerator and microwave, the door crusty with splattered food. I return to the desk and start rummaging through drawers.

When I open the second drawer, my body springs back. Inside is a handgun. Perhaps it's just here for the business. After all, if Carl planned on hurting me, he would have brought it with him to my apartment. I'm afraid to touch it, but I notice there is a stack of folders beneath. Using the edge of my sweater, I lift the gun by its handle, laying it flat on the desk, the chamber pointing away from me.

I dig the folders out, and start flipping through the pages. I'm not sure what I'm expecting, but what I find is photos of me. Pictures of me outside Mabel's school, at The Studio. The apartment. As I examine each image, my stomach sinks further. My hands begin to shake, forcing me to grip the photographs tighter.

Carl was following me. For weeks, by the looks of the photos, long before we went on our first date. I can tell because in one of the photos I'm wearing an orange sundress and heels.

That's the outfit I wore to the school fundraiser more than a month ago. He's been watching me this entire time. My body shivers, the thought of being watched, even in this moment, impossible to shake.

Beneath the photos are handwritten notes. There are a few notes about Matthew, where he works. His new girlfriend. But most of the notes are about me. Where I live and work, how I busy myself in the afternoons and evenings. He's written about what was said on our brief dates together. I see he has written the name Mabel, and my heart sinks. She shouldn't be anywhere near this. Carl clearly made it a mission to uncover as much about my life as possible.

The question is, why?

I close the folder, prepared to leave it in the desk where I found it, when something catches my attention, a detail I overlooked before. Written on the front of the folder is a name.

Richard Walsh.

My heart skips a beat. I sit on the rickety desk chair, my legs no longer capable of holding my weight. Carl has a connection to Richard. This can't be happening.

I have no idea how Carl Gates ended up dead inside my apartment.

But, Richard Walsh...

I know exactly what happened to him.

EIGHTEEN

LILLIAN

July—Two Years Ago

It started with a fight.

Maybe that's not true.

It started with a party.

When Voyage sold, Ted and Cat wasted no time celebrating their newfound success. They moved to the Seaside Cliffs neighborhood right away. *You have to move here,* Cat would tell me. *We can be neighbors!*

Cat didn't have trouble infiltrating the Anne Isle cliques. She has an aura attracting people to her. If it weren't for Cat, I never would have befriended Harriet or any of the other women in the neighborhood. I've always been overlooked. Only when people learned that I was married to the other half of Voyage did they care who I was.

Part of me liked the idea of living alongside my best friend and her fancy neighbors, but Matthew and I were on the same page about not blowing our windfall. When you grow up lower-middle class, as we both did, you find yourself constantly wondering when your luck will run out, and what we wanted more than anything, even more than a beautiful house, was a baby.

We spent most of his earnings paying off our student loans and outstanding business debt. I continued not getting pregnant. We poured even more money into fertility treatments, and after years of struggling to conceive, by the time Mabel finally came along, I didn't care where we lived or what material possessions we had; cradling her was like holding the entire world in my arms.

We stayed in a modest home for years before we decided to build a newer place in the Seaside Cliffs subdivision. There was one available lot at the edge of the neighborhood, nestled close to the cliff walks that gave the area its name. The price for the land alone was astronomical, but after all our years of saving, it was worth every penny. The view was spectacular, the rolling waves carrying on into eternity.

The building process took two years, and in many ways, became my full-time job aside from Mabel. She was nearly four by the time the house was finished, Voyage had an office downtown, and Cat and Ted had already divorced. There had been so much change in a relatively short amount of time.

We'd been in the Seaside Cliffs house for over six months, and had yet to throw a proper housewarming. The time felt right to celebrate, not only with each other, but with our old friends and new neighbors. For a brief, shining moment, everything in the world was right. Matthew and I were happy, maybe the happiest we'd ever been; we were even talking of trying for a second child.

"Don't we deserve this?" Matthew said to me. "We've worked hard to get where we are. It's time to enjoy ourselves."

The night of the party, I remember feeling anxious, like too much time alone with a toddler had hindered my ability to socialize. Maybe I wasn't wrong. Cat and Harriet were used to networking, but I was always most comfortable at home with

Mabel and Matthew. And even though I wanted to throw the party, I was nervous. About drinking, that my dress pinched in all the wrong areas. Jane had agreed to fly in and take Mabel to a hotel for the night; it would be my first night away from her, and it made me uneasy.

"It's going to be fine," Matthew comforted me. "Trust me, when the new baby comes along, we'll be dreaming of nights like this."

I relented, pushing my worries aside.

Once the party started, I fell into rhythm with the night. The caterer was passing around appetizers, our favorite songs rang throughout the halls, and every guest complimented the beauty of the house. After years living our lives on the periphery of Seaside Cliffs, Matthew and I had finally arrived at the epicenter.

Our guests were enjoying themselves, too. An hour in, and people's noses were already turning red, their bodies swaying with the music. Their happiness was contagious, and I could feel the energy with each fizzy sip of champagne, in every thump of the bass.

"We've waited too long for this," Cat said, cozying up beside me at the buffet table. "Finally, we're neighbors! Think of how much fun we'll have. We can have a party every week!"

"We might be getting too old for that."

"Speak for yourself," she said, bumping me with her hip. "Besides, you owe me for agreeing to play nice with *him*."

She pointed across the room, where Ted stood beside Matthew.

"They're business partners," I said. "It's not like we couldn't invite him."

"Could we have one night where the drama isn't about you and Ted?" Harriet said, joining us at the table.

"I said I was playing nice," Cat slurred.

"Speaking of drama," Harriet said, her head nodding across the room. "I can't believe they had the nerve to show up."

Harriet was staring at the Walshes. They were across the room, talking to some of the men from Voyage. Blaire was wearing an off-white cocktail dress, her hair pulled into a chignon. Richard was undeniably handsome in a black suit, an expensive watch on his wrist.

"We invited the entire neighborhood," I said. "Why wouldn't they come?"

"Didn't you hear what happened?" Cat asked.

I shook my head. My day had been devoted to getting ready for the party. My entire week, really. Gossip was never important to me, but especially then.

"Remember the new car they got last month?"

I nodded. Everyone in the neighborhood had seen Richard whizzing through the streets in his new convertible.

"It was repossessed. Apparently, it happened at the Southeast Shopping Center. Dozens of people saw. Rumor is there's even a video going around."

"That's awful."

I'd never had something like that happen, but Matthew and I had our share of money troubles before Voyage sold. I can remember the horrible feeling of having my debit card denied for insufficient funds, of having to live off sandwiches until the next payday. Having something like that happen so publicly, especially in a community like this, would have left me bedridden with embarrassment.

"I'm happy they came," I said. "They shouldn't be shunned over a misunderstanding."

"I say it serves her right," Harriet says. "Blaire has always acted like she's too good for the people around here."

"I heard Blaire was behind on making the payments," Cat said. "Richard is the one who works, and leaves her to pay the bills."

"Poor Richard," Harriet said. "It's a shame he has to suffer for his wife's mistake."

Cat nudged Harriet. "Maybe David can ask some questions downtown. Give us the scoop."

"He would never abuse his power like that," Harriet said, pushing Cat toward the kitchen. "But speaking of David, we brought a guy who works at the courthouse who is just your type."

The two scurried away. Part of me hoped whoever Harriet had selected for Cat would stick. I was ready for my best friend to find happiness again, and in the months that followed her divorce from Ted, I could tell she was only feigning content- ment. It was obvious from the way she'd brag about every date and sexual escapade. The more Cat told me about a man, the more convinced I was it was only a fling. It was when she played coy that I was convinced something more was there.

As the night carried on, I had conversed with several people from the neighborhood, some of whom I'd never spoken to before. I began to feel like I wasn't just Cat's friend or Matthew's wife—I was making my own mark in the community, and our housewarming party symbolized that.

Across the room, I spotted Matthew. I was preparing to join him when I heard someone say, "You have a beautiful home."

When I turned, Blaire Walsh was standing there. Richard stood behind her, sipping his drink. "Thank you for inviting us."

I tried not to think about the gossip stirring about her this very minute. "I'm happy you both could make it."

Blaire smiled and walked away, and I went over to the bar. I felt a warmth at my back, and turned to see Richard had followed me.

"Care to pour me another drink?"

"Sure," I said, grabbing the neck of the bottle.

"It is a beautiful home," he said, taking another look around. "Maybe I should get into apps."

"We've all seen your house, Richard. It's beautiful too."

"And this dress." He placed his hand on my torso, slid it down to my hips. "It really suits you. You should dress like this more often."

I stepped back, the feel of another man's hands on my body a violation. I held out his glass, even though it was clear he was already very drunk.

He stepped closer, his breath hot on my ear. "You know where I live, if you ever find yourself bored inside this big house."

I couldn't believe how brazen he was being, coming on to me inside my own home. Richard had the reputation of being a flirt, but his wife had been standing beside us only a moment ago.

"I think I have plenty of space right here."

"Everything okay?" It was Matthew. He'd wandered away from his friends, had joined us at the table. His eyes were on Richard's hand, which was still hovering dangerously close to my body.

"I'm talking to Lillian," Richard said, taking a step back. "Thanking her for being such a generous host."

Matthew could likely see the look on my face. He could tell I was uncomfortable.

"Are you okay?" This time, he directed the question to me.

"I'm fine," I said.

"I told you we were only talking." Richard's voice was loud, commanding the attention of the room. Heads started to turn, even the music became quieter.

Blaire appeared at his side. She gently pulled on his arm. "Richard, maybe we should—"

He ripped his arm away. Another step closer, and he was inches away from Matthew's face. "You can tell me if there's a problem."

I could feel myself shrinking. Matthew and I weren't used

to being the center of attention, at the center of controversy. We weren't used to big personalities like Richard. I felt for Matthew, fearful of how he would react.

"My wife said everything is fine," he said, his back straight. "That's all that matters to me."

Richard scoffed. Blaire tried touching his arm again, but he shrugged her away. He gave a mischievous smile then he stormed off. I'm not sure what direction he went; the party seemed to swallow him whole.

"What was that about?"

It was Cat and Harriet. They were standing behind me.

"I'm sorry about Richard." Blaire stepped forward. "He's had too much to drink, and it's been a difficult week. We should probably head home."

"Nonsense." Cat slid past me, wrapping her arms around Blaire. "It's a party. You need to enjoy yourself. He'll calm down."

Cat and Blaire walked arm in arm to the backyard. Harriet followed them, calling out, "What happened to the music?"

I felt a rush of gratitude for my friends and their ability to smooth things over, but my elation was quickly replaced with embarrassment. The champagne was starting to go to my head, melting my thoughts and burning my cheeks. The voices in the room were getting louder, too.

"I need some air," I whispered to Matthew, cutting a trail for the front door.

He followed me.

NINETEEN

LILLIAN

Now

My heart beats out of my chest as I rush out of the office, folder in hand. Hiding evidence is risky, but leaving it for the police to find would be more dangerous for me. I'm lucky they hadn't already searched Carl's office. These photos prove there is a deeper connection between Carl and me, initiate a trail leading back to my darkest secret.

I look at the name on the folder. Richard Walsh.

Before returning to the car, I slide the folder into the back of my jeans, covering it with my shirt. I sit in the driver's seat.

"So?" Cat asks, her feet propped up onto the dash.

"There wasn't much in there. Although it's clear Ben, or Carl, was lying to me." I start the engine, pulling onto the street. "And he had a gun."

"That's unsettling." Cat sits up straighter, fastening her seat belt. "Anything else?"

"Nothing useful." I'm careful to avoid eye contact. I can't tell anyone what I found in there. Not even Cat. The only person who needs to know is Matthew.

"Do you think you could stop playing detective now? I don't want you making this situation harder on yourself."

"Yeah, you're right."

I suddenly wish she was out of the car. It's too hard trying to act like I'm unfazed when I'm anything but.

"Besides, from what we know about this guy so far, he sounds like a low-life," she continues. "Crappy business. Serial dater. Cheating on his wife. He probably had a few people who wanted him dead."

"Cat!"

"I'm just saying! It should make you feel better. The real mystery is how he ended up in your apartment. Other than that, there's nothing connecting you to the guy."

The folder is stiff against my back, burning a hole into my conscience.

I wish Cat was right.

I storm into the house.

"Matthew?" The door slams behind me as I race into the kitchen. "Matthew, we need to talk."

He comes around the corner, a strange look on his face. "Lillian, we have guests."

Confused, I look behind him, and that's when I see Dylan and Detective Spelling sitting on the sofa. My hurry to tell Matthew about what I found at Carl's workspace retreats. I cling tighter to my purse, my pulse quickening at the thought of the stolen folder now inside.

"Detectives?" It sounds like I'm asking a question. I knew I'd be seeing them again, but I didn't expect it to be this soon. And I didn't think it would be here, in my home.

"We've gathered some more information we wanted to run by you," Spelling says, standing as I enter the room.

"Where's Mabel?" I ask Matthew.

"Rebecca took her outside for a swim."

"Rebecca?" Spelling asks. "Would this be the same Rebecca who was out with you on Saturday night?"

"That's right." Matthew gives me a worried look.

"One of us will need to get a statement from her before we leave." He looks at Dylan, then back at us. "Remind me, what is your connection to her again?"

"She's my girlfriend," Matthew says.

"That's funny," Spelling says. "When you told us you were out with a friend, you didn't mention she's the current girlfriend of your ex-husband."

"Why would I mention it?"

"It's just odd, is all. I have two ex-wives, and I can tell you they aren't getting together unless it's to bash me."

I have no interest in Detective Spelling and his love life, or his low assessment of mine. I only want to answer their questions so the two of them leave my house.

Mabel's house.

"Have you figured out how Carl Gates was able to get inside our apartment?"

"We don't know that yet," Dylan says. "But we have made some progress."

"Well, what is it?"

"Have you ever heard of the dating website Cupid's Corner?"

My stomach drops. Instinctively, my eyes fall on Dylan, but he's looking away. He already knows the answer to that question. It's the same website where I met him.

"Yes."

"After we informed Carl's wife of his death, she gave us access to his phone and computer records. Turns out, Mr. Gates connected with you on that website. Does any of this ring a bell?"

My heart starts thumping harder against my chest. Should I

ask to see another picture? Pretend I only now recognize him? Or would they be able to read right through me?

"I didn't realize it when I was at the station, but when I woke up this morning, once the shock had passed, I kept thinking the photograph looked familiar. I was going to tell you about it, I swear."

"So, you did know the victim?" Spelling asks.

"When I met him, he gave me a different name. He called himself Ben."

"You said you didn't recognize him—"

"I didn't! I was in shock and trying to get out of there as fast as possible."

"I'm talking about back at the station, when we showed you the picture of Carl."

"I thought maybe I was confused. Like I said, I didn't know him by the name Carl, and I couldn't figure out why he would give me a different name."

"How would you describe your interactions with Mr. Gates?"

"We went on two dates. The last one was over two weeks ago. That's it. I still have no idea how he ended up at the apartment."

"Did you have a sexual relationship with Carl?"

"No!"

"Do you meet a lot of men online?"

I glare at Dylan, feeling baited. So, that's the route we're taking. Tearing apart my sexual history?

"As I've already told you, I have a dating profile, something completely typical for a divorced woman in her thirties. And, yes, I met Carl on the site, but he gave me a different name. That's why I didn't make the connection."

"So, just to make sure, even though you went on at least two dates with the victim, he's never been inside your apartment?"

"Only two dates. And no, he's never been inside."

"I can vouch for that," Matthew says. "Neither of us bring dates into the apartment. It's part of our arrangement."

When he says this, Dylan's eyes light up. It's something small, but it will be enough for the police to start forming an opinion about me. They've caught me in at least two lies. I feel my body folding into itself.

Spelling looks back at his notes. "Thing is, when we showed a picture of the victim to your neighbor, Mrs. Haynes, she said she'd seen him before. With you."

"On our second date, he picked me up outside the apartment. But he never went in."

"You think it's likely she'd remember his face from such a brief interaction?"

"You'd have to know Mrs. Haynes. She's aware of everyone's business." I make a point of looking at Dylan. "And she never forgets a face."

"Saturday was your birthday, right?"

"Yes. Mine and my daughter's."

"You share the same birthday. That's sweet. Why weren't you with her on Saturday night?"

"I was during the day. I stayed at the apartment that night so my mother-in-law could visit with her."

"So, here's what I'm thinking. It's your birthday, and your daughter's, but you don't get to spend the night with her. You end up out drinking with, of all people, your ex's new girlfriend. The two of you get to talking about guys and makeup and whatever else. It suddenly dawns on you that you're heading home alone. So, maybe you pull out your trusty dating app and scroll through and find Carl. Maybe you invited him over."

"That's not what happened—"

Before I can finish my statement, Matthew is on his feet.

"What are you two trying to get at?" Matthew interrupts. "Are you trying to catch Lillian in a lie?"

"We're trying to get a clear picture of the night's events."

"I've told you everything I know."

"Yes," Matthew says. "It would be better if we talk after you have a clearer idea of what happened. From now on neither one of us will be talking to you unless we have a lawyer present."

Spelling gives Dylan a look that's part grimace. They stand.

"You know, you two really are a sight to see. The way you approach everything as a united front."

"Goodbye, Detective," I say, using all my strength not to react further.

"If you don't mind, I'm going to step out and talk with Rebecca," Spelling says.

"Follow me," Matthew says, walking out the back door.

Dylan and I are alone in the living room. As he sits across from me, his elbows on his knees, I wonder if he's thought at all about our date the other night, before the investigation took center stage.

"Have you told your supervisor about me?"

He gives me a strange look. "Yes. I have."

"And?"

"I'm still here, aren't I?"

His boss must have deemed our history inconsequential. After all, it was nothing more than dinner and a shared glass of wine. It felt like more to me, but that was before.

"Mommy!" Mabel comes running into the house, a towel wrapped around her shoulders. Her wet suit presses against my dry clothes, but I don't care. It feels so nice holding her in my arms.

"I missed you today," I say. "How was school?"

She ignores my question, asking one of her own. She points at Dylan. "Who's that?"

He waves, his smile friendly, but there's a discomfort in the room.

"Just a friend," I say, turning her in the direction of the

stairs. "Put on some dry clothes and we'll get started on homework."

I follow her to the stairs as Dylan's phone begins to ring. He answers, walking to the front door as he speaks. I only catch bits and pieces of the conversation.

"... still waiting on forensics... find the cause of death... hope we'll know something soon."

I take each step slowly, curious to hear what Dylan might reveal about the case.

"Gates. G-A-T-E-S. His record shows a few B&Es," Dylan says. "Burglary."

My nerves turn cold. Carl had a criminal history? And he was inside my apartment? An image of the gun I found inside his desk drawer appears in my mind, my knees buckling ever so slightly.

"And this is weird," I hear Dylan say. "He was cited for causing a scene at the police station. His brother died and he wanted to open an investigation."

Something inside tells me to stop, listen carefully to whatever is coming next.

After a brief pause, Dylan continues. "The brother's name is Richard Walsh."

TWENTY

LILLIAN

July—Two Years Ago

Navy skies above our heads, gray ground beneath our feet. We walked slowly at first, picking up the pace once our eyes adjusted to the darkness. With each step, we were transported away from the pulsing music, the reveling voices, the sting of embarrassment.

"What was that back there?" I asked, thinking back to the tense confrontation between Matthew and Richard. Everyone who witnessed it was stunned. "Tell me."

"Remember last week when Ted and I had a meeting with investors staying at Anne Isle Inn?"

"Yeah."

"I saw Richard there. And he wasn't alone."

"Okay..."

"He was with a woman. And it definitely wasn't Blaire."

"Oh." Richard was known for being a flirt, but I was surprised he'd actually cheat on Blaire. His advances on me at the party seemed out of character. "Did he see you?"

"I wish he hadn't. I was walking out of the restaurant just as he was heading into the elevator. Some girl was hanging on his arm. Ted was late, as usual, so I was the only one who saw."

"What did you say to him?"

"Nothing. Just a nod of the head and went about my business."

"And you think what he did back there, that was his way of flexing? Puffing up his chest?"

"I suppose. Rumors are one thing. Actually being caught? He had this look on his face, like he wanted to knock the memory out of me. I don't think Richard is the kind of guy who likes people knowing his secrets."

"What does he think you'll do? Run and tell Blaire what you saw?"

"Their marriage is their own business."

"It's actually very sad. Right before the incident with Richard, Harriet and Cat were talking about their finances. They said his car had been repossessed."

Matthew shook his head. "You'd think he'd be trying to solve his problems, not adding more."

We kept walking, our arms intertwined. The moon loomed above the trees, casting silver ripples over the water beyond the cliffs. It was a calming view, begging one to look both out and inward.

"I just don't get guys like that," he said.

"Like what?"

"Cheating on their wives. I can't imagine how exhausting it would be."

"Not everyone is as lucky as we are."

"We are lucky, aren't we?"

His lips were on mine, his hands around my waist. Alone on the cliffs, the lights from our home twinkling in the distance. The moon, the crisp air, the constant waves. I'd never felt happier, more complete.

"Stay right here," he said as he pulled away.

"Where are you going?"

"Back to grab some champagne. I'd like to make a toast."

"Here?" I looked around. "What about the party?"

"It's our party. We can leave if we want to. We won't stay out here all night, but I'd like my own little celebration. With just you." He pointed at the sky, smiling. "And the moon. The stars. The sea."

He was gone before a laugh even left my lips. Matthew could be so corny at times, and yet genuine. It was what made me fall in love with him, all those years ago back in college, before I had any idea who we might become or what we might accomplish. We'd achieved everything we ever wanted now, yet the core of our relationship remained. We still found happiness alone with each other.

My thoughts were interrupted by the sounds of footsteps. I was still smiling about the memories when I turned, expecting to see Matthew. Instead, I saw Richard Walsh staggering up the hill.

He startled when he saw me standing there. "We meet again," he said.

He was drunk. I could tell by the way he slurred his words, the way his balance wavered with every other step.

"What are you doing, Richard?"

He held out his hands. "All dressed up and nowhere to go."

"Blaire is still inside. Maybe you should join her."

"Fuck Blaire. She's the reason I'm in this mess."

I thought back to what Harriet and Cat were saying about the car repossession, how Blaire was the one who'd mismanaged their funds. Still, I was mortified that he would talk about his wife so harshly. I couldn't imagine Matthew ever talking that way about me.

"It's been a long night, Richard. A long week. Maybe you should go home."

"You could come with me." In a second, he had his hands on

me again, his sweaty palms on my bare arms. "We could have our own little party."

I pushed him back, more forcefully this time. "That's not going to happen, Richard. Ever."

"Lillian?" Matthew's voice called out for me in the darkness. A few more seconds passed before I could make out his face. His jaw tensed when he caught sight of Richard. "What are you doing here?"

"You again," Richard said. He spit on the ground, wobbled away from me. "You're one of those insecure guys, huh? Can't stand the thought of your wife talking to someone else."

"You're making her uncomfortable," Matthew said, his voice steady. "And you're drunk. I think it's time you went home."

"*Go home*, that's all people say. My house is going to get taken next, you know. You two just came into money. Give it another ten years. Wait until you're on the verge of losing everything, then talk to me about home."

I felt sorry for the Walshes. We barely knew them, only in passing, and whatever financial troubles they were having, it felt invasive that we were learning about them, like peering into someone's bedroom window, witnessing something we weren't meant to see.

Matthew put the bottle of champagne on the ground, the glasses falling beside it. He reached for Richard. "Here, I'll walk with you. You'll feel better in the morning."

"Get your fucking hands off me." Richard staggered, almost falling into me. I took a step back and fell, landing hard on the trail. He didn't even notice. His sights were on Matthew. "You must have felt like a big man in there."

"I was only trying to defend my wife."

Richard pushed him. Matthew stood upright, working against the slope of the ground to find his balance.

"I'm not doing this with you, Richard."

Richard punched Matthew hard in the stomach. The sound of their bodies connecting made me flinch.

"Stop!" I shouted. "What are you doing?"

But Richard was already rearing back, preparing for another blow. Matthew ducked, ramming his body into Richard's midsection. Both men fell, tussling with one another on the dirt. I stood, running in the direction of the house. I needed to find Ted or David or someone who could help—

A frightening cry rang out.

For several seconds, I stood still, afraid of what I'd see when I turned around. Something terrible had happened. The quiet gave it away.

When I turned, only Matthew was standing.

Richard had disappeared over the side of the cliff.

TWENTY-ONE

LILLIAN

Now

They're brothers.

That explains why Carl had a folder with Richard's name, why he went to such lengths to deceive me in the first place. He wasn't some jerk cheating on his pregnant wife; he was trying to figure out what happened to his brother.

Somehow, this stranger stumbled upon the biggest secret of my life. For the past two years, I've tried, and failed, to forget about what happened that humid July night. Most evenings, when I close my eyes, I imagine the dark landscape of the cliffs, feel my heart beating hard against my chest, hoping that Richard will reappear.

Of course, he didn't, and covering up his death is the worst thing I've ever done.

I'm reminded of what we did every time someone in town mentions his name. Every time I see Blaire Walsh and her three boys. To protect myself, I force a smile, but inside my guilt burns hot. If it weren't for Mabel, I'm not sure I could live with what I've done.

The guilt burns when I look at Matthew, too. Our actions that night tore our marriage apart. He's the only other person who knows the truth about what we did. Until now.

Carl must have known Matthew and I killed Richard, and I need to find out how.

Matthew walks in through the front door. After the detectives left, Rebecca decided she needed to go home, too. He walked her to her car. I did little more than breathe a goodbye. My thoughts warred between the horrors of that night and the severity of the trouble I'm presently in, paralyzing me.

Matthew locks the door and turns to face me. "This is getting bad."

"I know." My stomach aches like it's been punched.

His eyes roam around the room, looking everywhere but at me. "You should have told them about knowing the victim at the police station. Now it looks like you're lying."

It feels like I'm falling, and I guess I am. I land on the sofa, my spine sinking hard into the backrest. A medley of coincidences, sure. But the man inside our apartment was related to Richard, the man we killed. There must be a bigger connection.

"There's something else. When you were outside, I overheard Dylan talking to someone on the phone. I heard him say Carl's brother died two years ago."

"So?"

I exhale slowly. "His brother was Richard."

The color drains from Matthew's face in an instant. He stands still, staring at me from across the room.

"The man who died inside our apartment is related to Richard Walsh?" He begins to stammer. "How could he... are you sure?"

"That's what Dylan said. And I'm inclined to believe him." I reach into my bag, pulling out the folder I stole from Carl's office. I lay it on the seat beside me. "I found this today when I was going through Carl's things."

Matthew comes over, staring at the folder like it's some kind of mirage. He opens it, flipping through the photographs and notes. "What is this?"

"Carl must have known what happened to Richard. That's why he came after me in the first place."

"How? I mean, I didn't even know he had a brother. People have barely talked about Richard since..." He stumbles over his words. "Since his body was found."

"I kept trying to figure out why Carl lied to me. This is why."

"Where did you say you found this?"

"In his office at the car lot. Cat and I went by there today."

"You did *what*?"

"I was trying to figure out who Carl really was. I needed answers."

"You don't need to find them yourself. And take Cat of all people with you."

"Cat doesn't know about the folder. She doesn't know about any of this. Besides, it's a good thing I found this before the police did."

Matthew marches to the sofa and sits, cupping his chin with his hands. "Yeah, they don't know you're connected to Richard. That's good."

But I wonder how long it will be before they find out we were neighbors. It took them less than two days to find out I'd connected with Carl online. I have no idea where they're searching, who they're interviewing.

"Were you serious about getting a lawyer?" I ask.

"Of course, I'm serious. We should have hired one already."

"I didn't think they'd treat me like a suspect—"

"Of course, they're going to treat you like a suspect. It's our apartment." He cuts me off. "Maybe at first they weren't, but now that you've admitted to knowing the victim? Now that you've *lied* about knowing the victim? But they're acting as if you're the *only* suspect, which makes me nervous."

I don't appreciate Matthew's tone. It's quick and sharp and nothing like the man I know, but then again, we are under an enormous amount of pressure. Richard's name being added to the mix intensifies everything. When Matthew gets to thinking about something, his brain works so quickly his words struggle to keep up.

I feel the sudden urge to escape, but I have nowhere to go. A splash of water on my face, a few quiet moments, will help me think. I stand, walking in the direction of the hall bathroom.

I close the door and lean against the sink, the stone cold against my palms. Greige marble. That's what we decided for all the bathroom and kitchen counters. There used to be days when my biggest problem was settling on the right fabrics and materials to complete our perfect home. I never imagined, then, how our lives would end up.

Divorced. Grappling with not only one person's death, but two.

A memory of Richard enters my mind. The last glimpses I had before he went into the water, swallowed whole by the sea. Foolishly, I'd hoped his death was behind us, that it would live only as a terrible burden on my soul. Now, I worry Carl's death will lead the police to uncover the truth about Richard.

I close my eyes, shaking away the anxieties rising. Richard was an accident. One we resolved. But Carl? I didn't do anything. I didn't kill him. Someone else did, and I only need to keep myself together long enough for that person to be found.

When I return to the living room, Matthew has wandered back outside. The patio door is open, a silent invitation for me to join him.

"Do you have a lawyer in mind?" I ask, easing back into our discussion.

"Ted suggested Barry Walters."

"You can't be upset with me for leaning on Cat when you're involving Ted."

"I didn't take him on some sleuthing adventure. I asked for a recommendation. Besides, every part of our lives will be involved if we don't get this sorted. The company. Your job. Mabel." His jaw clenches as he turns, looking out over the pool. "Not to mention, the longer the police are sifting through our lives, the more time they have to learn about Richard."

"How do you think Carl knew we were involved with Richard's death?" I ask. "Could someone have seen us?"

"It was too dark. Besides, if someone saw what happened, they would have gone straight to the police."

He's right, but someone else has clearly uncovered our secret.

"Why didn't you tell me Carl had been at the apartment before?"

"He hasn't."

"Mrs. Haynes said—"

"You know how Mrs. Haynes is. She remembers everything. She must have seen him outside when he picked me up. That's all."

"That's good. If you weren't close enough to invite him in, they'll see you don't have a motive for murder," he says.

His question brings up another mystery. "How did Carl get inside the apartment on the night he was murdered? Do you think someone could have stolen our keys?"

"It's a possibility. I rarely have anyone over, besides Ted."

My stomach drops when I realize this is the moment I have to tell him. "There's something else."

"What?"

"I know we have the rule about not bringing dates into the apartment—"

"Lillian." He cuts me off again, closing his eyes in annoyance. "If you've been letting guys into the apartment, you need to tell me now."

"I'm trying." My voice sounds flustered. "And it's not *guys*. Only one."

"Who?"

"Dylan Logan. The detective."

Matthew's eyes bulge. "The one who was just sitting on our sofa?"

"Yes."

He lets out a dry, unbelieving laugh. "When? I mean, how?"

"We went on a date Friday. The night before the murder," I say. "We met on Cupid's Corner."

Matthew covers his mouth with his palm. "You've been dating the detective who is investigating Carl's murder? And you met him on the same website."

"It was only one date, but yes. It makes me worried they think that all I do is pick up guys online."

"Well, it does appear dating you has problematic results." He pauses. "That came out harsher than I meant. Should he even be on this case, given your connection?"

"We barely know each other. We were never... intimate."

"But it's all about how it looks, Lillian. And it isn't good," he says. "And why did you break the rules we'd set? I've not even invited Rebecca in."

I exhale. "I don't know. Dylan and I were having a good time and I wanted to keep the night going. Moving on has been easier for you than it has me. I wasn't going to let our stupid rules get in the way of my chance to find someone."

"The rules are what keep our arrangement working. It's what keeps everyone in our family happy."

"Maybe the rules aren't working anymore."

The words slip out quickly. I'm not sure if I mean them or

not. I felt unfulfilled in the days leading up to Mabel's birthday party, but I'm not sure if it was because of Matthew and our living arrangements, or if it's the residual grief over Richard's death that never seems to go away.

TWENTY-TWO

LILLIAN

July—Two Years Ago

It all happened so fast.

Isn't that what most people say when something traumatic happens?

I didn't know someone was behind me until I felt him grab my purse.

The car came out of nowhere.

Life can seem long and boring and tedious, until suddenly it isn't.

Richard vanished quickly, but the memory of that night is slow. Excruciating and brutal. Every detail cemented in my mind for the rest of time.

After he fell, I couldn't tear my eyes away from where he'd stood. I kept waiting for him to reappear, materialize from the crisp, cool air around us, even grab the rocky ledge with his hand, like a character might in a movie.

But there was nothing. Just the sounds of night around us. Trees whispering, waves crashing, my own breath, heavy and laden, contradicting the serene setting. Then Matthew spoke.

"Holy shit. Did he go over? Tell me he didn't go over. He was standing right there!"

The panic in his voice pierced something inside, forced me to accept what had happened.

"He fell," I said, my voice sounding nothing like my own.

"Richard!" Matthew took a step closer to the cliff, started digging in his pockets. He pulled out his phone, shining it below, but the light was like a firefly flickering in the surrounding blackness. "Richard!"

"Be careful." I pulled him back, not wanting him to get any closer. I'd just seen the cliff's danger.

He pulled away. "Richard!"

"Quiet. Listen."

We both held our breaths, listening for any sign of life. The night filled my ears. Then a voice. Voices. Shouting. Laughter.

The echoing came from the direction of our house, the party still raving. From the other direction, the side of the trail near the cliffs, there was silence.

"There are rocks and boulders," Matthew said. "He may not be in the water. He could still be down there."

"It's a thirty-foot drop. Even if he's not in the water, there's no helping him," I said. "He's dead."

"Oh my God." Matthew fell to his knees, leaned over so far his forehead was pressed against the rocky soil. "Oh my God, what happened? I didn't mean it."

"I know. It was an accident."

It was a tone I had never used with him before, which reminded me of cajoling Mabel when she'd skinned her knee, but thinking of Mabel in that moment hurt. Thinking of anything. It was like my life was over, starting anew right there on the side of the cliff.

"We have to call the police," Matthew said, when he finally raised up for air.

I tried to prepare for what we might say. How I would

explain to Blaire that her husband had fallen over the cliff. How I'd be forced to admit it was our fault. My thoughts were spinning, racing between Richard and Blaire and Matthew.

Back to Mabel. We could never let her know what happened. We could never let anyone know, or we'd risk losing the little girl we'd fought so hard to bring into this world.

"We can't call the police," I said. "If we do that, you'll go to jail."

His voice broke. "I wasn't trying to kill him. It was an accident."

"An accident where a man died!" I shouted. "The police don't look the other way when it comes to something like that. And you were arguing with him back at the party. Everyone saw. What if the police think you did this intentionally? They might think you pushed him."

As I replayed the moment, over and over again, I wasn't sure who did what. It was a rumble, a fight, and one person went over the edge. It just as easily could have been Matthew. Nothing could be done to save Richard, but all I could think about was how this situation could spiral, ruining the family I'd worked so hard to create.

"He attacked you," I said. "He wanted to fight."

Matthew was shaking now, going into shock. "I can't believe this has happened."

Another voice carried over from the backyard, followed by a new song blasting through the speakers.

"We can't stay out here all night," I say. "People are going to wonder where we went. Did anyone see Richard walking this way?"

"I thought he'd already left," he said. "Then, he was just here."

"Let's go back to the party. We won't tell anyone what we saw. We won't tell them what happened. They're all probably so drunk, they may not have even noticed we were gone."

"I don't know if I can," he said, staring out at the water. "I'm a mess."

"If we go back right now, no one will know we were here. They'll think he just fell."

"Oh my God. What if he's still down there? What if they find his body in the morning and—"

"We have to do this, Matthew," I cut him off, squeezing his shoulders with my hands to try and center him. "Think of your future. Mabel. Voyage. You didn't mean for any of this to happen, so we need to go back to the party like nothing did happen."

The words escaping my mouth frightened me. Never before did I think I could react so callously to the passing of another person. But in that moment, the only people I could think about were my husband and daughter. I didn't want either of them punished for a mistake. An accident.

I'm not sure which threat did the trick, but Matthew stood, shakily, and started hobbling toward the house.

"When we get to the house, go upstairs. Change into another white shirt, then take a few minutes to compose yourself. It's important people see us together. We don't need anyone remembering we disappeared halfway through the night."

Matthew didn't say anything. He followed me as I picked up the champagne bottle and glasses and led the way back. We snuck in through the front door, but the entire party had moved to the backyard—one of Matthew's co-workers was snoozing on the couch, the only person still inside. I gave Matthew a look, and he climbed the staircase.

I walked outside, found all of our guests around the pool. Matthew joined me a few minutes later. His skin was pale, but his cheeks were red. His expression was neutral. Anyone who saw him would think he'd had too much to drink, nothing else.

Ted clapped his shoulder, and pulled him away. The two began whispering.

I remained standing by myself, totally disconnected.

A voice drifted closer to my ears, pulling me back to reality.

"I said, thank you."

I turned, my every moment delayed, and saw Blaire Walsh standing in front of me.

"Thank you?"

"For the party. We should do it again sometime."

I watched her, using every muscle at my disposal not to react. I wanted to break down and confess, tell her what I already knew. *Your husband is dead. We killed him.*

"I'm sorry about Richard," she said, her eyes falling to the ground. "He gets like that when he's had too much to drink."

"Don't we all." I forced the words out.

Then I had another thought. If Richard's body was found, and the police suspected foul play, the first person they'd question would be Blaire. The woman standing in front of me. The longer she stayed at the party, the more convincing her alibi would be... if she ever needed it.

"Don't leave yet. The party is just getting started."

"But Richard's already home. I want to make sure—"

"He'll be fine. You deserve some fun," I said. "Come with me."

I locked my arms with hers, escorting her around the house until I found Harriet and Cat.

"There you are!" Harriet shouted. "Get over here. Cat was just giving us the scoop on Ted's latest Sugar Baby."

I forced another drink in Blaire's hand, keeping her enclosed in the circle of drunken gossip, listening and nodding when appropriate.

For the rest of the night, I mingled and smiled and eventually spoke, but it didn't feel like I was doing any of it. It was like I was hovering above myself, witnessing my own interactions, my gaze omniscient enough that I could see beyond the back-yard of the party, see over to the cliffs. I imagined Richard's body down below.

When everyone left, I listened as Matthew climbed the steps. Above, I could hear water running, could hear sobs, but I'd expended all my energy, and had none left to comfort him.

I sat in the living room, staring out at the backyard, waiting and waiting.

When the sun rose, I snuck out the front of the house and hurried to the cliffs.

I looked down.

There was no Richard, only jagged rocks and a hungry sea.

TWENTY-THREE

MATTHEW

Now

Black skies. Rolling waves. My own labored breathing. For months after Richard died, these were the memories I relived every time I closed my eyes. Last night, after Lillian uncovered the link between Carl and Richard, the guilt and paranoia returned in full force, threatening to overwhelm me. Both of us, really. We spent the rest of the night apart, each of us lost in our own private thoughts.

Now it's Tuesday morning, and I'm sitting in a lawyer's office, trying to calm myself.

I close my eyes, experience the sensations all over again. But this time it's different. I hear Lillian's voice.

Something happened. I need your help.

Richard's body was found six days after his death by a fisherman in the early hours of a rainy morning. The fear and worry that had consumed me since that night returned, as I suddenly feared the truth would come out about how he died. Would they be able to tell he hadn't fallen? Would they notice any cuts or bruising on his body?

Turns out, the elements had already taken their toll. It was hard for investigators to determine anything other than he had fallen into the water, and that his blood alcohol level was extremely high. Still, they had to investigate what happened. They spoke to anyone connected to Richard, and they spoke to me because he'd last been seen leaving the party at our house. Thankfully, I was able to keep them away from Lillian. She was so guilt-ridden in those early days, I'm not sure she could have withstood even a simple conversation with police.

I told them the truth—that Richard had been at our housewarming party and that he was very drunk—and the lie, that the last time I saw him he'd been walking away from the house. I sat there squirming, afraid I was already under suspicion, but to my delight, the cops didn't press any further. Everyone they'd talked with about that night said the same thing, even Blaire. Richard's death was labeled a tragic accident, and from that point on, my own guilt and shame started to dwindle.

I'm almost ashamed to admit it, but Richard's death isn't my biggest regret. Of course, I wish the night had unfolded differently, in a way that left him alive and away from my conscience. But if I'm being truly honest, which I rarely am these days, my biggest regret was the impact his death had on my relationship with Lillian, which is why I'm so desperate to help her now.

It was torturous watching the woman I loved wither away. Lillian had stayed by my side through everything. She had supported me, financially and otherwise, during those uncertain years when Ted and I were trying to get Voyage launched. Even during our struggle with infertility, she's the one who remained positive, steadfast in her belief that one day we would welcome a child into our lives.

I couldn't deny how deeply Richard's death changed us, and I wasn't surprised when she finally admitted she wanted to separate. I was upset, but not surprised. The couple we were before could have worked through anything, overcome every obstacle life handed us, but the people we were now? It seemed we could only find refuge from our guilt when we were apart; staying together risked us further damaging our already fragile psyches.

Divorce was the only way we could forgive ourselves for what happened that night, without the constant presence of the other person as a reminder, but I still went through a period of denial.

I tried wooing Lillian back. "Dating again" as all the relationship columns said. I'd send flowers to the dance studio, surprise her with a sitter for Mabel so I could take her out to dinner. It became clear these acts of adoration weren't reciprocated, they were even resented.

"What are you trying to do?" she asked me, after sending the sitter home, feigning a stomach bug.

"I'm trying to fix us," I said.

"The only way to fix what is broken between us is space," she said. "The way we've been living the past few months... it's not working."

"What about Mabel? What about our life together?" I pleaded.

"I'm doing this for Mabel," she said, her voice level. "Staying in a broken marriage will do more damage to her in the long run."

She was right, but admitting it didn't make it any easier. I felt hopeless having lost the one person who had stood by my side, knowing I couldn't confide in anyone else. I turned those negative feelings inward. I started drinking. Soon, that became the only way I could forget about my problems, forgive myself for the mistakes I'd made.

What's worse is I've made more mistakes since then. Some, Lillian doesn't even know about. Our conversation last night got me thinking...

"Matthew," Barry says, walking into his office. I hear his

voice before I register his presence, my mind still lost in the past.

"Thanks for meeting with me on short notice," I say, standing to shake his hand. I smile, and it amazes me how quickly I'm able to shed my nervous shell. I suppose I've had years of practice, acting like everything is fine.

"I understand you had some trouble at your rental property?"

That's all I told him over the phone. I sit back down, take a deep breath. Try not to hear Lillian's voice every time I blink. *Something happened.*

"I'm afraid it's quite serious," I say. "And it involves my ex-wife, Lillian."

I tell him everything Lillian told me over the phone, and only parts of what she told me later back at the house. I don't mention the connection between Carl and Richard. I don't want Richard being brought into this at all. Because even if we're able to prove Lillian had nothing to do with Carl's death, the last thing I need is the police department taking another look at Richard's disappearance.

"And you're saying she knew the guy? Went on a few dates with him." Barry's demeanor is hard to read.

"Yes. Of course, she didn't realize it at first. She was traumatized after finding him."

"Sure, sure."

"But now that she knows she had a connection with this man, she's afraid they might think she had something to do with his death."

"And all this happened during her night at the apartment?"

"Yes. Well, we're not sure when he died exactly. The police haven't told us that yet."

Barry knows about our co-living arrangements. One of our mutual friends, Karen, helped us agree on the terms, during the post-divorce mediation.

"Lillian called you after she dialed 911?" Barry asks, interrupting my thoughts.

"I think she called me first."

"Hum." He sighs. "Well, I understand why you're concerned. It doesn't look good for her. She knew the victim. And he was found inside the apartment you share. Which room?"

"Hers."

"Hum." That sound again. A filmy sweat covers my hands as I rub them against each other.

He scribbles down a few more notes before leaning back in his chair. He crosses his arms over his chest, appears to be thinking. Seeing him like this—speechless—makes me nervous.

"So... what should we do?"

"Before I agree to help, let me ask. Are you seeking representation for Lillian or yourself?"

"I... I don't know. Neither of us were involved."

"But right now, things look a lot worse for her than they do you. Both your names are on the lease for the apartment, which could make you both liable in a civil suit, but other than that, you aren't connected at all. The two of you are no longer a married couple."

"I know that." The sweat has somehow moved, is now dripping down the back of my neck.

"That means there is no privilege between you. If there's something you know or aren't sure about—"

"Come on, Barry," I cut him off before he can finish. "I know Lillian had nothing to do with it!"

"All right. Settle down. I just want to make sure I know who I'm representing. Where is Lillian?" The landline on his desk begins ringing. He answers. "...Ah, hello. Barry speaking."

I turn, allowing him privacy while he's on the phone. That's a good question. Where is she? I called her earlier in the day, and she didn't answer. I walk to the corner of Barry's office, narrow bookshelves lining the walls like pillars. I dial her number again.

"Pick up," I whisper, hoping the persistent ringing will cease. When it doesn't, I try to stifle my aggravation. I don't want Barry to see. I stuff my phone into my pocket and wait for Barry to end his conversation.

"I have a few appointments this afternoon. Let's meet later tonight. I'll come by your house and talk more."

"We'll be there, yeah."

"We." He chews on the word for a minute.

"Look, I know we're not married anymore, but Lillian is a friend. Mabel's mother. I'm only trying to help her."

"I respect that. But these are serious allegations, Matthew. If something ends up sticking... just make sure it doesn't cling to you, too."

I nod, quickly saying thanks and leaving. I'm both thankful for Barry's guidance and aggravated by his reaction. He's thinking like a lawyer, acting like a friend. But he knows Lillian, too. Surely, he can't think she's capable of murdering a man.

You *murdered a man*, says an angry voice inside, followed by the sound of breaking waves. I clear my throat, force the memories away.

People have never understood the devotion Lillian and I have for one another. They assume if we're this loyal, we'd still be together. But they don't know that my actions are the reason we fell apart. They don't understand that she's the one who protected me after what I did. I can't turn my back on her now, no matter how bad the situation looks.

This is my chance to repay her.

Something happened. I need your help.

Her voice haunts me, adding to my collection of ghosts.

TWENTY-FOUR

LILLIAN

Sleep last night came in flashes. I was at rest, then awake. Dreaming, then gasping. I need to get out of bed and start the day.

It's important we stick to routine. That's what helped us remain under the radar last time, and if I want to appear less guilty than I already do, I can't have any spells of depression.

Now, I remind myself that part of my routine is being alone. Finding peace within the silence. But there's no peace to be found now, only memories of Richard's body tumbling over the cliff, of finding Carl's body dead in my bed.

We got away with it.

Richard had been gone for nearly two months when that hideous sentence wormed its way into my brain. For weeks, I'd been a shadow of myself, barely able to get out of bed or cook dinner or practice handwriting with Mabel. During that time, each new day presented the opportunity for a knock on the door, police asking questions, shackling my wrists with handcuffs. Each night, I revisited those moments on the cliff. Richard was there, then he was gone, and my life changed forever.

When the fear of being arrested was finally replaced with that celebratory thought—We got away with it—I wasn't sure how to feel. Although there was a clear part of me that did not want anyone to find out what happened that night, there was still an obvious guilt. A man's life ended, and I did nothing about it. I didn't deserve the life I had, my daughter and my house and my husband, not when Richard Walsh's body was in the ground.

I didn't want to live with myself, but I had to keep living for Mabel. Hadn't it been my idea to return to the party like nothing happened?

I knew Matthew was struggling, too. There were subtle hints. His work hours had increased, as had his drinking. On the weekends, he no longer went golfing or played tennis. He stopped watching sports. Most evenings, he'd sit on the front porch staring at the cliffs in the distance, a beautiful view by anyone else's standards, but one that contained all the pain and suffering in the world for us.

We were both falling apart in our own ways, and we knew exactly what was the cause, but we couldn't do anything about it. Each time I tried to speak with Matthew about that night, tried to process my grief, the words would disappear. I couldn't bear to admit what we'd done. And he couldn't either, so we began speaking to each other only in Mabel's presence.

Summer turned to fall turned to winter. My life started to feel normal again. It had to be normal, for Mabel's sake. I became more involved at her school, offering my services when-ever they needed volunteer readers or parents to help with pumpkin painting.

Although I'm ashamed to say it, I made it to a point where I no longer thought about that night. Whenever I ran into Blaire Walsh in town, my entire body would shudder, but I simply arranged not to run into her, not to enter the same social circles.

I moved on with my life... until I saw Matthew, and then the memories would come rushing back. His struggles could no longer co-exist with my struggles, not if we ever wanted to move on with our lives.

Jane visited for Spring Break, which became a whole other stressor. We could pretend our marriage was fine for brief moments in public, but I knew it would be difficult to keep up the charade for someone staying with us. I allowed Jane to take Mabel to the park so I could have a few minutes alone with Matthew, uninterrupted, and then I told him.

"I think we should separate," I said. I'd practiced what to say in my head for weeks, but nothing felt as honest or direct as that statement.

Matthew didn't react at first. Then finally, "Separate or divorce?"

I think we both knew the answer. In a typical separation, the two parties would at least attempt a reconciliation. Go to therapy. Try to recapture what was lost. Those weren't options available to us. We couldn't tell anyone the truth about our problems unless we admitted what we had done.

Nothing could erase that night with Richard, and we both knew, even if we wouldn't say it, that it had ruined us.

"We have to find a way to move on," I said. "And I don't think we can do that together."

We heard Jane pushing open the front door downstairs, could hear Mabel giggling as she entered the house. That was the sound that broke us. The happiness we were most definitely about to ruin.

We both wept, the undeniable heartbreak we'd been trying to stifle finding its release.

Two years later, that same grief and loneliness has multiplied. I fooled myself into thinking we'd moved beyond what happened that night on the cliffs, but I suppose some events are so catastrophic you can never fully wriggle away from their grasp.

What I can't understand is how the truth could have been uncovered. I try to shift my thoughts away from the cliffs, back to the party itself, thinking of everyone in attendance. Is it possible one of them saw us? That this secret was never ours to begin with?

Once we wandered back to the house, it was almost startling how quickly the energy of the party seemed to stomp out the horror of what had just happened. No one seemed as though they'd just witnessed a man die—not even Matthew and myself.

Almost everyone we know was there that night. Including Blaire. Is it possible she knows what we did to her husband? But if she did, why wait so long to enact revenge? Perhaps whoever is doing this realizes it hurts more this way... to think our lives have gone back to normal, only to have them upended again.

All the same people attended Mabel's party this weekend. The same smiling faces, the same laidback attitudes. Was one of them plotting revenge even then? Could they have told Carl about our involvement, lured him to the apartment? But even if that was the case, why would they want to harm Richard's brother?

My phone rings with a call from Matthew.

"Where have you been all day?"

"At the house." I refuse to tell him I've barely made it out of bed.

"I hired a lawyer," he says coldly. "Barry will be coming by the house tonight to speak with both of us."

"Are you sure this is the right move?" I ask. Everyone insists hiring a lawyer is the smart thing to do, but I'm afraid it will make me look guilty.

"We have to be proactive," he says. "We already don't know who is working against us."

I end the call, my mind bouncing between what happened this past Saturday night and what happened over two years ago. Matthew is right. We don't know who is targeting us, but clearly someone is. The more I think about it, I don't believe anyone saw what we did. If someone didn't see what happened, perhaps they uncovered the truth later.

The question is, how?

TWENTY-FIVE

I sit on Mabel's bed, reading her a story, a light display shining across the ceiling in her room. For once, I wish she'd fight me about bedtime in order to postpone my meeting with Barry, but she falls asleep easily, so I gently close her door and head downstairs.

Barry looks like he's gained weight since the last time I saw him. He's well-groomed and smells like expensive cologne.

"Thanks for coming by the house so late," I say. "We're trying to keep Mabel unaware."

"That's for the best. And it isn't any problem. I've had one of my associates do some digging since this morning so we have a better idea of what we're up against."

"What did you find out?" Matthew asks, gesturing for Barry to sit on the living room sofa. He takes a seat next to him, while I sit across from them, my palms stuffed between my knees.

"First, I'd like to hear what happened from Lillian's perspective."

I go into the same story I've told countless times now, detailing everything that happened until I returned home from the police station. I tell him about the visit from detectives yesterday, how it was more confrontational.

"And that's why Matthew thought it was best to get a lawyer involved," I finish. "Everything seems to be pointing at me, but I have no idea how Carl got inside my apartment, let alone who killed him."

"You made the right decision," Barry says. As I spoke, he was relaxed, taking everything in. Now he leans forward, his elbows on his knees. "When people find themselves involved in a murder investigation, it's natural for them to feel overwhelmed and scared. I know it's difficult, but try not to worry about what might happen, and instead focus on the facts. We'll discuss everything the police have uncovered so far and talk through it."

Barry's steady approach eases my nerves, slightly. It's impossible not to worry about what might happen, but at least we have an objective voice guiding us.

"First, let's look at the cause of death. As I'm sure you could infer based on the amount of blood at the crime scene, the victim was stabbed multiple times. Nine puncture wounds, to be precise. There wasn't a murder weapon found at the scene, but there was a knife missing from the set inside the kitchen. Police believe that may have been the weapon that was used. Do either of you have another explanation for why the knife is missing?"

Matthew and I share a look, then shake our heads. I was so traumatized after finding Carl's body, I didn't even consider the weapon might have come from inside our apartment.

"Okay," Barry continues. "Now we have the time of death, which is a little trickier. Carl's body was cold and stiff by the time investigators arrived on the scene, which wasn't long after Lillian made the call to 911. That means he could have died anywhere from eight to thirty-six hours earlier."

"They can't narrow it down any more than that?" Matthew asks.

"It's not always easy to determine the exact time a person dies. Especially since there was evidence to suggest he bled out from his wounds. There's no telling how long he was on that bed dying, yet too weak to intervene."

The idea Carl knew he was dying and could do nothing about it frightens me. I wrap my arms around myself and squeeze.

"I wasn't inside the apartment most of the day. Surely, that will help?"

"Not necessarily," Barry says. "You have an alibi from the time you arrived at Mabel's party until you returned home, but Carl could have been murdered before that."

"They can't possibly think I'd murder someone just before hosting my daughter's birthday party."

"It would be a compelling alibi," Barry says. "Right now, we're only trying to piece together what the police theory might be. The victim's wife was out of town on Friday night and didn't return until Saturday morning, at which point she assumed he was at work. No one's come forward yet to verify Carl's location during that time."

I think back to my conversation with Alaina. She didn't seem like she could be involved in Carl's death, but I still know very little about her. It's convenient she was out of town when he was killed. Maybe she hired someone to kill him. Still, that doesn't explain why he was inside my apartment.

"And lastly, we have a statement from one of your neighbors. A Mrs. Loretta Haynes. She says she'd seen the victim at your apartment before."

I roll my eyes. "I already explained this. Carl picked me up for a date, but he waited in the breezeway. He never went inside the apartment."

"According to her he did," Barry says, looking at a pad of

paper with handwritten notes. "She told investigators she saw him exiting your apartment building over a week ago."

A chill spreads throughout my body. Mrs. Haynes says she saw Carl inside my apartment? But I've never invited him in. We'd ceased contact by then. She must be mistaken.

"If Lillian says he never went inside the apartment, I believe her," Matthew says.

His voice is firm, but there's a look on his face. I wonder if he's doubting me.

Barry raises his hands. "I'm only telling you what the police have against you. This case could unfold in a dozen different directions, and we need to stay aware."

"I've told the police the truth about everything." *Except Richard*, I think. I close my eyes and shake my head, willing this entire situation away. What I'd give to go back to Saturday afternoon, to that moment I was cuddling with Mabel on the couch. I wish I'd never returned to the apartment. I wish I knew exactly how Carl's murder is connected to what happened in the past.

It's ironic, really. For years, I worried I'd be punished for my involvement in Richard's death. Now it appears I'll be arrested for a crime I didn't commit.

TWENTY-SIX

LILLIAN

I haven't done anything.

I haven't done anything.

My mind continues to chant these words whenever paranoia sets in.

Last night's meeting with Barry didn't give me much confidence. If anything, he eloquently laid out all the reasons why the police think I'm involved in Carl's death, and there's little I can say to defend myself.

I haven't done anything.

And yet, I keep revisiting Saturday night, questioning my actions. Am I sure about the time I arrived at the apartment? How much did I have to drink? Maybe I left the door unlocked, and someone entered after I fell asleep. But I couldn't have slept more than a couple of hours. I think.

Why did I climb onto the bed? Surely, I should have recognized something sooner, before getting Carl's blood on my hands and clothes. Why didn't I call the police before I called Matthew?

If I can't make sense of what happened—if I can't trust my

own recollections—how can I expect anyone else to believe in my innocence?

Cat continues to comfort me via text. Even Rebecca has checked in to see how I'm feeling. *I'm fine*, I tell them, adding a bunch of false emojis to appear more convincing. In reality, I'm crumbling. I don't feel confident or innocent. I don't feel safe. There's a constant fear that this is my comeuppance for everything I've ever done wrong.

Mabel is my only motivation to keep going. It's not until school lets out that I feel the fog lift, and I celebrate the opportunity to be near her.

I'm in the pickup line at school. She slides into the backseat, and I turn to get a better look of her face. One glimpse of that snaggletooth grin almost erases the anxiety housed in my body.

"How was school?"

"Good." That's usually all I get out of her. She's looking out the window, lost in her own imagination.

"Did you practice today?"

"Yep."

"Tell me your line."

"Saturn is the only planet with rings like a hula hoop." She wiggles in her seat, doing her best to repeat the choreography.

I laugh. "Very good. You're going to be great."

Tonight is the kindergarten play for the fall semester. Mabel has been practicing her lines since last month, and I've been working on her costume just as long. I'm determined to attend and nothing, not even Harriet's rejection, can stop me.

No one has told me I can't go to the play. If anything, it would be more suspicious if I wasn't there. My presence will send the message I've done nothing wrong.

We rush home and I make something easy for dinner. Spaghetti and meat sauce. An hour later, as I'm loading the dishes from dinner into the washer, Matthew comes rushing into the house.

"You're late," I say.

"I know. Held up at the office. I'm trying to catch up on what I missed yesterday."

"We need to leave for the play in a half hour?"

"Damn." He looks around the kitchen, at the dirty plates from an early dinner. At the remnants from a last-minute costume revision on the counter. "I forgot."

"Mabel's getting dressed now. Rehearsal starts in twenty minutes."

Matthew looks behind him, as though someone might follow him into the room, but it's only us, standing alone in the kitchen of a house that used to be ours.

"About the play—"

"Don't tell me you have work."

"No. I'll be there." He puffs. "I was thinking maybe you should stay home."

"Are you serious?"

"They do one every semester. She'll have one in the spring."

"That doesn't matter. I want to attend all of them."

"I know. I just think with everything that's going on, it might be best for you to lay low. Mabel won't be able to see you're missing from on stage. And we can meet back here afterward. Share some ice cream."

My skin is burning with anger and shame. I bite into my cheek, using all the inner strength I can manage not to cry. Or scream.

"Things have changed," he says. "More people are talking about Carl and the apartment, and your name is in all those conversations."

What exactly has he heard? While I'm stuck inside the house during the day, a prisoner to my own thoughts and fears, he's experiencing another side of Anne Isle. I wonder what rumors are going around the office. The community. I wonder what is really being said about me.

"I don't care! It's my daughter's play. More people will notice if I'm not there than if I am."

He pauses. "I don't know if that's true."

"I've not done anything wrong." Saying the words aloud doesn't make them feel authentic, and that worries me.

"I know."

"Do you? Do you believe me?"

I think about Matthew in the wake of Richard's death. It was his lowest moment. And I was there for him.

Our roles have reversed, but how is Matthew treating me? Trying to distance himself, both physically and mentally. The person who would stand by my side no matter what is slipping away.

"You don't have to sit beside me," I say. "But I'm going to the play."

Matthew nods, but doesn't say anything else.

TWENTY-SEVEN

LILLIAN

When Matthew and I enter the auditorium, the crowd parts like the Red Sea for Moses. Every passing stare imprints onto my conscience, and I can feel the sting of being watched wherever I go. Even my cheeks burn.

It's not until I'm seated that I feel like I can breathe. Deep sighs exit my mouth, cool air filling my lungs. I've made it through the worst part. I can't control what the people around me think, only my reaction.

"You okay?" Matthew whispers beside me.

"Fine."

He nods, his head turning from side to side. I wonder who he's trying to find. I wonder what he's thinking. Does he feel sorry for me, that I'm suddenly the spectacle of the fall semester play? Or, is he embarrassed to be seen with me? Does he still wish I'd stayed home?

In the sea of hushed voices, one floats closer. "Excuse me."

It's Rebecca. She's dipping behind each seated guest, aiming for the empty chair next to Matthew. Once settled, she kisses Matthew on the cheek and smiles at me.

"Sorry I'm late."

"It hasn't started yet," Matthew says. "Mabel is backstage getting ready."

"She must be so excited." Rebecca looks at me. "You did a great job with her costume. I got a glimpse of the performers backstage."

The smile stretching across my face feels genuine. "Thank you."

I realize Rebecca isn't looking at me like the others in the auditorium. Her stare doesn't ask questions. She treats me like I'm the same Lillian she's always known. That's what I want. To be treated as if these rumors about me don't exist. There's an unspoken loyalty between us now. After she told me about her history with her ex, I realize she's more deserving than either Matthew or myself for a second chance at happiness.

The lights dim. Even if people want to keep staring, they can't. A spotlight points at the stage, where our attention should have been all along. On our children.

The program is as entertaining and clumsy as you might expect. Toddler-sized planets waddling around on stage. They sing songs, attempt choreography. Each child says their given line, some mumbling, others shouting. Mabel's line—*Saturn is the only planet with rings like a hula hoop*—rings in my head long after she's said it. My anxiety about being here is gone, replaced with pride for my daughter.

It's a happy feeling every parent seems to possess by the time the lights are lifted. Everyone is standing, cheering, focused on their child and nothing else. The rumors circulating about me are like any other type of gossip—entertaining in the moment, but quickly replaced. If I can just soldier on until the police find the real killer, I'll be back in Anne Isle's good graces.

I hope.

As we stand, Matthew looks at me. There's not a hint of regret in his stare, his insistence I stay home forgotten. He appears happy we're experiencing this together. His face is a reminder of the Matthew from a few days ago. The one I've known most my life.

The children take turns bowing, some having to hold onto others to ensure they don't topple over. Ms. Chess, their teacher, stands at the center of the stage.

"We'd like to invite parents to join us in the gymnasium for refreshments," she says.

I remain seated a beat longer, allowing the crowd to thin. This time, as people bumble down the narrow aisles, no one turns to look at me, and I feel myself relax.

"That was adorable," says a woman behind me. I turn to find Blaire Walsh waiting to exit her row.

"It really was," Matthew says, responding before he sees who is speaking. Once he registers Blaire's face, he stops. He's not been around her nearly as much as I have in the past two years. I can see his difficulty, as he tries to remain friendly with the woman whose life he ruined.

"Devon looks cute," I say, giving Matthew a few seconds to recover. "Great job with the costume."

"Thanks. Mabel was great, too."

We stand back, allowing her to pass. I wonder if Rebecca, who is standing between us, picks up on the awkwardness of the interaction.

"Should we grab Mabel and leave?" I suggest.

"Not yet," Rebecca says. "I was hoping to say hello to some of my former students."

She's clearly not picking up on the tension, but then, why would she? Rebecca isn't the subject of a criminal investigation.

It's fine, I mouth to Matthew, as we enter the main lobby.

The area is filled with parents waiting on their children. Some hold flower bouquets in their hands, and I wish I would have considered bringing something for Mabel. I'm making my way to the corner of the room when I bump elbows against someone else. When I look up, I'm standing beside David and Harriet Moore.

"Lillian," David says, looking at his wife uneasily. David is short and has a receding hairline, but he's always dressed in a custom-made suit. Tonight, he wears a red tie. A campaign sticker is pinned to his lapel.

"Mabel is cute as ever," Harriet says, her cheeks turning almost as red as the coordinating dress she wears. "You should be so proud."

"Well, I need to take off," David says to Harriet, kissing her on the cheek. "Tell Shelby I'll see her later."

He takes off without giving me a second glance, leaving the two of us alone. I open my mouth to speak, but my voice catches. Her rejection still hurts.

"Hi, Harriet," Matthew says, coming to join us. "Where's David?"

"Ah, cutting a trail back to the office." She plasters on that fake smile. "No time to rest with election day approaching."

"That's a shame," he says. "They're only young once, you know."

He takes my arm and leads me away before we can see her reaction. A warm gratitude expands inside my chest. Perhaps Matthew is more on my side than I realized.

"Thank you."

The doors open, and the children pour into the lobby. Each child runs to their parents. Ms. Chess is walking around the room offering miniature cupcakes and juice boxes to the performers.

No one is looking at me. Harriet and David aside, no one seems to care about my presence. I'm yet another mother, neighbor, friend. The rumors circulating aren't clouding people's perception of me; maybe they never were. Perhaps it was all in my mind.

"There you are."

I turn in the direction of the voice. Although the woman's face is familiar, it's not one I was expecting to see.

"Alaina?"

"So, you remember me?" Her voice is loud and deliberate. "I know your name now, too. Lillian."

Her tone, tinged with anger, is like a flare gun lighting up the night sky, grabbing everyone's attention. Every head turns in our direction. I try to speak, but I'm too stunned. My heart beats faster, bracing for what she's about to say.

"I was dumb enough to think you were some kind stranger," she says, tears beginning to fall. "But then the cops came asking questions and they showed me your picture."

"Alaina, let me explain." I force the words out, my voice low. "Let's go outside."

When I try to touch her shoulder, she shrugs me off. "Don't touch me. I mean, what kind of woman sleeps with a married man and then stops by to see his grieving widow?"

"I... I didn't—"

"They told me all about his online profiles. They told me you admitted to dating him, and that he was found dead inside your apartment."

People are beginning to stare now. Gasps break out across the room, followed by a solid, painful silence. There's a nauseous feeling in my stomach that urges me to leave, but there's no escape.

Matthew takes a step closer to Alaina.

"You the husband?" She places a hand over her pregnant stomach, protectively. "Do you know what your wife is into?"

"Let's not do this here," he says.

"I'll tell you what kind of woman she is," Alaina jeers. It's as though she's enjoying this. "A guilty one. A whore. You slept with my husband and then you killed him, and you thought I'd be too dumb to figure it out."

"No!" I shout, trying to drown out her accusations, but it's too late. I feel a tug on my leg, and look down to see Mabel staring up at me, the rings of her Saturn costume drooping beneath her hips. I pull her close to me, covering her ears with my hands. My eyes burn from trying not to cry, but it's bad enough Mabel has to witness this; she can't see me break down, too.

"Alaina, please listen to me."

All I want is to calm her down, but I know she won't listen when she's this angry. I reach out to her again, but before I can touch her, she raises her arm and slaps me across the face. The hit is sudden and unexpected. My cheek stings.

"That's enough." Matthew steps in between us, waving his hands in the hopes someone will come over and help. To my surprise, Harriet is the one who rushes to Alaina. She wraps her arms around her, whispering something only she can hear.

Alaina takes a step back, turning toward the other shocked faces inside the lobby. She points at me. "This woman is a cheater and a murderer!"

Some parents are frozen in place, unable to tear their eyes away from the scene, while others try guiding their children back into the auditorium. Alaina continues shouting over her shoulder. "Whore! Murderer!"

The words ring in my ears, weigh on my soul. Everyone watching. Everyone listening. And I don't know how to prove what she's saying isn't true.

Finally, Alaina relents. She collapses onto Harriet's shoulder, willingly walking with her to the door. Before she exits, she looks back at me, and our eyes lock. "You wanted to know how I'm holding up." She smiles, but not with her eyes. "Now you do."

The air in the room is sticky and warm. Because now I know it's not all in my mind. It's real. Mabel's teachers, her classmates, and my neighbors are all staring and glaring.

At me.

TWENTY-EIGHT

LILLIAN

The night breeze is a welcome greeting. I march to my car ahead of the group. Mabel hums a song, and I hope she's already forgotten about what happened inside. Matthew and Rebecca are silent, likely stewing over it.

Our cars are parked next to each other. Mabel skips toward me, embracing my legs. "Can I ride with Daddy?"

My chest clenches. Normally, I wouldn't question it. Sometimes she rides with me, sometimes him. But now I'm wondering if she doesn't want to be around me because of the scene with Alaina.

"Sure, honey." I wait for Rebecca and Matthew to catch up. "Let me talk to Daddy for a sec."

"Let's get you buckled up," Rebecca says, escorting Mabel to the other side of the car. Rebecca refuses to make eye contact, and I can't decide whether it's from embarrassment or shame.

Once the passenger door closes, Matthew whips his head in my direction, his skin a painful red, his brow glistening with sweat.

"I told you not to come to the play." His voice quivers with anger. He stuffs his hands in his pockets to try and calm himself.

"That's not fair. I had no way of knowing—"

"Who was that woman?"

It doesn't matter what explanation I give him for why I wanted to go tonight. It won't be enough. "Her name is Alaina. She's Carl's wife."

A wry chortle escapes Matthew's mouth. His hands have moved upward, resting on his hips, and he tilts his head to the sky. "Carl, as in the victim found inside our apartment?"

"Yes."

"How did she know who you were?"

"The police must have questioned her."

"No." He takes a step closer. "That's not what she said. She said you came to her."

My cheeks are burning again, and my stomach feels like it's dropped straight to the concrete beneath my feet. "I went to see her."

He rubs his forehead, making sure not to look at me. "Please tell me why you would do that."

"I was trying to understand why Carl lied to me about his life, and I wanted to see if Alaina recognized me. I thought maybe, if she found out he was cheating, she was involved."

"Cheating." The word lingers between us. "You said there was nothing romantic between you."

"There wasn't! We never even kissed. But she may not know that. If she found out her husband was on a dating website, she might have reacted."

"That still doesn't make sense, Lillian. She wouldn't track him down to our apartment and murder him there if your inter-actions with him were that innocent."

"Are you saying I'm lying?"

"I'm saying it doesn't make sense." A pause. "Now she knows who you are, and she thinks you went out of your way to deceive her. Which you did. It makes you look guilty."

"I know." There's a tossing in my stomach that refuses to

settle. I sit on the sidewalk to calm the sensation. "Everyone saw."

"Mabel saw."

I lean over further, trying to soothe myself. My sweet, inno-cent daughter. Her mind can't even fully process what Alaina was shouting about me, but she knows it wasn't good. She knows that a woman was targeting her mother in front of a crowd.

"You're right," I say. "I shouldn't have gone."

Matthew does what he usually does when I back down in a fight. He begins to feel guilty.

"I know it isn't fair, but I think we need to be careful about what we do in public, at least until the police solve Carl's murder."

I nod, thinking over what happened tonight. I want to believe Matthew is trying to protect me. Trying to protect Mabel. But there's a small voice inside that wonders if he's only dictating what I do in order to protect himself. I worry he's more concerned with protecting his own image—and the secret about Richard—than he is with proving my innocence.

I look up at him, but his face is turned to look ahead. I follow his gaze, noticing the unmarked police vehicle parking beside our cars. A nearby streetlamp catches a chrome accent, shooting a piercing ray of light in my direction. Matthew and I stand completely still, waiting.

Detective Spelling exits the driver's side door, Dylan exits the other. He's the first to speak.

"We heard there was a disruption at the elementary school."

I open my mouth to respond, but Matthew beats me to it.

"Yes. Alaina Gates. She caused a huge scene in front of my daughter and all her friends."

"I'm sorry your daughter had to see that," says Spelling, his voice sincere.

"That woman had to be escorted out of the building,"

Matthew continues. "She kept shouting at Lillian, accusing her of murder. Didn't you notice the woman was unhinged when you spoke to her?"

Dylan looks at me now. "We apologize on behalf of Ms. Gates, but surely you understand her husband was murdered. She's emotional. She's not been the most cooperative, even with us."

"She can't go around spreading rumors," I say.

"We received several calls about this incident from different witnesses. We wanted to make sure you were okay. See if you wanted to file a formal complaint."

"There's no need—"

"Yes," Matthew cuts in, taking a step closer to the police. "I would like to file a complaint."

"Well, since she targeted Lillian, she'd have to be the one to file a report."

I turn to Matthew. "What she did was wrong, but she is grieving."

"I don't care. Not when it comes to Mabel. That woman just assaulted you in a room full of people. If filing a complaint forces her to stay away from us, I think we should do it."

I imagine Mabel's face, those wide, wet eyes looking up at me as Alaina shouted.

Whore. Murderer.

"What do I need to do?" I say, my voice clipped.

"You'll need to come down to the station," Detective Spelling says. "We can write up an incident report and request a restraining order be put in place."

"Fine. I'll come tomorrow."

"Tonight would be better," Dylan says.

The sudden turnaround from both detectives, shifting from accusing me to making sure I'm okay, feels false.

"Should we call our lawyer?" Matthew says.

"It's up to you. You're simply filing a report about what

happened tonight. Ensuring Alaina stays away from you. I'm not sure how he can help."

But I'm not sure how much more I can handle on my own. I'm already to blame for so much. Even though I didn't murder Carl, it's possible he'd still be alive if it weren't for my own secrets. The familiar blend of guilt and shame return, and I have to fight to keep my composure.

I look back at Matthew, my eyes pleading. I don't want to do this, I don't want to dig any further into this mess, but he seems resolute. This isn't about me or him. It's about Mabel. About her protection. "Let me say goodnight to my daughter," I say. "I'll follow you there."

The cops nod, making no attempt to make me come sooner. That's a good sign. If they made me choose between saying goodnight to Mabel and coming to the station, I'd choose the former in a heartbeat. After what she witnessed tonight, she needs me.

I open the car door and hunker down close to Mabel, kissing her cheek. "I am so proud of you."

"Can we read a bedtime story when we get home?"

"I have somewhere I have to go," I say. "Maybe Daddy will read you a story. Or Rebecca."

"I want you," she whines, her hands playing with strands of my hair.

My chest squeezes tighter. I want nothing more than to come home with her, cuddle up in bed and forget that tonight ever happened. But it did happen, and if I want to protect her in the future, Matthew's right. I need to make sure Alaina can't come after us again.

"I'll be home as soon as I can," I tell her. "I promise."

I shut the car door, and she leans her tired head against the window. She's disappointed.

She needs her mother, smoothing her forehead, whispering that everything will be all right, even if it's not true.

TWENTY-NINE

MATTHEW

As soon as we enter the house, Mabel marches upstairs.

"Put on your pajamas," I shout after her.

I wander into the kitchen, emptying my pockets into the junk bowl, and lean forward over the counter. I breathe deeply, relishing a few moments of normalcy after this bizarre day.

Rebecca comes up behind me, starts rubbing the small of my back. I feel myself melting into her touch. "Are you okay?"

"I don't know. This all feels like it's getting too intense."

"Who was that woman back at the school?"

"Her name is Alaina. She's married to Carl, the man that died." It doesn't matter how many times these types of sentences leave my lips, it's not normal. I exhale. "I can't believe Mabel had to see all of that."

"She's a strong girl. She'll be okay."

Will she? Ever since she was born, I've put Mabel at the center of my life. Lillian has done the same. It's how we agreed upon this nesting set-up in the first place. We wanted to shield her from the complicated scenes so many children with divorced parents face. We didn't want her going back and forth between homes. We didn't want her feeling like she had to choose between us. She needed to know we were here for her, always in her corner.

The Florida offer appears in my mind again. A brief daydream of Mabel and I walking hand-in-hand on the beach, the sun beating down on our shoulders, salty air tickling our noses. Maybe change is what she needs after this, what I need. But I can't relive that fantasy without leaving Lillian behind, and I'm not sure she deserves that. I look up, and see Rebecca staring back at me, remember she's yet another person we'd be leaving.

"You should stay the night." I reach out my hand, pulling her closer to me.

"What about Lillian?"

"She has her own room."

"It might be better for the three of you to stay together." She grabs her bag. "Tomorrow will be a busy day at school. I could use some rest."

The past few days have been intense, and I feel a distance growing between us. We're used to Lillian being on the outskirts of our lives, and the past few days, she's been fully enmeshed.

"Is there something else bothering you?"

Her reaction tells me there is. "You don't need to worry about me."

"But I am worried. Is all of this with Lillian getting to you? You can tell me."

"It's not that. I mean, I am bothered by it all. Of course. But that's not what has been worrying me." She waits. "My ex was released from prison."

My legs suddenly feel weak. I sit on the barstool next to the counter. Rebecca rarely talks about her ex, and I try not to pry. "When?"

"Almost two weeks ago."

"And you're just now telling me?"

"I wanted to tell you sooner, but there was Mabel's party. Then everything at the apartment." She looks down. "You've had enough on your mind without worrying about my problems."

I stand, pulling her close to me. I kiss the top of her head. "Your problems are my problems."

I say this to comfort her, even if it doesn't feel completely honest. Rebecca and I have only discussed what happened with her ex once. Our relationship is still new, and I don't want to push her out of her comfort zone. Even now, with my arms around her, I sense her struggle.

"I always knew this day was coming," she says. "For the first time since his arrest, I feel like my life is normal again. As it should be. His release changes that."

"Has he contacted you?"

"No. He's not allowed to as a condition of his release. I'd like to think he's moved on, in his own way. I guess I'm just... afraid. I keep feeling like he's watching me. When I drive to school, when I'm home at night. And it's probably nothing at all. Just me being paranoid."

Afraid. Guilt washes over me, knowing I've not been there for Rebecca when she needed me.

"Stay here tonight," I offer again. "At least until you feel safe."

"No. Not with Lillian here. It's too complicated. I mean, sure, we all get along. But pushing sleepovers on one another is too weird."

My guilt grows. Because so much of my life is still connected to Lillian, I can't give Rebecca my all.

"How about this, then." I reach into my pocket and pull out my phone. "Let's share our locations. So, I know where you're at all the time."

"You don't have to do that."

"I want to. It would make me feel better, knowing you're safe."

She pulls out her phone and begins tapping the screen. She holds it out to me and smiles. "Done."

"You were wonderful tonight, by the way. Watching you work with the students, the parents. You kept your cool during the drama with Alaina. I doubt there are many situations you can't work your way out of."

She smiles. "It is getting late. I should probably head home. Let me know how Lillian's conversation with the police goes."

"Okay." I kiss her gently on the lips, watching as she walks away.

I climb upstairs, my footsteps light on the carpet, attempting not to wake Mabel if she's already asleep. Her bedroom door is open. I peer inside, the room dark except for the rotating night light.

I worry about Mabel, but I realize, in this moment, I worry about Lillian, too. She has very publicly been accused of murder, and I'm not sure she's strong enough to withstand the allegation. What if the police ask her more questions? She was shaken after what happened with Alaina, and she may not be able to handle investigators on her own.

Back downstairs, I dig through my wallet and pull out Barry's card. I contemplate whether or not I should call him, tell him about what happened at the play. He said to call him anytime. Did he really mean that? Or is it something important people say to make you feel protected?

My mind wrestles with what to do. It was foolish to suggest she file a restraining order by herself. I'm not sure I can trust the cops.

And, really, I'm not sure I can trust her.

THIRTY

LILLIAN

You shouldn't walk into an interrogation room and recognize the navy office chair, the water spots on the ceiling, the stale scent of coffee in the air. This is the second time I've been here in less than a week.

"You'll be comfortable here," Dylan says, as though he's reading my mind.

"Will I?"

"Trust me, you don't want to get stuck in the waiting room this late at night. You'll see everyone coming and going." He places a stack of folders between us, sits opposite me at the desk. "We just have some paperwork we need to fill out."

I wrap my arms around myself, even though I'm not cold. Simply, I'm trying to hold myself together, searching for a way to recall what happened earlier tonight while trying to ignore the shame and embarrassment of that moment.

Mabel. I think about her. Tucked into bed, her purple cover pulled to her shoulders. I need to finish this, so I can return to her.

"Can you walk me through what happened tonight?" Dylan asks.

Gone is the comfort of Mabel's bedroom. I'm pulled back to the present, to this familiar, dreadful place. I tell Dylan exactly what happened after the play. I recite the names she called me, the allegations she made. I mention other witnesses who saw the entire thing.

"Why did you reach out to Alaina in the first place?"

In all the time I'd been replaying what happened at the school, I'd overlooked the possibility I'd be asked about this. All the reasons I had sound better in my head than they do out loud.

"I wanted to see if she recognized me."

"And she didn't?"

"Not when I went to her house. That's why she confronted me tonight. She was so angry after seeing a picture of me, she just snapped."

Dylan exhales as he picks up the papers in front of him. He looks over his shoulder, then back at me. "You should leave all future investigating up to us."

"Well, you haven't uncovered anything. It's not in my nature to sit back and wait for answers. And everyone treats me like a suspect."

"Is that how I'm talking to you right now?" he says. "Like a suspect?"

"You're not treating me like I'm a victim. Which I am. A man ended up inside my home. He died there. It's very unsettling."

He stands, pushing back his chair. "I need to grab a few more signatures, then you'll be free to go. Alaina won't be allowed near you or your family."

When he leaves, he doesn't shut the door. I lean back, pulling my jacket tighter. At least that's one means of protection, keeping this woman who has clear reason to dislike me away from my family. I scroll through my phone, mindlessly waiting. Matthew hasn't texted. I click on the Facebook icon, but quickly exit out. There's no one in my social circle I want to check up on, not after the stares I received tonight. How quickly this event has changed the way I see the world, and worse, the way the world sees me.

Outside this room are gray cubicles on either side of the hallway. Every few minutes, there's the trill of a phone ringing, the gearing of a copy machine. The police station mirrors the set of *The Office* more than it does *Law & Order*.

Maybe that's not a good distinction to make. Maybe I'm getting too comfortable here.

Finally, I see Dylan rounding the corner, a stack of papers in his hand. Even from a distance, I can see how handsome he is. More thoughts I shouldn't be thinking.

He's walking in this direction, when suddenly someone stands in front of him. It's Detective Spelling, and although I can't see his face, I sense he's saying something important. Even from a distance I can tell the energy has shifted. Dylan's jaw drops, then his eyes look forward, landing on me. Spelling turns, and now he's staring at me, too.

They duck around a corner, obstructing my view. I sit up straighter, stretching my arms across the table. It was only a moment, but that nervous feeling has returned to my stomach.

When Dylan returns to the room, he stands in the corner, the papers no longer in his hands. Spelling joins him, shutting the door behind him, which gives me a sudden sense of claustrophobia. My presence tonight was supposed to be routine. Paperwork. But the mood of the room has turned more serious.

"Am I free to go?"

"Whenever you like," Spelling says. "But something has been brought to our attention, and we wanted to ask you about it."

My eyes flit across the room to Dylan, but his gaze is fixed on the floor, his arms crossing his body. There is an air of disappointment around him, so at odds with the way he seemed just minutes ago. I should get up and leave. But I'm curious. I have to know what they've uncovered. I need to know what's changed.

"What is it?"

Spelling places a picture of Carl on the desk. "We've already established you knew the victim."

We've been over this so many times, and now I'm frustrated. Spelling is pulling at straws, hoping for another opportunity to interrogate me.

"Yes."

"Did you know he had a brother?"

That last word makes my nerves stand at attention. My breath sharpens, and I have to use all the control in my body to keep from reacting.

"We didn't know each other enough to talk about family."

Spelling nods. "The two had lost touch over the years. Didn't really run in the same circles. But you know how family is, still always around. Carl's brother died a couple of years back."

My pulse settles. Maybe they haven't made the connection. Maybe they don't know.

"Uh huh."

Sounds. That's all that will leave my lips. I'm trying hard not to react. When I look toward Dylan, I see he's staring back at me, studying the reaction I'm fighting.

Spelling puts down another picture. "Do you know this man?"

I don't want to look. I hate myself for not leaving. But here I am, Spelling and Dylan staring down at me, another familiar face staring up. My eyes study it.

Richard's face.

"Yes. He was my neighbor."

"This is Carl's brother. Richard Walsh. Died two years ago."

"I remember," I say, keeping my voice level. "He fell from the cliffs in our neighborhood."

"It was more than just your neighborhood. He was last seen leaving a party at your house."

Spelling is an expert interrogator. He knows how to make an accusation without saying the words, how to let it linger.

He taps the first picture. "Carl was found dead in your apartment." He taps the second. "And Richard, your neighbor, was reported missing two years ago. Both have a connection to you." He waits, letting the tension build.

Then adds, "Now, what are the odds of that?"

THIRTY-ONE

LILLIAN

They know.

All the walls I've been building in my mind come crashing down. *They know.* They know about Richard. Carl is simply an afterthought. Even though his death is a mystery, I know I wasn't involved.

But I know Matthew and I are at fault for Richard's death. And if they've made that connection, there's nothing I can do to defend myself. I can't combat the truth.

"How well did you know Richard?"

Dylan asks the question, coming out of the corner and walking toward me.

"I... I told you. We're neighbors."

"Right." He leans over the desk. "But it's a strange coincidence, isn't it? Two suspicious deaths in the same family."

"Richard's death wasn't suspicious."

My voice is cracking. I can feel a ring of sweat breaking out across my forehead. Was this a setup? A way to let my guard down so they could get the answers they really want? I'm not sure how much longer I can...

A knock slices the tension in the room. The door opens, and Barry is standing on the other side.

"Everything okay in here?" he asks.

"She's only here to file a restraining order," Spelling says. "It's not an interrogation."

Barry makes a careful inspection of the room. "It looks rather official to me."

"Only a conversation."

"Has the paperwork been filed?"

Dylan stands straighter, dropping a document on the desk. "Just need a signature, then she's free to go."

"Lillian." Barry says my name like a child about to be reprimanded, nodding toward the paper on the desk.

I stand, my hand shaking so much I struggle with my own signature. The officers must notice. I drop the pen on the table, then look at Barry with pleading eyes.

"Come with me," he says, holding the door open. "Goodnight, detectives."

Night has fallen, only a few stars in the sky. Or perhaps, they aren't visible because of the bright lights beaming from the station. I follow Barry to his car, sensing he wants to put distance between himself and the building before he speaks.

"Looks like things were getting heated in there."

"I only came to file a restraining order. I didn't think I needed a lawyer for that."

"You always need a lawyer when you're talking with the cops," he says. "What were they asking you about back there?"

I should tell him the truth. He's my lawyer, the only person who could know the truth about Richard and help me find a way out of it. Make a case for self-defense, perhaps. But Richard isn't just my problem. He's Matthew's, too. I need to talk to him first.

"They were just revisiting what we've already discussed."

"Well, hopefully you learned your lesson." He opens his car

door, slinging his briefcase onto the passenger seat. "It's a good thing Matthew called me."

"Matthew called you?"

"How else did you think I knew where you were?"

I hadn't really thought about it. "What did he say?"

"He told me about what happened at that play and you were on your way to the police station. Guess he thought you could use some backup." He sits. Before closing the car door, he adds, "Next time I'd feel better if the phone call came from you."

I stand still, waiting for Barry to leave the parking lot. Matthew thought I needed backup? He didn't think I could handle a conversation with the police by myself, even though he was the one pressuring me to file the restraining order. The trust he has in me is quickly deteriorating.

There are more pressing issues than my ex-husband no longer trusting me. The police know Carl and Richard are related, and that they're both connected to me.

Which means they're both connected to Matthew, too.

THIRTY-TWO

MATTHEW

I roll from side to side, trying to find comfort in my bed. I'm still not used to sleeping alone, especially here. But it's not Rebecca or her bed I'm missing.

I miss sleeping beside Lillian. I don't even miss her, per se. I've accepted where we are, what our duties are to one another. But I miss the life we had, the simple one before I wrecked it.

My eyes are closed. I feel myself slipping into sleep when sounds from downstairs jolt me back to wakefulness. Lillian is home. I throw on my navy, terry-cloth robe and head downstairs. She's in the kitchen, pouring herself a glass of wine. We don't keep alcohol in the house. She must have stopped at the liquor store.

"How'd it go?"

She doesn't look at me. "I filed the restraining order, if that's what you're asking."

She looks pale and tired. Worried. Something's happened, and she's gearing up to tell me. "What is it?"

She sits on the barstool and takes a large gulp of wine before looking at me. "The police know Richard was our neighbor."

Hearing his name spikes my pulse, but I don't want Lillian to see. "That's not difficult to figure out."

"They know Carl and Richard are brothers. And they're making other connections. They read in an incident report that Richard was last seen leaving our house. Now, Carl has turned up dead in our apartment." She pauses. "Two crimes and I'm the only connection."

"Did they say that?" My voice is shaky now. "Did they use those words?"

"That's the point they were trying to make," she says. "The conversation was cut short when Barry showed up."

I exhale in relief. Knowing Barry was there to interrupt means Lillian couldn't have let much slip. She wouldn't have had the chance. I run a hand through my hair, feel the sweat building along my scalp.

"I thought you were there to file a report."

"I'm wondering if they even cared about that, or if they were trying to get me to come to the station with my guard down so they could ask me about Richard." She takes another mouthful. She's already finished the glass. She reaches for the bottle, ready to pour another. "Speaking of Barry, why did you call him?"

"In case something like this happened."

"If you thought the police were trying to trick me into something, why did you pressure me to go to the station in the first place?"

"I had no idea they were tricking you!"

"So, you called Barry because you couldn't trust me."

"Lillian, I trust you with everything." The words are sincere, even if I feel myself forcing them out. "I trust you with my life. You know that."

"I'm starting to wonder if that's changing. Ever since Carl's body was found, you've been questioning everything I say and do. It's like you don't believe me when I say I wasn't involved."

"I believe you." I pause. "I'm only trying to be as careful as possible. We're on a slippery slope, and this situation is only getting worse. You didn't do anything to Carl, but we both are responsible for what happened to Richard."

"Both?"

So much anger and accusation in that one word.

"We both covered it up."

She takes another sip of wine, and looks away. "We both covered it up, but it feels like I'm the only one dealing with the aftermath. I'm the only one they think was connected to both victims."

"I know it seems that way right now," I say to her, reaching for her hand. "But I'm right here with you. I am. I'm not going to let something happen to either one of us."

"I'm scared. After I found Carl, I was just confused. Considering all the connections to Richard, it feels like this is all deliberate. It feels like I'm being set up."

Does she think I'm the one behind this? She won't say it, but her stare, her words... she's losing trust in me too.

"They won't be able to trace what happened that night back to us."

"What if they do?" Her voice is shaky, fighting hard to hold back tears. "Carl was able to put it together, and he didn't even know us. That means someone else must have told him to look into us."

"Who would do that?"

"Maybe someone saw us that night."

"They didn't."

"Then someone else must know."

My stare fixes on the wine bottle, and I'm tempted to reach for a glass. Lillian doesn't know about the other mistake I made after Richard's death. Keeping this secret from her, worrying about how it might have played a role in what happened to Carl, is driving me nuts.

"Maybe it's time we bring Barry into this," she says. "Tell him the truth about what happened to Richard."

My jaw drops at the suggestion. "Are you crazy? We can't tell anyone."

"He's our lawyer. He can protect us. Maybe strike a deal before the police press charges. We could argue self-defense."

"That's easy for you to say. I was the one arguing with him when he went over the cliff. Coming clean about Richard might help you, but it certainly won't help me."

After keeping this secret for two years, coming forward would cause nothing but problems for us. She can't actually think that's the best decision. She's desperate, and that makes me nervous.

"I'm not sure how much longer we can keep running from this. It's clear someone knows what happened and they're using it against us. If the police find out—"

"They won't," I say, pulling her in for a hug. "I promise."

We need to end this conversation, at least for tonight.

I won't let the truth about Richard come out. It could ruin us both.

THIRTY-THREE

LILLIAN

I've been haunted by several events in my life. My infertility, each unsuccessful month as gut-wrenching and trying as the one before. Richard's death and the actions we took to cover it up, taking its toll on us both. Finding Carl's body.

Now, I can add the look on Mabel's face last night to that list. That's what first enters my mind when I wake up on Thursday morning.

The entire school witnessed Alaina's outburst, and the reaction that hurts most is hers. My little girl with the frightened face and watery eyes. Even if she's too young to grasp the trouble we're in, she can read tone. She saw the way Alaina shouted at me, the way the other parents cowered in fear and astonishment. And she saw me—her mother, her hero—at the center of it all.

For a moment, the memory eclipses everything, even the fact the police know I'm connected to Richard. Being embarrassed, accused, arrested for murder—all of that seems secondary to losing my daughter's respect.

That's why I'm willing to take hold of what little control I have. Instead of wasting away in bed, as my spirit longs to do, I get up and get dressed. I prepare a bowl of oatmeal and make sure Mabel's backpack is ready. When she comes downstairs with Matthew, I already have the keys in my hands.

"I can take her to school," Matthew says.

"No," I say. "I will."

He hovers close, whispering. "Are you sure that's the best idea? Considering what happened last night."

"Eat your oatmeal," I tell Mabel, smiling. I make eye contact with Matthew and lower my voice. "I won't walk her in. I'll let her out in the drop-off line. But I want her to see that I'm okay. How is she supposed to get over what happened last night if I can't?"

If there's one thing I've learned about parenting, it's this: children don't hear what you say, they watch what you do.

Matthew nods. "Okay. I'm going into the office. But if anything happens—anything at all—you call me."

"Sure."

I'm going to act as though nothing will happen. I'm going to act like this is a normal day in the life of our family, even if those days are numbered.

We listen to Mabel's favorite songs on the way to school. I sing along, dancing in the driver's seat, and eventually she joins in. I can almost see the weight of last night lifting. By the time we arrive at the drop-off area, Mabel is smiling and carefree.

"Have a good day," I yell through the rolled-down car window. "Remember we have dance practice today."

"Bye, Mommy." She waves. "Love you."

I say the words back, even though she can't hear me. She's already taking off, running to the open elementary school doors. She slows down to talk with a friend, and the icy grip on my heart begins to thaw.

She's going to be okay, I tell myself.

I've pulled out of the parking lot and onto the main road when my phone begins ringing. It's Cat. She must have heard about the drama last night. Although I don't feel like rehashing the ordeal so soon, I'm not in a position to be pushing away the few friends I have left.

I answer.

"Have you talked to Matthew?"

"I saw him this morning at the house."

"Police are at Voyage." Her voice is high-pitched and jittery. "They're questioning the employees. Ted's fit to be tied."

"Voyage?" I balk. "Why would the police be there?"

"I don't know. It has something to do with the murder investigation."

But why? I'm at the center of all this, not Matthew or Ted or their business. Maybe the police are trying to put pressure on Matthew by interfering with his life. Or maybe the police know something I don't.

The time is ten past eight, according to the dashboard clock. The front lobby doesn't open for another hour. "How do you know?"

"I have a friend at the front desk who drops information anytime something interesting happens," she says. "She said the police were there when she arrived this morning."

Matthew should be on his way to the office, or just now arriving. What will he think when he sees Voyage is littered with cops? And Ted. I can't imagine the amount of anger he must have at me. At both of us.

"Why do you care what's going on at the office?"

"According to our divorce agreement, the business still pays my bills, too. And yours," she says. "Besides, it's fun knowing whenever Ted is in hot water. This is different because you're involved. I wanted to give you a heads-up."

My mind is racing, my palms beginning to stick to the steering wheel. This has gotten out of hand. Regardless of what the police know, they clearly think I'm involved. And now, thanks to Alaina, the entire community does, too.

"Have you heard anything about last night?" I ask Cat.

"No," she says. "What happened?"

Cat is big on gossip, but because she doesn't have kids, sometimes information is relayed to her second-hand if it involves the school crowd. So, I tell her about the awkward altercation, and how I'd reached out to Alaina on my own before that. She sounds aghast that the woman, despite her grief, would lash out so publicly, especially in front of Mabel.

"It's not right," Cat says. "The police aren't even finished investigating. It's only a matter of time until they find something that will clear your name."

"I hope." My voice is deflated, the magic from my morning with Mabel fading. I'm back to reality. "Let me know if you hear back from your friend at Voyage."

"I will. I might ask around about Carl and Alaina while I'm at it. The nerve of that woman," she says. "Whatever happened to innocent until proven guilty?"

Those words stay with me, even after we've ended the phone conversation. It's a just concept. As people, we've never really waited to get the full story before making assumptions. We judge people, expecting them to fit into whatever role we've pre-constructed. The court of public opinion is often too eager and swift, prematurely deciding who is innocent, who is guilty.

I hope, in this instance, the public makes the right call.

Then I think of Blaire and her boys. I imagine what their lives must have been like in the past two years, without a husband and a father. Maybe I deserve to be punished more than I'm willing to admit.

THIRTY-FOUR

MATTHEW

I arrive at the office at a quarter until nine. I wasn't lying when I told Lillian I had work to do. I've been distracted all week, don't even know about the outcome of Ted's meeting with the potential investors. But I'm also ready for something to take my mind off what's happening. I need to replace last night with something predictable and safe.

For as long as I can remember, when the rest of the world has been crumbling around me, work has been the constant that keeps me going. Even during my drinking days, I still made Voyage a priority.

And yet, when I walk inside the office, I'm greeted with strained faces from my employees. There's a suspicious tinge in the air, and for a moment, I wonder if I'm losing my mind.

I head to the front desk. "Mandy, what's going on?"

Her eyes are wide, thick dark lashes stretched almost to her eyebrows. "The police are here."

"The police?"

"They're speaking with Ted right now. And they also asked to speak with you."

I look up the stairs, but am afraid to move. This can't be happening here. This drama can't infiltrate work, my safe place.

I storm up the stairs, heading in the direction of Ted's office. Sure enough, he's inside. I spot the detectives talking to him through the glass walls. I duck around the corner, trying to hear what's being said without being seen.

"...I told you, we've had a limited interaction since they divorced," says a voice. It's Ted. "We're cordial, but I can't tell you much about her anymore."

"And Carl Gates? Are you familiar with that name?" It's the younger cop, Detective Logan, talking. "Maybe you or Matthew had business dealings with him in the past."

"Never heard of him."

"Maybe you'd recognize him. Take a look."

There's a pause, and I assume the police have a picture for Ted to review.

"No. I don't know him."

"One other question," Detective Spelling butts in. "Are you familiar with Richard Walsh?"

My stomach drops when I hear his name. Lillian was right. They're pursuing this connection. Carl leads them to Richard, which could lead them to me.

"Yeah," Ted says. "I know him."

"How?"

"We used to be neighbors. My ex-wife and I were friendly with him and his wife, Blaire. I wouldn't say we were particularly close," Ted says, his voice level. "What's he have to do with any of this?"

"What can you tell us about his death?"

"Must have been... two years ago. He was drunk and stumbled over the cliffs in our neighborhood. It's a dangerous area, especially at night."

Spelling doesn't offer any more information than that. A smart move, if it weren't working against me. We need to minimize the connection between the victims somehow, otherwise I'll have a lot more trouble headed my way.

"Sorry, I can't help you with that either. Now, if you'll please leave. It's intrusive having cops walking around the place."

I zip around the corner into the office. "Morning, Ted." I feign surprise when I look at the two detectives. "Excuse me. What are you doing here?"

"We had a few questions for your business partner," Detective Logan says.

"And you, too," Spelling adds.

"Lillian and I have been clear. We won't be talking to you without a lawyer present."

The detectives exchange a look.

"All right. We'll be in touch," Spelling says. He looks back at Ted. "Thank you for your time."

I stand still, allowing the detectives to pass. I wait until they've started descending the stairs before shutting the office door and turning around.

"Why were they here?"

"You tell me why they're here!" Ted shouts, his voice shaking with anger. "I mean, what the fuck, Matthew? The police questioning me at work, in front of all our employees."

"What did they want to know?"

"They were asking questions about you and Lillian and that godawful apartment." He waves a finger at me. "I told you not to get involved with this. Let Lillian fight her own battles."

"I am. Clearly, they're going after her harder than I realized."

"No, they're going after you harder than *I* realized. You need to distance yourself from this before you take me and Voyage down with you. How do you think investors will react when they hear one of the co-founders is tied up in a murder investigation?"

"We have a lawyer. You heard me say it. Everything will get sorted, we just need time." I say the words aloud, hoping they'll ring true.

"They asked if I knew the man who was killed. Carl. And they were asking about Richard Walsh." He exhales.

There's a beat, and I wonder if Ted will keep pressing, but he places his hands on his hips, waiting for an answer.

"Just trust me to handle this. Lillian didn't murder anyone, and once that's proven all this will go away."

Ted lets out a sarcastic laugh, turning so that his back is toward me as he paces the room.

"You'd tell me if something else was happening, right? If there's anything I need to know."

"You know I would."

"Good," he says, but he sounds unsure. "But please, for the love of God, think of someone else besides Lillian. Mabel or me. Yourself! Your devotion to this woman is going to bring us all down with her."

I grit my teeth to prevent myself from responding. I leave his office, enter my own, sit behind my desk, completely clueless over what my next step should be.

THIRTY-FIVE

LILLIAN

I hang up the phone, my throat raw from trying not to cry.

Matthew was irate that the police came to Voyage. Ted's fury must be even greater. I never imagined that this situation would stretch its vicious roots, attaching itself to so many people.

I'm so distraught, I'm reluctant to answer the next phone call that comes in. I don't recognize the number. I take the call anyway, and a dispatcher at the police station informs me my apartment has been released and I'm free to return.

My chest swells with this little victory. I'm banished from everywhere else, it seems. Returning somewhere familiar, even if it's the same place where this trouble began, is comforting.

The drive isn't long, and I find myself having a greater appreciation for the landmarks I pass. Just last week, life was normal. Now, it's like everything is slipping away.

When I arrive at the apartment complex, there are no longer police cars crowding the lot. It's as if nothing happened at all. Like I've stepped back in time, to a less complicated moment in my life. Even Mrs. Haynes is outside, allowing her dog to tinkle. She stands still when she sees me approaching the building.

"Back already?"

"It feels much longer than it's been," I say. The two of us haven't really ever talked much, just passing comments, which aren't even always friendly. But she was the first person there for me that night. "Mrs. Haynes, I wanted to thank you for waiting with me until the police arrived."

She nods, as though debating how much to engage. "It's been a strange scene around here the past couple of days." She looks down at her dog. "Hoppy didn't like having all those cops around. Too much foot traffic."

"I'm sorry about that, too."

"He doesn't like being around so many new people. And there seemed to be a new one every hour, except for those two in suits."

"Detectives Spelling and Logan."

"Yeah. The older one won't shut up. At least the younger one is easy on the eyes."

I can't be bothered with thinking about Dylan right now. I'm more worried about what we learned during our discussion with Barry—that Mrs. Haynes told police she'd seen Carl exiting my apartment.

"Mrs. Haynes," I begin, "the police say you once saw Carl leaving my apartment, but that can't be true. He picked me up for a date, but he never went inside the building."

"You weren't with him at the time. I told the police that. But I distinctly remember it," she says. "I never forget a face. He walked right into me without even offering an apology."

"When was this?"

"I don't keep a diary, dear. I just know what I saw."

She sounds too confident for me to keep questioning her, but if Carl was inside our apartment before his death, he didn't enter it with me. How did he get inside? Could Matthew have a connection with him he's not telling me about? Perhaps she's simply mistaken, has Carl confused with Dylan or Ted or another guest.

As Mrs. Haynes commits so much to memory, how could she not have seen anyone entering or exiting the apartment that night? If anyone was to pick up on something suspicious, it would be her.

"Do you remember anything from last weekend? Anything that might explain what happened?"

"If I did, I would have already told the police."

"Right. It's just, they're not telling me much."

"That's how investigations work, dear. Especially if they think you're guilty."

"I'm not guilty." It feels good to declare it out loud. I take a deep breath, repeat the words: "I'm not guilty."

Mrs. Haynes faces the building, then looks back at me. "Saturday night was my great-niece's birthday. She's about the only person who takes the time to visit me anymore, so we went out to celebrate, even if that meant spending the evening with my hag of a sister." She shakes Hoppy's leash. "We went to Thai Palace down the street. Should have known better. They've got the best panang curry in town, but a horrible wait on the weekends. It was after ten o'clock before I returned home. Hoppy had to relieve himself on the back porch while I was gone, poor thing."

"What about earlier in the day? Did you see anything?"

"I never saw anyone coming or going. Not until I heard you screaming."

I exhale in frustration. Out of all the nights for Mrs. Haynes to be away from the complex, it had to be that one.

"Thank you. And I'm sorry again, for the intrusion."

I start to walk toward the stairs when she says, "I guess it wasn't all bad. It's the most excitement I've had in years."

Mrs. Haynes speaks her mind, a trait I'm beginning to think

develops with age. She won't come out and say I'm innocent, but at least she's not treating me like I'm guilty, as my own peers do.

I stand outside the front door, yellow ribbons of caution tape coiled up on the ground, like snakes. I take another deep breath before walking inside.

This place has never felt like my home—that's back in Seaside Cliffs with Mabel—but it feels more disconnected now. It has been disrupted by strangers, the air tinged with the still-present scent of death. I wander around the living room first, taking in the upturned sofa cushions and emptied cabinet drawers.

I work up enough courage to enter the bedroom, finding the mattress and bloody sheets have been taken, probably for some type of forensic testing. The violent centerpiece of the room is gone, but streaks of blood remain on the walls and ceilings.

A memory of finding Carl's body flashes in my mind. The confusion. The darkness. The fear.

The familiar quiet of the apartment returns as I realize I'm the only person responsible for cleaning the mess. So, that's what I do. I clean and I clean and I clean. I try, fruitlessly, to put everything back together the way it was before.

It takes several hours before the place looks more like a home than a crime scene. My clothes smell of sweat and bleach, my hands are raw from scrubbing surfaces with various cleaners. I'm rearranging the last of the furniture, reconnecting the electronic devices left unplugged by the police.

The entertainment center is large and difficult to move—I remember it took two men to bring it into the apartment after I purchased it, but I'm trying to wriggle my way between it and the wall, so I can fix the internet connection.

As I'm sliding away from the wall, my foot catches on a cord. Some devices fall onto the newly mopped hardwood floors.

"Shit," I say, assessing the damage. There's an overturned router and DVD player. Nothing appears damaged, until...

There's a small rectangular piece on the floor about the size of a USB drive. I pick it up, wondering where it must fit in this mess of electronics, but it doesn't appear to be broken. There's a label on the bottom of the device, and when I read what it says, my stomach drops.

MicroSpy.

I'm certain I've never seen this device before, and although I still don't know what it is, exactly, the word *spy* makes me nervous. I pull out my phone and research the brand name. Sure enough, it's a recording device, a bug.

What is it doing inside my apartment? Did the police leave it here on purpose? They may not have enough to arrest me, but that doesn't mean they aren't tracking my every move. They could be trying to build a case against me at this very moment.

My nerves are so rattled that when the alarm on my phone goes off, I startle, dropping the MicroSpy bug on the floor. It's time to pick up Mabel from school. I stash the device in a Ziploc bag and put it into my purse to investigate later.

I lock up the apartment and scurry down the concrete steps leading to the parking lot.

THIRTY-SIX

LILLIAN

Someone is spying on me inside the apartment. If not the police, then another person. I find myself looking over my shoulder, the paranoia almost suffocating. I try not to obsess over it as I drive to Mabel's school.

She slides into the backseat of my car, tossing her backpack to the side. Her cheeks are flushed and her hair, which was this morning styled perfectly, is in disarray. Such is life for a lively kindergartner.

"How was your day?" I ask, forcing my voice to sound as cheerful as possible.

"Good."

"Tell me one thing you learned."

I started this back when she was in preschool, and her answers have become more detailed over the years. She begins telling me about the shapes they're learning about in math class, how she was able to color them with crayons. As she speaks, there's no hint of distress in her voice, no sign that someone might have given her a hard time about last night. I'm relieved. Not only are children resilient, but they easily forget.

Adults, however, never do.

We pull into the parking lot of The Studio. I'd considered not letting Mabel go to ballet practice, especially after Harriet told me my presence wasn't the best look for The Studio. However, I'm trying to stay resolute in my commitment to rise above the drama.

So, I'm going to take her. The dance duffel is already in the trunk, packed with tights and slippers and a pink leotard. Normally, I'd walk inside with her, busy myself around the front desk during her class. I won't go that far, but Mabel will go to class. She will carry on like everything is normal because for her, it is.

At least for now.

She hops out of the car, walking around back to the trunk to grab her bag. I meet her there, grabbing the spare hairbrush and ties I keep in a Ziploc bag.

"Let me pull back your hair," I say.

"Aren't you coming with me?"

I look at the front doors, seeing no sign of Harriet.

"Not today. I have a few errands to run," I say. "I'll fix your hair and then you can run inside and get dressed. I'll be right here when you finish up."

She doesn't question the decision, her head bobbing as I try to pull her hair into a bun, securing the wisps of delicate baby hair around her face.

"There." I pose her in front of me and smile, give her a kiss on the cheek. "You look perfect. Ms. Harriet can help with your clothes, if you need it."

She hurries along, entering the building alongside one of her classmates. The little girl's mother holds the door open. I'm quick to get back inside my car, not wanting to be spotted by the other moms. Instead of driving away, as I should, I remain parked. I watch the parents walking in with their daughters. Smiles on their faces, maybe a little tired around the eyes, but still happy. Just last week, I'd been one of them, and it hurts that I no longer feel any connection to them.

In a flutter of thought, everything hits at once. The bug inside the apartment and the questions it raises. The embarrassment of last night. My eyes water. I'm so used to holding back tears, all my emotions really. I don't want to seem suspicious. I don't want to give Mabel a reason to worry. But here, alone in my car, I let the tears fall, thankful for this brief moment of release.

Someone starts tapping on the driver's side window, and I jump. I startle even more when I see the person standing beside my car is Blaire Walsh. I roll down the window.

"Blaire?"

"Devon decided he wants to start dance. It's his first class," Blaire says, looking at The Studio entrance, then back at me. "I couldn't help noticing you seem upset. Is everything okay?"

"Yes, I'm fine. Just a little emotional."

Blaire smiles, and it's hard to tell if the look contains sympathy or pity. She looks down. "You know, I saw what happened last night. At the play."

I clear my throat. It stings even more, knowing this woman I've hurt so deeply witnessed my embarrassment. Then again, if anyone has earned the right to judge me, it's Blaire.

"I've actually been wanting to talk to you," she continues. "I'm not sure if you know this, but the person who died this weekend... he was Richard's brother."

How do I react? Do I tell her the police already made me aware? Or, do I act surprised? Unable to think clearly, I opt for the latter.

"I didn't know Richard had a brother."

"We weren't close or anything. Even before Richard died." She raises her head now, looking across the parking lot. I wonder if she's trying to stop herself from tearing up. "I'd actually only met him once. Richard and Carl had the same mother, different fathers. They didn't really grow up together. A few years ago, they had a falling out."

"And Alaina. His wife. Did you know her?"

"No. They hadn't been married that long, from what I understand," she says. "I don't know why I felt the need to tell you. I guess it just seemed odd seeing you around town, hearing about what people were saying, and not mentioning it."

I know little about Blaire, but this is obvious: she's always been kind. Even now, she's wanting to make sure I'm okay. If only she knew how involved I was in her husband's death...

"Those things Alaina was saying about me. They weren't true. I wasn't having an affair with Carl."

Blaire nods. "I believe you. I know we're not close, but I've never thought you were the type of person to wreck someone else's marriage."

"Thank you." I look away. I'm not deserving of Blaire's praise. Because of me, her husband is dead.

"I guess..." She pauses, as though struggling to wrestle out what she wants to say. "I guess, I just wanted you to know that it doesn't matter what people are saying, not everyone is against you. I know that's what I'd want to hear if the tables were turned."

A lump forms in my throat, and I fight hard to swallow it down. "Thank you for telling me that."

She looks back at the building. "Maybe at next week's practice we can go inside together. Chat while the kids practice pirouettes?"

I chuckle, genuinely. "I'd like that."

She waves, stepping away from the car and inside the building.

If she only knew how much anguish Matthew and I had caused her, she'd be the last person giving me hope when I need it most.

THIRTY-SEVEN

LILLIAN

I drive along the coast, the deep waters of the Pacific ahead. There are several stops along this route, perfect for tourists hoping for an unobstructed view of the sea. At this time of day, the skies are clear, the sun sparkling on every ripple and wave.

I'm killing time while Mabel is at ballet practice. Normally, I'd spend my hour behind the desk doing paperwork, occasionally peering through the studio door watching the children practice pliés. But I'm no longer welcome there.

And I have nowhere else to go. The apartment is out of the question, especially after finding the bug. I can't stop thinking about it. Could the police have put it there? Are they that desperate to build a case against me?

Or, it could be worse. The only other person with access to the apartment, to my knowledge, is Matthew. Could he be keeping tabs on me? He's been acting strange ever since Carl's body was found, and although I want to believe he's wrestling with the same paranoia I am, I can't shake the feeling there's something he's keeping from me.

A year ago, that question would have never popped into my mind. A week ago, even. Since Saturday, everything has been off-balance, loyalties shifting. I never would have thought Harriet would abandon me, or that Blaire Walsh would be there comforting me during my time of need.

When I'm not thinking about the bug inside the apartment, I'm revisiting my conversation with Blaire. She seemed sincere. She always does, which only tightens the knot of guilt inside my chest.

The investigation into Richard's death ended as quickly as it began. Not long after his body was found, there was a funeral.

I didn't want to go, but Matthew insisted.

"All of our neighbors are going," he said. "We don't want to be the only ones that don't."

And that logic angered me because deep down, I believed our absence would raise questions. We should be looked at with suspicion. Richard's death was our fault, and we deserved some form of punishment.

But as always, my mind went back to Mabel. Perhaps being arrested would cleanse my own soul, but where would that leave her? Matthew was right. We'd committed to keeping what happened a secret—from the police and everyone else—and we had to see it through, which meant attending.

Matthew was right again about all our neighbors being in attendance. Harriet and David sat toward the front. Cat sat in the back, with some of the other single housewives. Many neighbors had brought their children, hoping they could be a comfort to Richard and Blaire's boys, but I left Mabel at home with Jane. I refused to let her be a witness to the pain we'd caused.

Music blared from the organ as people took their seats. The last person to enter the church was Blaire. A man I'd never seen before was helping her down the aisle, her grief so strong she could barely walk.

Before taking her seat, she paused at the casket. She leaned over, placing something inside, then her knees buckled, as she let out more sobs.

My neck and cheeks turned hot. It felt like the eyes of everyone in the church were burning into my flesh, but of course, no one was looking at me. No one could tear their gaze away from Blaire, the woman who had lost everything.

The minister started speaking, but his words were distant and blending together. The entire room, it seemed, was folding into itself, collapsing around me. When the congregation stood to sing the first hymn, I ran out of the church.

Matthew followed me outside. "Are you okay?"

My breaths were so rapid and shallow, it made it impossible to speak. I shook my head.

He looked back at the church, then stepped closer, whispering. "You can't do this here. People are going to wonder why you're so upset."

"Let them wonder!" I shouted, blocking his arm when he tried to wrap it around my shoulders.

The ceremony continued without us, the doors closed so no one could hear, and yet I still felt exposed. All my shame and guilt on display.

Matthew tried again, pleading. "Maybe you were right. Maybe coming here was too much for you, but I'm begging you. Hold it together."

I didn't have a compelling argument. All that escaped was a shallow sob. This time when he wrapped his arms around me, I didn't have the strength to fight him off.

"I know it's hard." His mouth was pressed against my ear, his breath warm and wet. "I'm struggling, too. Every day. But we just have to stay strong a little bit longer. This is almost over."

I pushed away from him, marching in the direction of the car. I knew Matthew was hurting, had witnessed his struggles first-hand. But there seemed to be an end date for his grief.

After the body was found, after the investigation ended, after the funeral... at some point he'd be able to move on from what we'd done.

I knew in that moment I never would, and I believe that's the very moment our own relationship began to crumble.

He went back inside, while I waited in the car. I couldn't stand to see Blaire again. I'd never be able to wipe that heart-breaking image of her from my memory.

And Blaire is still here, torturing me every time I see her. Now that I think of it, I've been around her several times in the past week. First, at Mabel's party. Then at the school play. Today, she just happened to be in the parking lot to witness my little breakdown. Anne Isle is small; it could all be coincidence, but what if it's something more?

No one would have a greater motive for revenge than Blaire. Because of me, her husband is dead, she's raising three boys by herself. And now an earlier thought returns. What if someone saw us? Blaire was at the housewarming party. For all we know, she could have wandered around looking for Richard, witnessed the entire altercation on the cliffs. Perhaps she's the one behind all this, tightening the tension until I break and come clean about what happened that night.

But why would she wait all this time? Two years. And I remember being with her in the moments after Richard's death. She seemed rattled and embarrassed by his behavior earlier in the night, but she didn't seem distraught. Nothing like the broken woman I remember from his funeral.

And how does Carl fit into that theory? Blaire claims the two weren't close, that the brothers barely had a relationship. Of course, maybe that's just the story she's spinning. It's not like Carl is around to say otherwise.

I think back to my conversation with Mrs. Haynes. She was adamant about seeing Carl leaving my apartment *before* this weekend—more than a week ago, she said. As much as I'd like to believe she's mistaken, her admission leaves me unsettled. Matthew and I are the only ones with keys. Could someone we know have given him access? Stolen one of our keys and made a copy? Exactly how long has this plan against us been in place?

My thoughts are on an endless loop. I turn on the radio, trying to quiet my mind, when I see the clock. My hour alone is almost up. I turn the car around, driving back in the direction of The Studio, away from the rolling sapphire seas, and all the secrets they keep.

THIRTY-EIGHT

LILLIAN

I return to The Studio five minutes before Mabel's class is due to end. Harriet is standing outside, tapping away at her phone. I wonder who is manning the front desk in my absence. I pull into a parking space, but remain in my car.

She walks over to the car, tapping on the window, not unlike Blaire Walsh just an hour ago.

"Could we talk for a minute?" she asks, her voice distorted through the glass.

I take a deep breath and switch off the ignition. I wait for her to take a step toward the sidewalk, so I can open the door and step outside.

"Is everything okay with Mabel?" I ask. As far as I'm concerned, she's the only topic worth discussing with Harriet.

"Yes, fine. Happy as ever." Her cheeks are pink with that fake congeniality I'm used to watching her display toward other "friends" and neighbors, but never me. I'd foolishly thought our friendship was sincere. "I wanted to talk to you about the other day."

"There isn't much to say. You don't want me around The

Studio," I say. "I hope that doesn't mean Mabel isn't invited either."

"Of course not!" Her voice is filled with false outrage. "I love Mabel as though she's my own. You know that. And I care about you, too. That's why I wanted to check in."

"I don't need anyone checking in on me. What I need is for people to stand beside me, acknowledge the fact I wouldn't kill anyone."

As the words leave my lips, I feel entitled, powerful. Then I recall Richard, how easily he disappeared over the side of the cliff, and my confidence falters. Perhaps I don't deserve to be trusted.

"I'm sorry, okay? I wanted to apologize for asking you to leave The Studio the other day. It was no way to treat a friend."

Harriet has said a lot over the years, but I rarely hear her admit she's wrong. It makes me more willing to continue the conversation, but I can't forgive her so easily. I've always been told you learn who really cares for you in moments of desperation, and Harriet was quick to turn her back.

"I appreciate the apology," I say, "but I think you're right. Taking a step away from The Studio is probably best right now."

"Stepping back from The Studio or me?"

"Both," I answer, honestly.

Her voice begins to break. "I guess I deserve that. I just wanted you to know I truly am sorry. You didn't deserve what happened to you at the school play."

I'd almost forgotten she'd seen what happened. Everyone in the building saw. Alaina made sure of it. Then another memory from that night appears, one I'd almost forgotten.

"Do you know Alaina?" I ask.

"I've seen her around." She seems to stand up straighter. "I wouldn't say we're friends."

"Well, I seem to remember you comforting her that night instead of me."

"I wasn't choosing her over you. I was only trying to help," she says. "It was quite the scene."

The embarrassment from that moment stings, even now. I try not to think about it, focus instead on this connection between Harriet and Alaina that I didn't know existed.

"How do you know her?"

Harriet hesitates, like she doesn't want to answer. "She's a member of David's support group. Spouses sometimes attend. I met her there."

Alaina was in AA. That's why Harriet didn't want to tell me. Spilling the guest list at his weekly meetings takes away the anonymity. Then again, maybe there's another reason Harriet wanted to downplay their friendship.

"She's almost nine months pregnant. What was she doing in AA?"

"She hasn't lived in Anne Isle very long. Maybe a year. She started coming to the meetings before she was pregnant. I guess it doesn't hurt to keep up the habit. A lot of people still attend, even if they've been sober for years."

I think of Matthew. He's been sober for almost a year. When is the last time he went to one of David's meetings? Is it possible he knew Alaina from there? Or Carl?

"What about her husband? Did he ever attend?"

"No. I never met him. I didn't put everything together until I saw her at the play when she was screaming about her husband dying. Saying he was found inside your apartment." She shivers at the memory. "I thought seeing a familiar face might calm her down. She doesn't know many people here, especially in Seaside Cliffs."

But she knows Harriet. And David. This means Alaina—and Carl—might have connections to my other neighbors, too.

"I'm happy you were there for her," I say, tensing my jaw. "You need rely on friends when times are hard."

Harriet exhales. "I said I was sorry! I've been dealing with so much lately with David and his campaign and... everything. I took my worries out on you, and I shouldn't have."

David and his bid for mayor hardly matter to me, not when my freedom and reputation are in jeopardy.

"He's been drinking again," Harriet says, before I can end the conversation. "The stress of re-election has been too much for him."

"I'm sorry, Harriet," I say.

I may not be able to forgive her for the way she treated me, but I empathize with her about David's drinking. It's not easy to watch a person you love injure themselves with an addiction. I remember the worry I had for Matthew in the months after our divorce was finalized. His drinking became so constant, I feared he'd get breathalyzed or destroy his health, lose everything we were trying so desperately to save.

Harriet is the one who gave me the names of local resources that could help him. Even if she betrayed me in the wake of Carl's murder investigation, she has proven to be a good friend in the past. Maybe she really isn't acting like herself.

"We're dealing with a lot right now too. I'm trying to distance myself from, well, everything." I touch her shoulder. "But if things get really bad, and you need someone to talk to, you can call me."

"Thank you." She's crying now, tears streaming down her cheeks.

THIRTY-NINE

MATTHEW

Ever since the detectives left the office, I've felt eyes watching me. At best, the police presence merely piqued the interest of our employees. At worst, this investigation could put a large dent in our business.

Most people treat Voyage like a winning lottery ticket, and in some ways it was; the company's success changed our lives overnight. Truthfully, selling the company is where the real work began. Ted and I are still running, the finish line yet to be determined. We need several good years before we can even think about moving on to something else, let alone retiring comfortably.

One big scandal could sink us, and we'd never get another shot.

Now, I'm starting to wonder if this mess at the apartment will end up doing the one thing we didn't want from the start. Wiping us clean. Tanking the business. And, worst of all, the truth about Richard could come out.

Ted avoids me the rest of the day. He's a workaholic, but also, I believe he's staying in his office because he wants me to see how committed he is to the business we created. If Lillian or Richard or any of it brings me down, it will bury him, too.

To say I'm relieved when five o'clock rolls around is an understatement. I run down the stairs, into my hot air-filled car, and only then do I feel I can really breathe. On the drive home, I consider what our next steps should be. Is Ted right about distancing myself from Lillian? Should I obtain my own lawyer, one that can work in my best interests instead of ours? I owe everything to Lillian. Much more than Ted even realizes.

But I'm also keeping secrets from her. If she knew about the mistake I made after Richard's body was found, I'd lose what little faith she has in me.

When I arrive home, the house is empty. Mabel has dance class on Thursday afternoons, and Lillian is probably determined to keep her schedule the same. I'll give her that; the woman knows how to persevere.

My phone rings with a video call from Mom. I've only talked to her once since she left, to make sure her flight landed. I answer. I can tell she's in the garden, the light streaming awkwardly into the lens of the phone.

"Is Mabel home from school yet?" she asks. "I promised her I'd show her my flowerbed."

"At dance. I'll have her give you a call when she gets home." But as I say the words, I sense my mother already knew this, and it's precisely why she picked this moment to ring.

"How are things?"

That last word is overflowing with innuendo.

"If you're asking about the investigation, I don't have much to tell you. Police are still looking into everything."

She nods. "You don't think you could get into any trouble for this, do you?"

"I wasn't there, Mom. For God's sake, you were my alibi."

"And Lillian? How's she holding up?"

"They're looking into her. Hard. But Lillian is a strong woman. She's holding her own."

She looks at the phone dead-on. "You'll let me know if I need to come back to town, won't you? I can stay with Mabel while the two of you... sort things out."

"It's appreciated, but Lillian and I can handle this."

"*Lillian and I*. The way you talk, it sounds like the two of you are still married."

"You didn't want us getting divorced in the first place. You've not treated her the same ever since."

"Only because I don't believe in divorce."

"It's not the Easter Bunny, Mom. Divorce is real, and it's there so both parties can move on with their lives."

"Which, from where I'm sitting, neither of you are doing." She pauses. "I mean, if you two get along so well, why not just stay married?"

I shake my head. I'll never get her to understand. Not only are her ideals on marriage antiquated, she couldn't fathom how devastating Richard's death was. The toll it took. We both changed, individually and as a couple. The fact we were ever able to put our lives back together is a complete miracle, and now it's falling apart all over again.

"We'll let you know if we need you, but Lillian and I can handle this."

"There's something else I wanted to talk to you about. I meant to bring it up before I left town, but then so much happened."

"What is it?" I'm irritated, as my tone makes clear. It's been a long day and this conversation with my mother is only making it longer.

"I talked to Ted at Mabel's party. He told me about the offer."

I feel my blood turning warm beneath my skin. That

bastard. He couldn't be patient, and now he's brought my mother into it.

"How come you didn't tell me the board wants you to relocate to Florida?"

"Because it's not going to happen. Our lives are here in Anne Isle."

"Ted seemed to like the idea. He says you're the holdout."

"Ted doesn't have kids. He doesn't have responsibilities. I wouldn't expect him to understand—"

"Mabel would love it down here, and you know it. Don't you think it's time you move back home?"

"*This* is our home. And Lillian and I aren't together anymore. Deciding to move isn't that simple. How are we supposed to raise Mabel if she's in one state and I'm in another?"

"This is the precise reason the two of you need to distance yourselves from each other. You say you divorced so you can move on, but she's holding you back. You'd rather stay there with her, even if coming home is the right decision for the company. Not to mention, for me."

Out of all the ways Ted could have decided to put pressure on me, this is the worst. Moving to Florida would put us forty-five minutes away from Mom. She'd love being around Mabel more, and me.

"I still haven't talked to Lillian about it," I say. "I'm not going to move hours away from my daughter."

She clears her throat. "Considering the past week, it wouldn't be hard for you to gain full custody. I mean, Lillian is a suspect in a murder investigation. Not to mention, you're the sole provider for the family."

Anger washes over me so quickly that I have to grasp the countertop for balance.

"You aren't suggesting I use this situation to my advantage?"

"No, of course not." She's trying hard to sound helpful. "But Mabel would have everything she needs here."

"Except her mother!" My voice is raised now.

"Her mother could very well end up in jail. And then what will you do? The offer will be rescinded. Mabel will be heartbroken. And she'll be stuck living there with all of it. Maybe the timing of all this is more of a blessing than you're giving it credit for."

"I'm not making any decisions without talking to Lillian," I shout.

"Talk to me about what?" Lillian says, as she walks in the front door. Mabel is a few steps behind her, her backpack on one shoulder, the dance duffel on the other.

I wasn't expecting them home so soon. I hang up and lay the phone flat on the counter.

"Talk to me about what?" Lillian repeats.

FORTY

LILLIAN

Matthew is standing in the kitchen. His face is red and there are droplets of sweat along his hairline.

"Daddy!"

Mabel pushes past me, giving her father a hug.

"How was school, darling?"

When he speaks to her I can sense it. Something is wrong. There's no break from the stress. Every time I talk to anyone, it seems, more pressure is being added.

"Run upstairs and start on homework," I tell Mabel. "I'll be up in a sec."

I watch her leave, waiting until I can no longer hear her footsteps to speak. "What is it?"

"It's just, well—"

"Is it about the investigation? Have you talked to Barry?"

"No, it has nothing to do with that."

My chest feels light with relief. But I'm still wondering why Matthew appears so agitated. "Whatever it is, go ahead and tell me."

"It's about the business."

"I'm sorry the police showed up there today. I can't even imagine what Ted said—"

"It's not that, either." He exhales. "We received an offer a while back, and I've been waiting to tell you."

"An offer?"

"We have a new investment offer. The board wants Voyage to expand. A new office, new employees, new materials. It's a big deal, something we didn't expect to receive for at least another five years. It's all Ted's been talking about for weeks. The payoff would be substantial."

"That's great."

I'm happy for him, especially after this string of bad news. Then I consider his demeanor. I wonder if my connection to Carl's death has somehow ended up costing them the deal.

"Yeah, it is great." Matthew looks down, one hand on his waist. Whatever he plans on saying next, it's clear he doesn't want to say it. "They want Voyage to relocate to Florida."

"Okay, so—"

"If we accept the deal, we'd have to move there. The entire company, including me."

"Oh." My mind moves quickly now. An image of Matthew leaving. And Ted. Neither of them being around anymore. I look at the stairway, and think of Mabel. "So, you'd be moving to Florida?"

"Yes. Which puts a dent in, well, everything."

Once the shock and sadness disperse, something grittier takes hold.

"How long have you known about this?"

"A month."

"I see."

"I've wanted to talk to you, but so much has happened. I couldn't find the right time."

"If you move, that will disrupt everything. We won't be able to continue co-parenting Mabel. We'd probably sell the house.

All the things that made us decide to start nesting in the first place."

"I know."

"So, do you want to do it?"

His pause scares me.

"It's best for the company. Ted definitely wants to do it." Finally, he looks at me. "But moving wouldn't be fair to you."

"You're damn right it wouldn't be. Not to mention Mabel."

"I know."

"That's, what, ten hours away? She'd be split between the two states. All the things we said we didn't want for her would end up happening."

"I know."

"She's safe here. Secure. The happiest child of divorce I've ever seen. You moving the company will ruin all that."

"That's why I haven't made a decision. I couldn't, without talking to you."

"I'm not hearing you say you don't want this. It sounds like you resent me for being in your way."

"It's not that. But, yes, it's a hard decision. If I was doing what was best solely for me, the decision would already be made."

My eyes sting with tears. I've lost so much in this past week —my reputation, my respect. All of that pales in comparison to losing my daughter. And even if she were to stay here with me, when she did leave, she'd be gone for days, weeks, maybe months at a time. It's not even happening yet, but I can already feel my body yearning for her.

"You think moving is what is best for you?"

He turns, pacing in front of the sliding glass door that leads into the backyard. "I don't know anymore. Right now, I just want to be as far away as possible from Anne Isle and this whole investigation."

For the first time during this conversation, I agree. Between the police investigations and the possible acquisition of Voyage, it seems everything would work out for Matthew right now if I weren't in the picture.

Then I think of the recording device inside the apartment. If it's not the police keeping tabs on me, could it be him? Was it inside the apartment long before Carl was murdered? He's already kept the possibility of moving the company from me for a month. How long has he been keeping secrets?

"The police know Richard and Carl are brothers, and they could very easily circle back to how Richard died and how we were involved. That's what we should be talking about right now. Not whether or not Voyage is moving to Florida," he continues. "What are we going to do if the truth comes out? We can't both go down for this. We need a plan."

"What do you mean we can't both go down?"

"Where would that leave Mabel?"

"And you think because the police already suspect me of murdering Carl I should take the fall for Richard, too?"

"You're the one who keeps suggesting we tell a lawyer the truth about Richard. You keep talking about self-defense. If anything, I'm afraid you'll throw me to the wolves to save yourself."

"Wow. You really think that little of me," I say, my anger so raw, I can't stop myself. "This isn't fair. I'm not the one who was arguing with Richard. I'm not the reason he fell."

"Are you saying it's my fault?" Matthew's eyes bulge, his jaw drops. "My first reaction that night was to call the police. You're the one who said we should cover it up. Yes, I was fighting with Richard, but it's your fault we have to carry this secret with us the rest of our lives."

"You don't really mean that," I say, but I'm afraid it's true. Maybe everything would have been easier if we'd told the truth about what happened that night.

"Maybe I do, Lillian. You're the one who brought Carl into our lives."

"Because I met him on a dating app? We've already established he was chasing *us* down. He had the pictures and notes to prove it. All of it was kept in a folder titled *Richard*! Carl knew what we did, and since he wasn't there to see what happened, someone must have told him."

His demeanor changes. Both hands are on his hips. "What are you saying?"

"I know I didn't tell anyone what happened to Richard." I pause. "Did you?"

He shakes his head, turning to look out the window, so I can't see his face. "Of course, I didn't tell anyone."

But I'm not sure I believe him. I don't know that I trust anything he's said, or his motives resting beneath the surface. We've hit a low point tonight, each blaming the other for what we could have done, but it's clear I'm in a far more dangerous situation than he is, and what bothers me most is he seems okay with that.

"I don't think we should be under the same roof anymore," I say. "I'm going back to the apartment."

"Are you crazy? Carl was murdered there less than a week ago. It's not safe."

But I don't feel safe here, either. I can't trust Matthew. "The apartment has been released. I was over there today cleaning."

Matthew grabs his keys off the hook by the door. "Stay here tonight. Get some sleep. We'll talk in the morning."

"Are you going to the apartment?"

"I'll stay with Rebecca," he says.

I storm up the stairs, not really concerned where he stays, as long as it isn't here.

FORTY-ONE

MATTHEW

Rebecca doesn't answer when I call her, but her location shows she's at home.

I pull up to the curb beside her house, taking a few moments to sit alone in the car before I walk inside.

I'm still bothered by my argument with Lillian. This wasn't the way I wanted her to find out about the new offer for Voyage. I understand she's upset at the idea of me, and possibly Mabel, moving away. That coupled with everything that's happened in the past week must leave her feeling abandoned.

The last thing I want is for her to feel like I'm casting her aside. Everything I've done since she found Carl's body has been the opposite of that—I've been trying to protect her.

How does she repay me? By insisting it's my fault Richard died, totally ignoring the role she played in covering up his death. And although she didn't come out and say it, she seemed to be insinuating I'm somehow setting her up. Orchestrating all of this so I can move to Florida with a clear conscience. The Lillian I know wouldn't think this way; perhaps she's so desperate with how the situation is spiraling, she thinks it would be easier to confess.

My own secret replays in my mind. How would she react if she knew what I did after Richard's death? I'm afraid all this mayhem might lead back to that single mistake, but I don't want it to be true.

We've reached a point where I have to start thinking logically, stop being led by emotions. Now that the police are starting to ask questions about Richard, we have to be prepared for what will happen if the truth comes out. I'd like to think if we stick to our story, neither of us implicating the other, then the police will have nothing against us. But if that doesn't work, we could both end up getting arrested, leaving us in prison and Mabel alone. Maybe Ted and my mother are right. It's time I stop worrying about Lillian and start protecting myself.

I approach Rebecca's front door and knock. After a couple of minutes, she answers wearing a robe. A towel is wrapped like a turban atop her head.

"Matthew, what are you doing here?"

"I tried calling," I say. "Care if I crash here tonight?"

"Sure. I must have missed your call when I was in the shower."

She holds open the door, and I walk inside. Her house is much smaller than either my house or apartment. It's a quaint, two-bedroom home, but I enjoy the coziness. It reminds me of the small house Lillian and I shared before Voyage made it big.

"Is everything okay?" she asks. "You know you're always welcome, but I wasn't expecting you this late."

"It's just tense at the house right now," I answer, honestly. "Lillian and I haven't lived under the same roof in quite some time, and we both need some space."

"Has something else happened with the investigation?"

"Not really."

Rebecca doesn't know about the Voyage offer either, and I don't feel like bringing it up tonight. If she reacts the same way Lillian did, I won't have a place to sleep. Besides, I can't say what I want to do yet. A week ago, my decision was clear. There were too many people in Anne Isle I didn't want to leave behind.

Now? I'd be lying if I said the idea of a fresh start didn't appeal to me.

"I still feel awful about the other night," Rebecca says. "Don't tell Lillian, but it's all the teachers have been talking about at school. It certainly didn't paint her in the best light."

"That woman was making accusations that weren't true."

"I know," she says. "But people like to talk."

Lillian knows that, too. Which is why I'm still angry she decided to track down Alaina in the first place. She should know better than to try and insert herself into an active investigation, but Lillian is headstrong, and I'm worried her impulsive decisions will only continue to cause more problems for us.

"We filed a complaint against that woman. She won't be causing more trouble." I place my hands on her shoulder, urging her to sit. "And we're going to schedule another meeting with our lawyer to work out next steps."

I realize Rebecca is still standing, refusing to make eye contact. "Our lawyer?"

"Yes. Why? Rebecca, is something wrong?"

"Don't you think it's time you get your own lawyer? Separate yourself from Lillian a little bit?"

I take a step toward the kitchen. My hand is itching for the open bottle of wine on the counter, but I open the fridge and take a bottle of water instead. I chug half the bottle before I respond.

"What's making you say this?"

She exhales. "What happened the other night was really eye-opening. That and seeing the way people have reacted to it. They really think Lillian is guilty—"

"She isn't!" I shout, cutting her off. She takes a step back from me.

"I know. I mean, I don't want to believe she's guilty. But really, who else could have been responsible?"

Anyone who knows the truth about what we did to Richard, I think, but I can't tell Rebecca that. I'm surprised a little gossip at school would spark such a big turnaround. Just last week, Rebecca and Lillian were on their way to being friends. Now Rebecca is asking whether she killed a man.

"I'm standing by Lillian."

"And I respect that." She comes closer, resting her hand on my chest. "The last thing I want to do is get in the middle. I don't want you to feel like you have to choose between me and her. But I'm becoming more uncomfortable. I mean, no one knows what happened inside that apartment. I don't think we can follow Lillian blindly. Not when there's so much evidence against her."

I'm trying to remain open-minded, but I feel my jaw clenching. Rebecca is supposed to be on my side, which means believing in Lillian. Now she's yet another person trying to caution me.

"I know Lillian. She could never murder a man in cold blood."

"I didn't want to believe my ex was a violent person either," she says. "But he was."

"It's a different situation—"

"I know it is. All I'm saying is, when you have history with someone, sometimes it's hard to see their flaws. My friends and family tried bringing red flags to my attention. The ways he tried to control me. How he tried to disrupt the happy parts of my life. But I was so close to him, I couldn't see it until it was too late. I don't want your feelings for Lillian to cloud your judgement."

"I don't have feelings for Lillian. Not like that."

"You were together for more than a decade. You share a daughter. Lillian has always been lovely to me. I can't imagine her doing something so brutal, but you never know how a person might react when they're put in danger."

I think back to that night on the cliffs. I never would have thought I could be responsible for ending a man's life, but that's the situation I was put in. Could Lillian have found herself in similar circumstances? Am I really missing what everyone else is able to see?

"Can we not talk about Lillian tonight? Or the investigation or anything?" I pull her closer, and she rests her head on my chest. "Nothing would make me happier than to spend a night with my girlfriend."

"I'd like that, too," she says. "Just promise me you'll think about what I said."

"I will. In the morning." I lean in for a kiss. "I never get you all to myself anymore."

Rebecca is a patient woman, and in many ways, I don't deserve her. She raises her head to look at me and we kiss. The worries of the past week melt away, and I feel a wave of desire course through me.

"How about I lock up and we head to the bedroom?" she says, a mischievous glint in her eyes.

"You go ahead. I need to grab some things out of the car. I'll lock up for you."

She skips into the bedroom, while I return to the balmy evening outside. It's darkened considerably since I went inside, and the streetlights are aglow.

As I'm walking to my car, I notice a black truck parked directly across the street. The engine is running, but it's at a standstill. I wonder, was it here when I arrived?

I walk around to the back of the car and pull my overnight bag out of the trunk. I always have a go-bag in the car, have ever since Lillian and I started taking turns at the Seaside Cliffs house. It makes it easier when I forget toiletries to have an extra set on hand, and right now it works for my impromptu sleepover with Rebecca.

I slam the lid to the trunk. When I turn, I notice the black truck is still idling in the road. I stop and stare for a minute, my senses heightened. The car starts moving, the engine revving as it speeds down the quiet street in front of Rebecca's house.

I try to get a glimpse of the driver, but it's too dark. All I see is a flash of a man's face and an exposed arm covered in tattoos. I certainly don't think I've seen him before, and yet he feels familiar. I look back at Rebecca's house, wondering if she has any idea who would be scoping out her neighborhood, when it hits me.

Her ex.

Rebecca told me he was released from prison and she'd mentioned feeling frightened. Could it have been him? He's not allowed to contact her directly, but nothing is stopping him from keeping watch on the house.

"You coming back inside?"

Rebecca is standing in the doorway. She's now wearing pajamas, her hair falling over her shoulders in wet clumps. For a split second, I flash back to a memory of Lillian in our little old house. I sometimes forget how much the two look alike.

"Be right in," I say, watching as she walks inside.

Then another idea grips me. Rebecca's ex has been out of prison since before Carl was murdered. If I'm not being paranoid, and he really was sitting outside her house just now, could he have been watching her since his release? Has he been watching me?

I know he physically assaulted Rebecca, but I pull on my memories for any other details she's told me. I know he was controlling, and often turned abusive whenever she tried to leave him. In fact, their final altercation, the one that landed him in prison, was prompted by their breakup. What if he's seen me with Rebecca—or worse—seen me with Lillian?

He could have easily gotten them confused, from a distance. What if he followed Lillian to our apartment thinking she was Rebecca? Or maybe he was trying to confront me and instead found Carl? He's the only person I know with a history of violence. Lillian and I could be wrong. This situation may not be about Carl or Richard—it could be yet another tragic misunderstanding.

Perhaps this is only the theory I wish to believe. It would certainly be easier to accept than any of the other theories we've floated in the past couple of days, even if it means Rebecca and I are in more danger than I realized.

I look up and down the street, suddenly aware of how easy it is for anyone to find you if they try hard enough. On the surface, Rebecca's ex should have no reason to want to do any of us harm, but I know that he's violent. What if he's not ready to see Rebecca move on? Earlier this week she'd told me she was scared.

It's at least worth mentioning to Barry, even the police. It might give them another route to investigate, one that would lead them away from Richard and us. I click the lock button on my car, listening to the high-pitched beeps. I go back inside Rebecca's house, making sure the front door and windows are locked before joining her in the bedroom.

FORTY-TWO

LILLIAN

The morning sun streams in through the bedroom window, but my thoughts are still lost in a fog. My life won't go back to the way it was before. I've lost my job, my apartment, my friends. Even my room at the house feels like a guest room I'm renting out.

And now Matthew is no longer on my side.

Two things bonded us, even after the divorce: Respect and trust. We've both told little lies to each other over the years, but the deception has escalated, creating a deeper divide, pushing us away from each other.

I don't think Matthew trusts me anymore. And I don't know if I can trust him. For the first time in my adult life, I'm alone.

A sickening thought creeps in, too disruptive to ignore. Just last night, he accused me of wanting to turn him over to the police. He admitted that moving to Florida would be best for him. The only outlier in his perfect plan is me. Could he be trying to get me out of the way, and Carl's death is part of that plan? What if Matthew is behind all of this? Maybe me taking the fall for Richard's death has been the idea all along. I don't want to believe it, but the possibility is there.

I have over a decade of memories that counter the thought. The head-over-heels whirlwind that was our dating in college. Our wedding. The sacrifices we made in those early years, when we didn't know whether or not Voyage would ever take off, but it didn't matter because we had each other. The painful years of infertility.

Mabel.

All those moments, all that history, couldn't be erased in his pursuit for a better future, could it? Matthew of all people couldn't abandon me this way, frame me for a crime I didn't commit. Especially after I stood by him in the wake of Richard's death.

I sit up and pull my purse onto the bed. I was so tired last night; I didn't even take the time to charge my phone. As I'm searching for it, my hand brushes against something else. The Ziploc bag containing the recording device I found inside the apartment.

The police could have planted bugs, which means they're more convinced of my guilt than I originally thought. The only person I know who has access to the apartment is Matthew. If he's been spying on me inside the apartment... it could mean a lot of things. None of them good.

His words from last night come back to me. *We can't both go down for this. We need a plan.*

Right now, my only plan is to uncover who is spying on me and why.

I stand on the sidewalk across the street from the police station. The temperature has dropped significantly since last weekend, when Mabel and her friends were splashing around in our back-yard pool. My arms are covered in chill bumps, as I rub my hands over them for warmth.

Most of the people scurrying inside barely take the time to

raise their heads. This works to my advantage, because I don't want to be seen by anyone, especially Spelling. There's only one person I'm hoping to catch off guard, and it doesn't take long for him to arrive.

Dylan exits the building, raising his head to survey the scene. He sees me standing across the street, and stops.

"What are you doing here?" he asks when he walks over.

"I wanted to talk to you."

"Then call the station."

"I have to show you something." I lift the Ziploc bag containing the bug. "Tell me what this is."

He grabs the bag, rubbing his thumb over it. "Where did you get this?"

"I found it when I was cleaning the mess your crew left behind," I say. "Are you spying on me now?"

"This doesn't belong to the police department, if that's what you're suggesting."

"Then how did it end up inside my apartment? You just searched the place. Surely, your team would have found it if it were in there before."

"Exactly where did you find it?"

"In the living room. Beneath the DVD player."

He nods, looking over his shoulder at the station. We're the only two people left on the street.

"We didn't tell you this, but we found a recording device like this during our search. Identical to the one in this bag."

My lungs feel suddenly filled with hot, heavy air. He's confirming the devices were inside the apartment before Carl was murdered. Who would do that? Better yet, who could do that? Besides Matthew.

"Why didn't you tell us?"

"We were trying to see if we could track where the information went, but we can't. It connects to a live feed, and we're unable to trace it. We assumed that either you or Matthew had placed the device inside the apartment to keep tabs on the other." He pauses. "So, you're saying this isn't yours?"

"Of course, it isn't."

"What did Matthew say when you found it?"

"I haven't told him."

Dylan's expression says it all. He's waiting for me to draw my own conclusions. My initial reaction is to defend Matthew, but then my fears from earlier come back. What if he knows more about Carl's presence in my apartment than he's letting on? In the chaos following Mabel's party, I haven't even stopped to consider where he was the entire day. He left that night to pick up pizza with Jane and Rebecca, but he could have snuck away from them. He could have been at the apartment, and I would never know it.

"You should have told me what you found. I could have at least been prepared before I moved back into my apartment."

"We're not obligated to tell you anything about our search. All relevant information will go to your lawyer. I don't think he'd appreciate you tracking me down to ask questions, by the way," he says. "We searched the apartment thoroughly. This one must have slipped past us."

I should be happy that the recording device doesn't belong to the police department, but I'm not. I'm left wondering if Matthew is the one invading my personal life. What was he trying to find?

"Any other questions?" he asks. "You know, it's actually common for criminals to insert themselves into active investigations."

"Is that an accusation?"

There's that loaded expression again. "If you're concerned with looking guilty, you should stop investigating on your own. Leave it to us."

"Have you stopped to think what it's like to be in my position? I have no idea what happened the other night, and yet everyone from your partner to my former friends have already labeled me guilty."

"No one is saying you're guilty—"

"They are! Just two days ago Carl's widow screamed it in front of my daughter and all her friends. And now I have to worry about who was spying on me and why. I'm only looking for answers because I want all of this to go away."

Dylan looks down. His bottom lip is tucked in as he debates what to say. "We told you to give it time, and no one said that would be easy. But we have to gather more information before we can clear you."

"Well, let's hope by the time you've found the answers you're looking for my life isn't completely ruined." I attempt to walk away.

"Look." He reaches out and touches my arm, gently. My nerves come alive. "If I were you, I'd quit worrying about Carl and the investigation. I'd worry more about who is in your inner circle."

"What's that mean?"

"We've already established those recording devices were there before we searched the place. Possibly before the murder. You need to really think about who you can trust. And who had access to your home."

Matthew. His name repeats in my head on a loop.

I look up at Dylan, only just now realizing his hand is still on my arm. "Are you trying to help me?"

"That's all I'm trying to do."

This is the first time I've felt he might be in my corner more than I realized. He's a cop; it's not in his nature to ignore the facts, many of which seem to be pointing at me, but I'm starting to get the feeling he just might believe me after all.

"Take my card." He lets go of my arm and fishes through his wallet. "This is my direct work line. From now on, call me if you have any leads. Don't put yourself in danger trying to solve this thing. That's my job."

It's sound advice, but there's still only so much I can tell Dylan, and I won't stop searching for answers until I've found who is responsible for putting Carl's body inside my bedroom.

FORTY-THREE

MATTHEW

I'm sitting in my car, the radio off, the air-conditioner blasting. In front of me is the law offices of Byron and Pierce. My appointment begins in five minutes, but I'm reluctant to walk inside.

I don't want to do this, but it might be the only choice I have left.

Ted gave me the name of another lawyer—an even better one than Barry, he says. When I told him what I was planning, that I was hiring someone to represent solely me, I swear I saw a glint of humanity in his eyes.

"You're doing the right thing," he told me. "For yourself and the business."

What I don't tell him is my nervousness that I might be more at fault than I care to admit. At first, everything seemed to be pointing toward Lillian. She knew Carl. She was the one in the apartment that night.

But after seeing Rebecca's ex outside her house, I can't stop wondering if maybe I was the real target all along. What if he's been tracking Rebecca and me? What if he went into that apartment because he wanted to do me harm? I need to go over my theories with someone—a professional—and consider next steps.

I also can't shake the fight with Lillian. We've never gone after one another like that, not even in the wake of Richard's death. Back then, we were clinging to our secret together. Now, it no longer feels like we're a team. The trust between us is broken. Lillian could decide to come clean to the police about everything. Sacrifice me to save herself. Having my own attorney serves as a protective barrier against what could happen.

Even if this is the right choice, the smart choice, it still feels very wrong. I keep telling myself that things won't change. In an ideal world, Lillian will no longer be a suspect in Carl's death. We'll both return to our normal routines, unscathed. But if that doesn't happen, if the police keep pestering Lillian, trying to tie her to Carl's death, they could uncover the truth about Richard.

Stop stalling, says an impatient voice inside. It's like ripping off a Band-Aid. This way, I'll be protected. Maybe Lillian will never even have to know.

I step out into the waxy afternoon air, closing the door behind me, when my phone rings. Lillian. A hot jolt of unease stuns my spine, like she knows what I'm doing.

"Are you at the office?" she says when I answer.

"I, uh, am running some errands for work." Maybe she does know where I am. She's out of breath, gasping. I hear the muffled sounds of a car radio in the background. "Is everything okay?"

"No. I didn't tell you this yesterday, but someone bugged our apartment. I found a recording device when I was cleaning."

"Someone is recording us! And you're just now telling me."

"We were arguing about other things last night," she says. "Anyway, I spoke with the police. It's not their device. So, whose is it?"

"I... I don't know. Why would someone want to record us?"

"Maybe they were trying to catch us talking about Richard."

It strikes me how careless it is for us to be discussing this over the phone. I begin pacing the parking lot. "We should talk about this face to face."

"Or maybe... it belongs to you."

My head turns fast. "Are you accusing me of bugging you?"

"Well, it doesn't belong to me. Or the police. Who else could have planted it?"

"Maybe the same person who snuck Carl into the apartment without you knowing about it."

"Carl didn't know anything about me until a month ago," she continues, as though she didn't hear my last response. "He was barely in contact with his own brother. If he found out about what we did, someone must have told him. Which means someone else knows."

A month ago. Something about that timeframe stops me in my tracks, confirming my deepest fears. My mistake. I hadn't put it together before, or maybe I'd been avoiding the truth. I slump against the car, a cruel realization forming in my mind. My throat is drying rapidly, my words choking their way out. "You think... you think someone else knows what we did."

"If no one saw us, they must have found out another way." She pauses, and each silent second is another strike against my heart. "Matthew, is there something you're not telling me?"

"No, of course not," I answer, a little too quickly. "You know everything."

But it's a lie. I made a crucial mistake after Richard's death, and I fear that is the catalyst for what has happened in the past week. My heart is beating hard against my chest, waiting for her to speak.

She sighs, a deflated sound. Her newfound doubt gives me hope.

"You're driving yourself crazy looking into this. You need to stop," I warn her. "Head back to the house. Mabel will be out of school soon. The two of you should catch dinner, maybe get ice cream."

"Yeah, I'll do that."

I'm not sure I believe her. And I'm afraid my tone will give away my own intentions, that I'm trying to distract her.

"I'll see you at the house tonight," I say, ending the call.

I take a gulp of crisp air, but it doesn't seem enough. Sweat is building along the back of my neck, beneath my arms. I look back at the law offices of Byron and Pierce, no longer planning to go inside.

Hiring my own lawyer would be neither my first or worst betrayal.

I've already betrayed Lillian.

We're not the only people who know about what happened to Richard that night. I couldn't tell her I told someone else, believing wholeheartedly that person would never betray me. But that timeline... one month ago. Maybe I was wrong. Maybe I already know exactly who is behind all this.

I re-enter my car, crank the engine and drive away.

FORTY-FOUR

LILLIAN

I know Matthew—his motivations, his insecurities, his faults. It's a rapport that's been nurtured over the years, from late adolescence into adulthood, from starry-eyed dreamers to professionals to parents. It's an intimacy so sincere I once believed nothing, not even divorce, could tear us apart. He knows me, and I know him.

And that's how I know he just lied to me.

I could tell from the delicate tenor of his voice when he said the words: *You know everything*. His quickening of breath, audible through the phone.

I think back to our argument last night, when I asked if he told anyone what happened to Richard. He turned away from me, hiding his face. His response—*Of course, I didn't tell anyone*—was false. It's a lie I can feel in my bones, in my soul. Matthew has betrayed me. He told someone.

Could he have told the police? His mother? Ted? Rebecca? After years of putting each other first, who could be so important that he placed them above me?

Himself. If he intended on taking the fall for Richard's death, he would have told me. He'd admit to going to the police, turning himself in, resolving this matter before it destroys our lives.

But he isn't doing that—he's still lying—which makes me fear he's placed the blame on me, probably because he figured out that the longer this carries on, the higher the risk becomes that we'll both go down.

Another possibility: Maybe he's the person who reached out to Carl in the first place.

There was hardly any information in the folder I found in Carl's office about Matthew and his life. All the evidence pointed to me. Matthew could have supplied Carl with everything he needed to know. He could have been behind all of this, from the very beginning.

The betrayal is palpable, an acid-like warmth coursing through my body, tingling my skin. Even my earlobes burn. Maybe, instead of fighting against Matthew and the police, I should learn to accept my fate.

An innocent man died, and we covered it up. For two years, we've allowed his wife and children to believe a lie.

Even if I didn't give Richard his final blow, or murder Carl in my bed, I'm not blameless.

I committed the crime of withholding answers, and the day of reckoning has come.

The phone rings and rings. For a brief, selfish moment, I hope he won't answer. I hope this choice will be taken out of my hands. Just when I'm about to end the call, the line connects.

"Detective Logan." Dylan's voice is official, yet welcoming.

"It's Lillian." There's a pause, a space between what I wish I was calling about and what I actually am. "Will you be at the police station later? I want to come by."

"Uh, yeah, I'll be here. We're waiting around on some

reports, so we don't plan to leave. We tried making contact with your lawyer—"

"No lawyers," I cut him off. I let out a slow exhale. "See you soon, Detective."

"Lillian, is everything okay?"

He sounds concerned, not as a detective, not as someone eager to close the case, but, almost, like a friend.

"See you soon," I repeat, and I hang up the phone.

I've done a lot of thinking in the past couple of hours, and what I've landed on is that I am alone. The police aren't on my side. Neither is Matthew. Sure, I'll always have a few friends in my corner, but none of them can shield me from what's coming. And even they might turn their backs on me if they learn the truth about what Matthew and I did.

I've let the events of that night haunt me. It's torn apart my marriage, installed this never-ending paranoia that one day everything just might come crashing down. And it appears that day has come. I'm tired of running from the inevitable.

It's time to pay for my sins.

But before I go to the police station and tell Dylan and Spelling the truth about how Richard died, how I believe it connects to whatever happened to Carl, there's one person I need to speak to first. Someone who deserves the truth above everyone else.

I exit my car, and walk across the street. The concrete steps leading to the front door are lined with manicured shrubbery, the leaves green and alive, but the buds beginning to fade. I approach the front door and knock.

Blaire Walsh answers.

"Lillian, this is a surprise," she says. Her smile is genuine, but a little caught off guard.

"I thought I might take you up on that cup of coffee," I say. "Do you mind if I come in?"

"Sure." She moves back, welcoming me. "This is usually the

quiet part of the day, before the boys get out of school. I'm happy you decided to join me."

I follow her inside, taking note of all the homey details as I pass. The white stone floors are gleaming, in an almost unnatural way. The walls are painted beige and caramel, the effects reminding me of a warm autumn day. As we wander into the living room, I take in other details—the white carpet (how does she keep it clean with young boys?), the plush furniture, the large stone vases homing plants in the corner.

Above the fireplace is a series of pictures of Blaire and the boys. They look like they've been taken sometime in the past year, based on their ages. They're each smiling, Blaire's arms wrapped around her children protectively. There's no Richard. His absence sends a painful pang inside my heart.

If I'm going to do this, tell the police the truth about what happened, then Blaire Walsh deserves to know first. In some ways, we've victimized her most.

"How do you take your coffee?" Blaire asks. "Or, is it too late in the afternoon? I could brew us some tea."

"I'm always ready for coffee," I say. "Black, please."

"I agree." Blaire turns, opening a crème-colored cabinet and retrieves two mugs. She seems delighted to have a visitor, a friend. Her enthusiasm makes what I'm about to tell her even harder.

I clear my throat, my eyes roaming the room, landing again on the pictures above the fireplace.

"Beautiful photos," I say, trying to relieve the tension building inside. "How have the boys been?"

"They're better and better each day. It was an adjustment, you know, after Richard died. I think we're all finally finding our place."

"It couldn't have been easy on them," I say. "Or you."

Blaire stops moving. Her back is to me, so I can't see her face. I wonder what she's thinking, if she's trying to pull from that well of strength that has helped her survive these past two years.

"You were so nice to me the other day in the parking lot," I say, flailing. "You didn't have to be. It made me start thinking about how difficult the past two years must have been on you. Without Richard. It's a marvel how you've been able to hold everything together."

My words have clearly provoked a reaction. She turns now, her cheeks streaks of red across her tan skin.

"We've had our moments. If anything, his absence has given me an appreciation for everything I do have."

It's an admirable answer, one that speaks to her modesty. And now the conversation is lagging again. Something inside presses me to keep going, tell her what I came here to say. Before I can, Blaire starts up again.

"The first few days were the hardest. All I did was wait. Wait for Richard to come home. Wait for his excuses for why he left in the first place. After a while, the anger simmered down and I began to worry. Then, I was waiting for an explanation, a call from the police or the hospital. It never occurred to me that he'd died. That he'd never again walk through that door."

She smiles now, giving off the aura of a teenager recalling their first love.

"I'd never met a man like Richard before. He was different from my own father in so many ways. He took risks and enjoyed being the center of attention. There was this light on him at all times, and being near him gave me a little light, too. My father never liked him. He was convinced Richard was after me for the wrong reasons."

"What do you mean?"

"My father is a very wealthy man. I know by the time we moved here, Richard had made a name for himself. I know people in town wonder how we're able to keep the house, able to survive at all without his income. The truth is, I bought this house. I paid off the mortgage years ago, with money from my trust fund. The boys and I have always been taken care of. Whatever money Richard made, well, that was just to flatter his ego."

Blaire's right. People in town assumed the Walshes would go under, end up moving away after Richard died. Most people talk about Blaire like she's a gold digger, a green-eyed housewife who married for money and nothing else. Even Harriet and Cat have made comments.

"Why do you work at the salon?" The question comes out faster than I intended, and it sounds judgmental.

She shrugs. "I wanted to do something to fill my days while the boys are in school. It's not much money. But it gives me something to do, and I think it sends a good message to the boys. I don't want them to be like Richard. I don't want them to think they have to marry into money or inherit it, that they'll come by it easily."

I understand her point. It's the same reason I started working at The Studio. I wanted Mabel to see me as more than some woman feeding off her father's success. This is the most I've ever talked to Blaire Walsh in one sitting, and we have more in common than I realized.

"I don't only work at the salon." Blaire stands, walks over to a bureau and opens it. "When I was younger, I wanted to be an artist. I earned a degree in art history. Before the kids came along, I used to sketch all the time. Then, it all stopped. Recently, I've started up again. Would you like to see?"

I shift in my seat. "Sure."

Blaire carries over a sketchbook. The pages are filled with colorful drawings of woodland animals in vibrant settings. There are words written on every page, and I realize it's a poem.

"I've been working on this in the last few months," she says. "I thought about putting them into a children's book. I know, that sounds silly."

"It doesn't. I love reading with Mabel. I do it every night before she goes to sleep."

"I do the same with my youngest. Did it with the older ones, too. Richard was never into that sort of thing." She smiles, but it's strained and sad. "For so long, it was like I was waiting for him to come back. Finally, it feels like I can start living my life again."

She takes back the sketchbook. I think she's going to return it to the bureau, but instead she turns her body away from me. She begins to sob.

I place my hand on her shoulder. "Blaire, are you okay?"

Her voice is disruptive static, crackling when she speaks.

"It's just—and trust me, I know this makes me sound like an awful person—but I thank God every day that Richard died."

FORTY-FIVE

LILLIAN

There's a pained pause after what she's said. I watch her, taking in her stiff posture, her eyes filled with tears. Then, she laughs, self-deprecatingly.

"I can't believe I said that out loud."

Now I'm the one who is stiff, unsure of how to react. Out of all the things I thought she might say, it wasn't that.

"You must think I'm some kind of a monster."

"No, I don't."

I don't really know what to think, but Blaire Walsh is no monster. She's not saying these words to be cruel; if anything, I sense she's speaking from a place of hurt. She's ashamed.

"Like I said, everything was so wonderful in the beginning. My parents never liked him, and we had a few problems there, but I really believed Richard loved me. After we got married, he started to change. He became obsessed with making money, building his own business. He was constantly trying to keep up with the Joneses. It was so unnecessary. I told him we could buy half of the Seaside Cliffs subdivision if we wanted. He didn't have to work so hard, set his hopes so high. But he was determined to make a name for himself. For *us*, or so he said.

"But Richard wasn't very clever when it came to business. He kept searching for what was easy and fast, not what was profitable. There's no telling how much money I invested in him over the years, trying to be supportive. The few times he did get ahead, he'd lose it. After a while, I don't even think he was trying to work anymore. I think all his business dealings were an excuse for him to get out of the house so he could meet women."

"You knew about the other women?" I catch myself. "I mean, Matthew mentioned seeing him once. With another woman. It was so out of character, I thought he must have misread the situation."

"No, I knew about the women. Probably not all of them, there were so many. And I know how everyone in Anne Isle talks. After a while, it became easier to pull back from the social scene. It seemed like everyone was either sleeping with my husband or gossiping about who was." She shakes her head, then locks eyes with me. "You were always kind to me. Genuine. That's one of the reasons I reached out to you the other day."

"Richard had a reputation of being a flirt. A charmer. I never thought he was actually cheating."

"After a few years, I didn't even care. It was just part of life with him. But he'd gotten so careless toward the end. Sleeping with women from the neighborhood, women I thought were my friends! Like Harriet Moore."

"Harriet?"

I'm shocked. I never felt she and David had a particularly happy marriage, but I didn't think she'd sleep with a married man, especially someone local.

"I caught them once. She begged me not to tell. She said it would be a scandal for not only her marriage, but all of Anne Isle."

My jaw drops in a mixture of shock and disbelieving laughter. That reaction is so self-indulgent, so insincere. So Harriet.

"That was big of you. If it were me, I'm not sure I could have held my tongue."

"It wasn't worth it. Telling people what I saw would have caused problems for Richard, which only caused more problems for me."

"I'm so sorry, Blaire. Harriet is my friend," I say, having to fight the urge to use the word *was*, "but I didn't know about them."

"That's why I keep to myself. I'm better off with enemies than friends like that." She wraps her arms around herself. "I've never admitted it to anyone before."

I know why I avoided Blaire after Richard's death, but why didn't I make more of an effort to know her before? Was it because she'd been deemed unnecessary by the likes of Harriet and Cat? Perhaps if I'd been less concerned with following their lead and more concerned with making genuine connections, Blaire and I would have become friends sooner. Maybe none of these horrible events would have unfolded the way they have if I hadn't been so shallow in the past."

"What about your parents?"

"With what little pride I had left, the last thing I wanted to do was admit to my father he'd been right about Richard all along." She rolls her eyes, then her stare hardens. "The affairs weren't even the worst of it."

She stands abruptly and walks to the window across the room. The curtains are pulled back, providing an unobstructed view of the backyard. There's a large playground in the center, two metal benches on either side where I imagine Blaire sitting and watching the boys play. She keeps staring out, as though deciding whether she should continue.

"Richard wasn't just emotionally abusive," she says, finally. "He hit me, too."

She comes back to the sofa and sits, this time putting more

distance between us. Her eyes are focused on the rug, as though looking at me will steal what little courage she has left.

"Richard's ego was too much. Anytime he made a bad deal or I confronted him about one of his affairs, he'd take it out on me. At first it felt small. He'd shake my shoulders during an argument, grab my arm. Sometimes, I'd be the one that started the fight. I even convinced myself that I'd provoked him, that it wasn't his fault. Then, it became worse. He started smacking me. It would all happen so fast. He'd go from being the man I loved to this... monster. And when he drank, everything became much, much worse."

"Blaire, I had no idea."

Reflexively, I want to ask why she didn't tell someone sooner, but I stop myself. It's an easy question to ask, but a difficult one to answer. I can see how difficult it is even now, when Richard has been gone for two years, to be honest about what happened. No wonder she was afraid when he was still alive, living with that unbearable presence every day.

"No one would have believed me. Richard was handsome and charming and charismatic... all the reasons I fell in love with him worked on everyone else, too."

"There's never an acceptable reason to hit you."

"I know. And if I'd been younger and stronger, I would have left. I swear I would have. But by the time it got really bad, the boys had been born. I kept thinking I owed it to them to stick it out, that in time Richard would change. But when the boys got older, it only got worse."

There's a lump in my throat. "Did he... did he hurt the boys?"

She closes her eyes and shakes her head. "Never. I would have left if he'd done that. But they were getting older, starting to hear us argue. There were a few times I know they saw things they shouldn't have, and I was worried about what that would do to them. The last thing I want is to raise more boys like Richard." Her eyes turn wide, aglow with memory. "I sometimes still think about the night of your party, when he was grabbing at you. Do you remember?"

The lump sinks to my chest, and my body wants to recoil. "I do."

"I was mortified. I'd seen him act that way with women before, and they'd usually welcomed it. The men would look the other way, *boys will be boys* and all. But when he grabbed you like that, it was all I could do not to go after him myself. Of course, Matthew got there first."

I feel my body starting to sweat. I've remembered that night with absolute clarity for years, and it worries me to think Blaire has, too.

"After he stormed off, I was dreading going home. Richard wasn't used to being called out like that. Between that and the drinking, I knew it would be a rough night ahead. But when I got home, he wasn't there. I figured he'd come home the next morning, but he didn't. And then the police showed up a week later."

I remember when Richard's body was found. I was so fearful the truth would come out, that someone would be able to tell what we did. All they saw was a man who had had too much to drink and took a stumble. With each passing day, our culpability in his death seemed to go away.

Until Carl turned up dead.

"You know, his brother thought something more sinister had happened. Carl insisted Richard wouldn't have gone out that way. That there had to be more to the story. Sometimes I think the only reason he moved here was to prove himself right. He certainly didn't spend time with his nephews."

"You don't believe Carl?" I ask. "I mean, you don't think something might have happened to Richard?"

"I don't care if it did! And I know it's awful to say, but our relationship had gotten so bad, and I was so used to it, I don't know if I ever would have had the strength to leave." She smiles through tears. "Ever since he died, our lives have been so much happier. Richard never would have allowed Devon to take dance classes, or been there for the boys when they needed him. The kids are thriving, and I think it's because they knew deep down their father wasn't a good man. I think they understand I'm the only one who truly loves them like a parent should.

"And I'm no longer looking over my shoulder, afraid of what trouble Richard will cook up next. I feel safe. I've even started drawing again." She looks down at the sketchpad. "It's like him dying gave me hope."

"I'm sorry for what he put you through, Blaire. I wish I had known sooner. I wish more people knew what kind of a man he really was."

"It feels good saying it. I've kept it inside so long." She clears her throat and wipes the delicate, damp skin underneath her eyes. "You won't tell anyone—"

"No, never. It's your story to tell."

She nods. "I hope my story ends up being much greater than that. And to answer your other question, no, I don't think something bad happened to him. Bad things rarely end up happening to guys like Richard. It was an accident. It was like my prayers were finally answered."

She squeezes my hand and the tightness in my chest releases. Like everyone else in Anne Isle, I believed Richard was a loving father and husband. For years, I've grappled with guilt over what we took away from Blaire and the boys, believed I'd never find redemption for the role I played in his death.

Now I've been confronted with the truth of who Richard Walsh was. I've witnessed the pain in his wife's eyes as she recalled his abuse, and seen the hope she has to finally live life

in peace. The change in her demeanor has transformed something inside me, relieving this weight I've carried the past two
years.

Because any guilt I had for what we did to Richard Walsh is
now gone for good.

FORTY-SIX

MATTHEW

My pulse is pounding as I rush upstairs, swinging left in the direction of Ted's office. I can see through the large glass windows the room is empty, but I enter anyway, as though Ted is in there, hiding beneath his desk, behind a door.

I look at my watch. Half past three. There's not a logical reason why Ted wouldn't be here. We plan most of our meetings in the mornings and early afternoons, and he usually works until seven o'clock on an average day, long after the rest of our employees have returned to their families.

I retrace my steps, stopping at the front desk.

"Mandy, where's Ted?"

"He's gone home for the day."

"Home?" I look at my watch again. "It's not even four o'clock."

"That's what I thought." She looks around the room, lowering her voice. "Between you and me, he seemed a little off."

"What, like he was sick?"

"More like he was angry."

"What was on the agenda today? Did he have any meetings?"

"He's been in his office most of the day," she says. "Maybe he just needs a break."

"Yeah, maybe." But I know Ted. I've known him far longer than Mandy or anyone else on our payroll. He doesn't take breaks, and when I spoke to him earlier today, he seemed elated I was hiring my own attorney, was absolutely giddy about giving me the number. What could have happened in the past few hours to make him leave? Perhaps he knows I skipped my appointment with Byron and Pierce.

"Do we have anything this afternoon?" I ask.

"No."

"Good. Hold my calls," I tell her. "I'm going to swing by Ted's. Make sure he's feeling okay."

I walk out of the office, the mid-afternoon sun casting rays across the cars in the parking lot. The light hurts my eyes. I duck inside my own car and sit still, trying to think.

I'm not just worried about Ted... I'm worried about what he's doing, what he might have already done.

I look up, back at the building, and it's as though I've fallen back in time. It's no longer daylight, but night, and all the people clustering around the building are gone. I'm remembering a night from over a year ago, when it became clear my marriage to Lillian was no longer salvageable.

I was drunk. I showed up at the office, fumbling to unlock the front door. I knew Ted would be there, and I needed him. The waiting area was dark, as was the second floor, except for Ted's office, which was glowing bright. As predicted, he was working late.

Ted startled when he saw me, then he smiled, nodded at the bottle in my hand.

"I didn't know we were having a party." But when he stepped closer, his demeanor changed. Maybe he caught a whiff of my sweat, or saw the despair on my face. "You okay there, buddy?"

"She's leaving me."

I collapsed into the chair in front of his desk, held my head in my hands, and sobbed. Ted was stunned at first. We'd seen each other through our best and worst moments, but this... this was different.

"Maybe it's not as bad as you think," he said, trying to be optimistic. "You two are going through a rough patch. It's normal after having kids, from what I hear. You'll work it out."

"No." I leaned up, my swollen face staring directly at his. "Our marriage is over. And it's my fault."

"You can't do that to yourself," he said. "Even if you two go your separate ways, it's never on one person. Don't let her put it in your head you're to blame."

"She's not putting anything in my head!" I screamed. "I know this is my fault. Because of what I did!"

The sobs returned. Ted waiting a few seconds before asking, "What did you do?"

"Remember that party? The one we had after the house was completed."

And I told him. Drunkenly, stupidly, told him about everything that happened. I told him how we walked along the cliffs, trying to blow off steam, and Richard confronted us there, and that when he did... I told him it was an accident. We panicked, fearing people might think his death was some kind of revenge for the way he acted at the party. We were worried for Mabel, the business, ourselves.

So, we covered it up.

When I finished, the bottle in my hands was empty, and Ted had poured two glasses of whiskey. His glass was almost finished.

"It sounds like you two didn't have a choice," he said. He couldn't say *you did the right thing*, because we didn't. What we did was wrong, and the price Lillian and I had paid was our marriage.

Ted listened to me that night without judgement or disgust. He was my oldest friend and, even though Lillian and I had promised to never tell a soul about what happened, that night, I had to get it out. Keeping it inside was killing me—had already killed my relationship—and Ted comforted me. To his credit, I talked for more than an hour before he brought up Voyage, the potential hit it could take if the truth about what we'd done ever came out.

"Thank you for trusting me," he said. "But you have to move on from this. You can't tell anyone else."

"I won't—"

"I'm serious. Lillian and I know, but that's it. We can hold you together."

And it was true. After that night, I found it easier to accept everything that was happening. I found it easier to move on. I struggled with drinking for a few more months until I decided to get sober. The combination of my drinking and my guilt was a liability we couldn't risk. Lillian would be irate if she knew I'd made the mistake of telling Ted.

He never mentioned it again, although I know he came close when he realized Carl was Richard's brother. He must have been thinking about what Lillian and I did, that this was all connected.

But now I worry Ted is the one behind this. He's the only person I told, the only person who could have sent Carl toward us. Toward Lillian. What's hardest to ignore, is the timing. Ted wants to move the company, and he knows the only chink in the chain is Lillian. Could he have orchestrated all this to get her out of the picture?

I crank the engine and pull onto the highway, speeding in the direction of Ted's house.

FORTY-SEVEN

LILLIAN

Mabel sits in the backseat, talking nonstop about her day at school. I'm trying to give her the attention she needs, but my mind is bogged down with too many thoughts. The conversation with Blaire Walsh plays on a loop, my emotions bouncing from fear to outrage to relief.

And I can't get ahold of Matthew. I've tried calling him three times, but each call goes straight to voicemail. My loyalties to him have been tested in the past couple of days, but he deserves to know the truth about Richard Walsh; it might clear his conscience, as it has mine.

When we arrive at the house, there's a car in the driveway, but it's not Matthew's. We're grabbing our belongings when someone exits the front door, hands out wide.

"Grandma!" Mabel shouts, skipping up the steps and embracing her.

"Jane?" I don't even try to mask my irritation. "What are you doing here?"

"I thought I'd surprise my favorite girl," she says, bending down to kiss Mabel's cheek.

Or is she surprising me? And Matthew? Did he know she was coming?

"You've been gone less than a week."

"I don't have much else to do home alone," she says. "I thought the two of you could use an extra set of hands given... everything."

My teeth grind against each other and I inhale tightly. "Mabel, go on inside. Change clothes and I'll make you a snack."

She obeys, leaving me alone on the front steps with Jane.

"Does Matthew know you're here?"

"No. I kept offering, but he insisted the two of you had everything handled on your own. I'm his mother, Lillian. I know when I'm needed."

"You are not needed," I say. "How did you even get into the house?"

"I have my own key."

Since when? Matthew never told me that. Does she have a key to the apartment, too?

"The thing is, Jane, it's been a hectic week, yes, but that doesn't give you the right to show up at our home uninvited."

"I don't need an invitation to visit my son, Lillian. In case you've forgotten, this is his home, too."

Could Jane have a motive to want me out of the picture? If she knows there's a possibility she could have Mabel all to herself, could she be involved? She rarely visits town this often. Now that I think of it, she was in town when Carl died. Even the night Richard died. Could she have come back to the house during the party and seen what we did? Or maybe Matthew confessed to her, and now she's using the information against me.

She looks ahead, focusing on something in the distance. I turn just in time to see an unmarked police car pulling up to the curb. It's Dylan, and he's alone. I sigh in frustration.

"See, your hands are quite full at the moment," she says, piously. "I'll take care of Mabel while you get things sorted."

I refuse to respond. I'll deal with Jane later. Right now, I march toward Dylan, meeting him on the sidewalk.

"You said you were coming by the station—"

"Well, something came up." I correct my tone. My outlook has changed since talking to Blaire, but it's not like I can tell him I no longer plan on confessing to murder. "I had to get Mabel from school."

"I wanted to talk to you. There's been a development."

"Do you know who murdered Carl?"

"We haven't made it that far," he says. "I need to ask. Are you prescribed any sleeping pills? Anti-depressants?"

"No. What's that got—"

"Did you take any drugs that night?"

"No. I barely drink anymore, let alone take drugs. I told you that the night of the murder. What does this have to do with anything?"

"I told you we were waiting on some lab reports. The liquor you were drinking the night of the murder was laced with something."

"Laced?"

"Sleeping pills. We didn't find any pills inside the apartment or evidence anything else had been tampered with. Just that bottle."

"What are you saying?"

"Someone wanted to make sure you were disoriented when you returned home that night. It could have been so they could commit the murder themselves, or maybe because it had already happened."

I'm stunned, another layer of violation on top of this whole mess. "You're saying you no longer think I killed Carl?"

"I'm saying there were enough sleeping pills in that bottle to make you sleep through a tornado. It could have even killed you, if you drank enough."

"I only had one glass." I didn't need anymore. I was already drunk from my night with...

Before I can finish the thought, Dylan asks, "Where did you get that tequila?"

There's a sinking feeling in my gut, a tightness in my chest.

"It was a gift for my birthday. From Rebecca."

FORTY-EIGHT

MATTHEW

Ted's condo is a far cry from the mansion he owned with Cat, but it's still luxurious in its own right. It's located directly on the beach, in a quiet part of Anne Isle nestled away from the tourist and business districts. It's so far out, I had to drive nearly an hour to get here, and during that time, I've worked up my anger.

I pound on his front door, shifting my weight from foot to foot in impatient irritation.

Ted opens the door. He's still dressed in his business clothes, but I notice his tie has gone slack around the neck and he's holding a bottle of Dos Equis in his hand. There's a grimace on his face.

"It was you, wasn't it?" I push my way inside. Ted steps back, clumsily, sloshing beer onto the gleaming wooden floors. "You're behind all this."

"What the fuck are you talking about?"

"You're the one person I told. The only person who could have set all this up."

He puts down the beer, stands straighter. He puffs out his chest like he's about to hit me, a reaction I haven't seen from him since our college days. Perhaps, on some level, this confrontation has been building since then.

"What exactly are you getting at?"

"I told you about Richard!" I scream. "You're the only person I told, and you've decided to use my biggest secret in order to take Lillian down."

Ted's fists are contracting, and for a second, I think he really might hit me. Then he turns, making his way to the living room and sits, his back to me.

"You're so concerned with Voyage," I say. "It's all you've ever cared about. You put it before Cat, before me. You knew I would never pick up and move to Florida as long as Lillian was in the picture, so you told Carl about what happened in the hopes he'd go after Lillian."

"I've never talked to Carl a day in my life."

"Then you had someone else do it. Either way, he knew we were responsible for Richard's death. He'd been following us for weeks. Since right around the time we received the offer to move Voyage. Hell, maybe you hired someone to kill him inside the apartment, just so Lillian could take the fall."

"Are you really accusing me of murder?"

"You were my best friend. I trusted you. And you're using the biggest mistake of my life against me. You must be crazy if you think I'm going to let Lillian go to jail over this. I'll sink the business before I let that happen."

"The business is already sinking." He stands now, walking across the room and pulling something out of a dresser drawer. He throws it down. "It's safe to say I'm not the only person who knows what happened to Richard."

I look down at the table. Inside a Ziploc bag, there's a round gray object. I have no idea what it is, or why Ted is so angered by it.

"What is this?"

"I found it beneath one of the chairs in my office. It's a bug."

"Bug?"

"A recording device. Someone is spying on our conversations."

"And you think I put it there?"

"No." He shakes his head, walks across the room, making sure the curtains on the window are pulled shut. "I think the police put it there. They must have planted it that day they came to interview me. There's probably one in your office, too. I tried looking before I left, but I couldn't find anything. I was so upset, I had to leave."

"The police can't do that, can they? Plant bugs without your consent?"

"They can do anything with a warrant. And if they think they have enough evidence tying you to Richard or Carl or both, they'll find a way to make the charges stick." He finishes the bottle in one gulp. "If they arrest you for murder, the business is done. We're both fucked."

I sit now, my eyes still staring at the little device on the table. Why would the police bug the office? They couldn't have concrete proof of Richard's death unless it came from Ted or Lillian. They are the only ones that know.

"Did you tell anyone about Richard?"

"No. Why would I try to hurt you? My best friend. My business partner."

"You're the only person I told."

"You keep saying that, but I'm starting to wonder. You were a mess there for a few months, back when the divorce was happening. Drinking every night, crying at the drop of a hat. If Lillian had been a little more menacing, she probably could have taken full custody and a lot more money. Of course, I guess she had her own secrets to protect."

"Lillian wouldn't do that." I clench my eyes shut. "Why are we even talking about the divorce? It's got nothing to do with what's happening now."

"My point is, how do you know you didn't tell someone else? Go on a bender and start running your mouth? You were so wasted that night in my office, I'm surprised you even remember it."

"I... I didn't tell anyone else."

But the suggestion worries me. He's right. For a few months, I was in limbo, hovering between drunk and sober, sanity and despair. Could I have told someone else about what we did and not remember? Mom? Rebecca? It's a strange feeling, not being able to trust yourself.

"We've already made more money from the business than I could have ever imagined," Ted says. "If we don't go to Florida, I think it would be a dumb move, but it's not going to break us. Break *me*. I wouldn't stab my best friend in the back for a few extra bucks."

Ted isn't the type of person whose ego easily bruises. My accusation has wounded him, tested the bonds of our nearly twenty-year friendship.

"Someone knows about Richard. That's what started all of this."

"Then I'd take a closer look at your inner circle. You know what I think is really bothering you? That your womanizing, wild-card business partner has more sense about this than you do."

I'm about to respond when my phone starts ringing. I pull it out of my pocket and stare at the screen.

"Let me guess," Ted says. "Lillian."

"She's been calling nonstop. I wanted to confront you before I talked to her."

"Well, if I were you, I'd sort things out with her. I'm no longer involved. With any of this." He slides his hands through the air. "I'm doing what I've been begging you to do since this started. I'm distancing myself."

I can feel my heartbeat pulsing inside my head, my palms

sticky from sweat. I silence the call, looking back at Ted. He looks like a shadow of the friend I once knew.

"Even if the police did plant those bugs, it won't implicate you. You've done nothing wrong."

"Don't I know it."

He's angry with me. Angrier than he's ever been. But I can't deal with this right now. I have to talk to Lillian, tell her that the police might be invading our lives more than we realized. My body shudders at the thought.

"If you talk to the police—"

"I won't." He takes another sip of his drink. "Any communication will be through my attorney. Only a fool would do otherwise."

Maybe Ted is right. I've been foolish, but I'm still wondering how much I can trust him. He could still be at fault, holding his hand until the last card has been dealt. His words haunt me. *How do you know you didn't tell someone else?*

I have to find out the answer to that if I want to know who is behind all this.

FORTY-NINE

LILLIAN

How could it be Rebecca?

We're driving down the road in Dylan's car, and similar variations of that question keep repeating inside my head. How? And why?

Even with the proof in front of me, I still find it hard to accept she's behind all this. I know she gifted me the drugged liquor, but I still can't figure out why she did it. Her connection to Carl remains a mystery, and even greater than that, what about Richard? I'd assumed all this somehow linked back to him.

Maybe it still does.

Maybe my earlier theory was right, that whoever killed Carl knew about what happened to Richard. Could Matthew have told Rebecca? My skin feels hot, tingles crawling all over me. I know Matthew and Rebecca are in a relationship, but I didn't think that would override his loyalty to me—or his own self-preservation.

Then, another idea drifts into my mind, making my stomach sink further. What if Matthew and Rebecca are in on this together? She could have left the liquor, but what if he put her up to it? He might still be trying to pin Richard—and Carl's—death on me. That queasy, lonely feeling returns. I lean forward, resting my stomach atop my thighs to try and make it go away.

"You okay?" Dylan asks.

"No." The worst possibility is that Matthew is involved, but I can't tell him about that. "I can't believe Rebecca would try to drug me. We're friends."

"It is a strange situation, isn't it? She's dating your ex-husband."

"We're not teenagers, Dylan. Adults don't go around hating each other just because."

"Love and money. Those are the two biggest reasons people kill. That's what twenty years on the force has taught me."

"But Matthew and I don't love each other. Not like that. Not anymore. And Rebecca loves Mabel. She knew her before she knew either one of us. My God, she was her teacher."

"Motive, on the surface, seems easy. Love, revenge, greed. When you try and apply it to someone you know, it clouds things. You have no idea what Rebecca is really thinking, how she really feels about you being such a big part of her boyfriend's life. She wouldn't be the first person to want the first wife out of the way so she could start over.

"That's where detectives come in. We can analyze a scene objectively, consider all the people involved and their motivations. We tend to pick up on details others don't, even when it comes to the people they are closest to."

"What about Detective Spelling? What are his thoughts on all of this?"

"He knows about the liquor and agrees it helps validate your story," he says. "What you have to understand about Spelling is he's suspicious of everyone. You can't take it personally."

"Just another part of being a cop?"

"His type of cop. I'm a little bit different." The car comes to a halt. He clears his throat and looks across the street. "Is this the place?"

It's Rebecca's house, a one-level brick with a large window beside the front door. The panels are yellow, the roof gray. There's a curved walkway leading from the front door to the sidewalk, and it's lined with shrubbery that I imagine looks colorful and vibrant in the spring. The home is charming and quaint, exactly what you would imagine for a young teacher.

A criminal? *Murderer?* Not so much.

Dylan asked where she lived, and I offered to show him. Beyond that, I'm not really sure what he plans on doing.

"Stay in the car," he says, unbuckling his seat belt. "I'm going to see if she's home."

"Won't you take her to the station?"

"Eventually. Spelling is on his way here. He'll give her a ride." He opens the car door, letting in a gust of wind. "Thanks for showing me the place."

I watch him walk to the front door, holding my breath. Part of me still doesn't believe she could be involved, but I also can't ignore the trail leading back to her.

My phone buzzes, and when I see the name on the screen, my heart skips a beat.

It's Rebecca.

I look at the house. Dylan is still standing by the front door. He steps to the left, cupping his hands around his face and trying to peer through the darkened window. Could she be inside? Is she avoiding him?

I click on the message, but there are no words. Only an image.

My heart starts beating faster, fear and adrenaline working overtime, as I look down at the screen and see a picture of Richard. It looks like it's been pulled from an internet profile.

Time stills as I sit there, alone in Dylan's police car, staring at the face.

Then, the words come.

Meet me at the apartment. No police.

The threat is understood. Rebecca knows about Richard, and even if I still can't piece together why she's targeting me, she's giving me the opportunity to find out.

"Guess she's not here," Dylan says, as he sits back in the car. His expression changes when he looks at me. "Are you okay?"

My throat feels tight; I struggle to release the words. "Yeah. It's just a lot to digest."

"I'm going to take you with me back to the station. Until we talk to Rebecca, we can't be too careful."

I nod, shakily. "Okay."

I should tell him, I know I should. Meeting Rebecca on my own is dangerous; I still don't know what she is capable of or what she wants. I could bring Dylan to her right now, end all of this.

But she knows about Richard. I can't protect myself and our secret at the same time.

I try to level my breathing as Dylan pulls onto the road, driving in the direction of downtown. I'm clutching the phone with my hands, feeling it grow hot from my grasp.

"If Matthew calls," Dylan says, "don't say anything about Rebecca. It would be better if he hears it from us."

Unless he already knows. Rebecca clearly knows about Richard, and she couldn't have found out any other way. My fears might be right. They are in on this together, and I'm being played.

The car slows as Dylan enters a gas station parking lot.

"Mind if I grab a soda?" he asks, already putting the car in park.

I shake my head, determined not to make eye contact. It feels like every emotion is on the brink of bursting.

As soon as Dylan exits the car, I receive another message.

Now!

I hear Rebecca's voice screaming at me, imagine a clock ticking as time runs down. I look back at the gas station. Dylan is standing inside in the line. I can't wait any longer, and I can't let him know where I'm going.

If Rebecca reveals the truth about Richard, then we've lost everything.

I open the car door and slink outside. I jog down the street, trying to get far enough away that I can hail an Uber and head straight to the apartment, unseen.

FIFTY

MATTHEW

By the time I arrive at the house, the sky is that purplish hue between twilight and nightfall. I imagine Lillian and Mabel sitting at the kitchen table, working on homework and eating the last bites of their dinner. It's a comforting thought, a memory from the past I pull upon to help me squash the uncertainty of the present.

But when I walk inside, I only find Mabel sitting at the table. A wad of spaghetti is twirled around her fork. She drops it when she sees me.

"Daddy!"

"Hi, lovebug. Where's Mommy?"

"She took off with that detective." It's Mom, standing by the sink, washing dishes by hand. "Been gone for more than an hour."

I wipe my face with my hand, like her presence isn't real. "Mom, what are you doing here?"

"You need me, so I decided to come."

"When did you arrive? How did you..."

She wanders closer, throwing a dishrag over her shoulder. Her voice is low, so that Mabel can't hear. "The two of you are a mess if I've ever seen it. Mabel needs some kind of stability while you get your affairs in order."

"Our affairs?"

Is she talking about Carl, or more? Does she know about Richard? Could I have told her long ago and not even remembered?

"Mom, I—"

Before I can finish the statement, there's a knock at the door. Mabel jumps up from the table, wandering toward the foyer.

"Honey, sit down. I can get it."

I turn on my heels, cutting her off before she makes it to the door. When I open it, Detective Logan is standing on the porch.

"Is Lillian here?"

"My mother said she was with you."

"She was. She waited in the car while I was inside the gas station. When I returned, she was gone. She's not answering her phone."

I look back into the house. Mabel is at the table, and Mom is standing right behind me.

"Go on," she says.

I sigh and walk outside, irritated that Mom took it upon herself to return, but thankful for her in the moment. Once the door is shut, I ask, "What's going on? Why was she with you in the first place?"

He tells me about the results of the lab testing, how it appears someone was trying to drug Lillian that night. There's a brief moment of relief—this is the closest we've come yet to proving another person is at fault for Carl's death—and then the other shoe drops.

"Lillian says Rebecca gave her the alcohol," he says. "For her birthday."

Something inside sinks. Maybe it's my hopes, or my heart.

"I don't understand. Rebecca wouldn't want to hurt Lillian. They'd gone out with each other that very night."

"Did they usually do that sort of thing? Go out for drinks?"

"No... no, but it was Lillian's birthday. And my mother was in town and..."

I'm struggling to make sense of what he is suggesting. I don't know why Rebecca would want to drug Lillian, let alone murder Carl. There's never been any bad blood between the two of them.

Carl. Richard. What if Rebecca knows what we did? Ted's words from earlier come back again: *How do you know you didn't tell someone else?*

Could I have confided in Rebecca, and not remembered? Could she have somehow found out the truth? She's been a part of our lives for so long now. She could have been looking into us and neither of us would have suspected.

Dylan's words interrupt my trance.

"It's a pretty common excuse. New girlfriend is jealous of the old wife. Maybe Rebecca has a connection to Carl, one we don't know about."

"Rebecca wasn't jealous of Lillian."

As I say the words, I wonder if they're true. On the surface, the two always got along. They even appeared to be friends, but didn't Ted and everyone else tell me how bizarre that was? How it's not normal for two women to get along when the common link is a man they both love. Maybe they were right. Maybe Rebecca was jealous. Lillian isn't an easy act to follow, and maybe it would be easier for Rebecca to have her out of our lives for good. I don't want to believe it, even if there's a ring of truth to it all.

"I don't think Rebecca could be behind this," I insist. Who am I trying to convince, him or me? "She wouldn't want to hurt either of us this way."

"Well, we need to find Lillian. And Rebecca, too. I already went by her place, but she wasn't home. Do you have any idea where either of them could be?"

I think, my mind buzzing with so many possibilities it's hard to focus. On anything. Then—

"I don't know where Lillian is." I pull out my phone, clicking through my apps. "But Rebecca and I share our locations."

"That's good," Dylan says. "Does it say where she is?"

My throat is dry when I speak, my heart sinking lower. "She's at our apartment."

FIFTY-ONE

LILLIAN

The inky, dark sky is starless. The lampposts in the apartment complex parking lot cast yellow light on the cars. I step out of the Uber hesitantly, questioning my decision to come here alone. Should I go inside? Should I call the police?

Confronting Rebecca on my own is dangerous. She is likely the person who killed Carl. But then I remember the photo she sent me of Richard. If she knows what we did, I can't get the police involved without sealing my own fate. Meeting her, as she requested, and finding out what she wants, is my only option.

Walking up the concrete steps to the second floor, I feel like a criminal walking to an execution. I'm scared, but beneath that fear is a burning curiosity. I want to know why Rebecca is involved. I need to know why she deceived me, pretended to be my friend so she could frame me for murder.

Dylan's theory sounds too simple. Surely, she wouldn't go to such lengths to get me out of the picture, to have Matthew all to herself. He's already hers. I gave him up a long time ago.

Now, I realize my curiosity involves him, too. I need to

know if he's working with her to bring me down, if he's betrayed me after everything we've been through together.

I reach for the handle and twist. It's unlocked. I step inside the apartment, closing the door behind me.

It's dark. The moon peers in through the large windows, covering the rooms in streaks of pearlescent gray. I can make out the silhouettes of furniture, and nothing else. I flick the light switch on the wall, but nothing happens. Either the bulb has burned out or it's been deliberately tampered with.

Fresh fear spreads throughout my body.

"Rebecca?" I call out.

Silence. For a second, I debate turning around and leaving, but if I do that, she could tell the police what happened to Richard. She might go down for murdering Carl, but she'll take me with her. In this moment, losing my life doesn't seem as bad as losing my freedom.

I tiptoe across the living room, making my way to the lamp in the corner of the room, feeling my way through the darkness, afraid someone will reach out and grab me. Maybe this is what she wants. To get me inside, disoriented and alone, so she can attack.

After what feels like minutes, I make it across the room, and pull the dangling cord attached to the lamp. The light is minimal, but it's enough for me to see my surroundings. My peripheral vision catches something beside my feet.

I jump back, almost knocking the lamp over. I scream.

On the floor, lies Rebecca. She's face down, a puddle of blood beneath her. Even though she's the one who brought me here, even though she's the one who has been threatening me, my instincts take over. I kneel beside her, placing my hands on her warm flesh.

"Rebecca? Are you okay?"

She doesn't answer. The blood is everywhere. The smell of

it is overwhelming. Her body is still, which makes me think it might be too late, but I pull out my phone anyway to call 911.

"Don't move."

Someone is standing behind me. I hear the words, but they aren't what alarm me. What sends shivers crawling up my spine is the voice. I know it. I've heard it countless times over the years, in countless ways. In happiness, sadness, despair. The voice is so familiar, I don't bother following the orders.

I turn around.

"Cat, what are you doing here?"

FIFTY-TWO

LILLIAN

Cat is standing in the doorway of Matthew's bedroom. She's dressed in black leggings with a black sweater, a matching cap on her head. It looks like a costume.

Except for the knife in her hand. That looks very real, and she has it raised, the blade pointed at me.

"I really didn't want it to come to this," she says.

"Come to what?" My brain struggles to wrangle my thoughts with the intensity of this moment. "Why do you have a knife?"

All she says is, "It was supposed to be Carl. He was supposed to come after you."

"You knew Carl?"

"I sent him after you. I wanted you to pay for what you've done."

"What are you talking about?"

"Richard!" His name escapes her lips in a roar. "You killed Richard!"

Air stalls in my throat. How does she know? Why is she doing this? What's the connection between Richard and Cat?

"I love him," she says, her voice starting to tremble. "And he loved me."

"You were sleeping with Richard?"

"He's the only person I cared about since things fell apart with Ted. My last shot at happiness. And you took that chance away from me."

"But Richard was married. Blaire—"

"He didn't care about Blaire! She didn't make him happy. He was stuck with her. Just like I was stuck for years without realizing it. When we found each other, it somehow felt like all the shit Ted had put me through was worth it. We were going to be happy together."

The revelations come fast, each one hitting harder and harder. "How... how did you know what happened?"

"I didn't for a while. Like everyone, I thought he'd fallen. And I was heartbroken. Richard loved me. And then one night, I stopped by the Voyage office. Ted was being a dick with his alimony payments, as expected. I was going to confront the bastard in the place he cared about most. But Matthew beat me to it. I could hear him outside the door. He was moaning about you and the divorce and how his life had gone to shit. He was crying. Red-faced, snot-nosed crying! And that's when Matthew told him. The real reason why your marriage fell apart."

Matthew confessed. He couldn't keep it in. All the times I thought I was there for him, kept him intact, he'd already slipped. And he told Ted of all people.

"What happened was an accident—"

"Oh, I heard all about it. How he was drunk. Got into an argument with Matthew. How you got rid of his body, after you whacked him over the head."

My skin goes cold. Me? I never hit Richard. My back was turned when he...

"Cat, that's not what—"

"You threw him into the ocean like trash. The man I loved. My last chance at happiness." She raises the knife, her hand shaking violently.

I throw up my hands. "It was an accident. Everything that happened that night was an accident, and we've felt horrible for so long."

"Oh yeah, I can really tell. The business gets better and better every year. Matthew and you are the golden divorced couple of Seaside Cliffs. You have Mabel and a shag pad and a beautiful house." She pauses. "You get to be happy, and you don't deserve it."

She's getting angrier. I realize I have to keep her talking. "How did you get involved with Carl?"

"Richard told me once he had a brother. He said they weren't close and I didn't think much about it. When I realized Carl had moved to the area, I thought maybe I could make him useful. It's not like I could go after you myself. I didn't want to spend the rest of my life in jail. So I sought out Carl.

"I tracked him down and told him his brother's death was no accident, and I knew who killed him. Turns out he had a lot of unresolved issues with his brother. He was more than happy to take down the person who killed him. I convinced him to go online and try to connect with you.

"But Carl wanted to make sure what I told him was true. That you were the right person. He started looking into you. Looking into Matthew. Following the two of you around like you were his little hobby. And he couldn't just have one lousy date with you. He had to make sure you were the one who killed Richard, that I wasn't just telling stories. I'd told him I used recording devices to spy on my ex, and he wanted to plant them inside the apartment. He thought he might catch you talking about what happened. I slipped the key off your ring, and he made a copy."

Carl is the one who bugged the apartment. And Cat is the one who gave him access. Not Matthew or the police. I think of all the things I found in his trailer. He'd been following me for weeks, because Cat put him on my trail.

"He kept waiting and waiting. He wouldn't confront you about it until he was sure. I kept pressing him. We got into a fight and he said he was going to take back the bugs and call the whole thing off. So, I confronted him. Here."

"You stabbed him?"

"That wasn't the plan. We kept arguing and then he... he came at me. He put his hands around my neck, acted like he was going to strangle me. I ran into the kitchen and grabbed a knife. For protection. But once I started stabbing him, I couldn't stop. I was so angry. At him and you and everyone else who refused to let me be happy. I hauled him to the bed and pulled the covers over him. I didn't know what else to do. I grabbed the bugs and left, kept trying to think of what I needed to do.

"I thought, maybe I could find a way to make it look like you killed him. It was your birthday. Back home, I had a bottle of Casamigos. Your favorite liquor. I spiked it with some sleeping pills, thinking it might be enough to make you confused about what happened. And then I dropped it back by the apartment before Mabel's party."

All this took place in the hours we were getting ready. Cat showed up later, like everything was fine.

"The tequila was in a bag from Rebecca."

"When I came back, there was already a present for you by the front door. It was from her. Almost too perfect. I slipped the bottle into the bag, thinking I'd be able to blame it on her if anyone found out.

"Once word got out that the liquor was laced, I knew it was only a matter of time before all this led back to me. And I couldn't let that happen. I told her to meet us here. That we needed her help to sort the whole thing out." She looks down at Rebecca's body. "And now you're here."

"What are you going to do? Say I killed Rebecca?"

"Yes. But I'm going to say you attacked me first."

And with that, she rams the knife into her left arm.

FIFTY-THREE

MATTHEW

My lungs ache as I rush up the steps, heading for the apartment.

"There you are."

It's Mrs. Haynes. She's standing in the doorway of her apartment, her body half-concealed by the door. It takes a moment to realize she's not speaking to me, but to Detective Logan behind me.

"I heard screaming," she says. "I already called the police."

Logan pushes past me, leading his way into the apartment. I follow him.

"Drop your weapon," he shouts.

I take another step inside, shocked at the scene before me. Lillian and Cat are in the kitchen, struggling. When they see us, they separate, each leaning on opposite sides of the small space. They're both panting, and, it looks like, bleeding. Cat holds a knife in her hands.

A few steps away, in the living room, I see something on the floor. It's a body, it's...

"Rebecca!"

I rush toward her, but Logan takes a step in front of me, cutting me off.

"Lillian killed her!" Cat screams, stepping back, her body flat against the wall. She's still holding the knife, and there's blood oozing from a fresh cut in her arm. "I came here to try and stop her, but she attacked me."

"I didn't," Lillian shouts. She's hunched over, covering a wound on her leg. "Cat did. She was behind all of this."

Cat? Why would she want to hurt Rebecca? Or Carl? Why would she be after Lillian, her best friend?

Detective Logan isn't listening. His weapon is still raised, pleading with Cat to drop the knife.

"She's a murderer," Cat cries. "She killed Richard!"

My blood turns cold. I look at Lillian, her bloodstained hands held up in a surrender position. The stain of blood on her thigh grows.

"Just put down the knife," Dylan says, ignoring Cat's accusations, "and we can talk this through."

But Cat is inconsolable, crying and panting.

"You don't understand," she says. "He was all I had left. She deserves to pay for what she did to him."

"Richard didn't love you," Lillian tells her. "He only cared about himself."

"You didn't know him!" Cat screams.

"*You* didn't know him," Lillian repeats, but there's a soothing element to her voice. "None of us did. He was an awful person, especially to Blaire. He abused her."

Cat's mouth drops. "You're lying."

"I'm not. Blaire told me. She said the best thing that ever happened to her and the boys was Richard dying."

I know Lillian is trying desperately to de-escalate the situation, but her voice is too resolute to be a lie. I don't know when she talked to Blaire Walsh, but she speaks as though this information will resonate with Cat.

"Blaire is a liar. She couldn't accept the fact he didn't want her anymore." Cat's breathing heavily, and briefly lowers the knife, like her mind is fighting hard to process what she's just heard. "He loved me."

"You weren't the only person he was sleeping with," Lillian says. "There were other women in the neighborhood. The week of the party, Matthew saw him with a different woman at a hotel. He was using you, just like he used Blaire and everyone else in his life."

"Stop lying!"

Lillian shoots a look at me for help.

"I saw him," I say. "He was with someone else."

"You'll say anything to protect her," she says. "It's a lie."

"It isn't!" Lillian cries. "You have to realize you're risking everything for a man who didn't love you the way you did him."

"Put the weapon down," Detective Logan repeats, taking a step closer to the kitchen. "Now!"

"You have to stop lying," Cat says, her anger renewed.

She lunges forward, aiming the blade at Lillian, who tries to move out of the way.

Everything happens so fast, each second its own excruciating moment in time, until the gun goes off, silencing it all.

FIFTY-FOUR

LILLIAN

My body rumbles, tilting from side to side. I open my eyes, see another face close to mine. It's a man, shining a light.

I'm in an ambulance.

Have I been stabbed? Am I dying?

I realize I'm only thinking the words. I'm too weak to say them. The questions race through my brain, one after the other. The thoughts exhaust me. I close my eyes again, hoping when I wake, I'll finally have the answers I crave.

The sterile scent of antiseptic stings my nostrils. When I open my eyes, gone are the cramped confines of the ambulance. I'm in a hospital, the walls painted gray. Dylan sits in an armchair beside my bed.

"You're awake."

My voice cracks when I try to speak, but I have to know. All I remember is Matthew and Dylan running into the apartment, little else. "What happened?"

"Cat stabbed you before we arrived," he says. "She lunged

at you again, and you took a nasty hit to the head when you jumped out of the way."

Memories flood back. Cat inside the apartment, everything she said about Carl and Richard. The gut-wrenching realization that she was the person trying to destroy my life.

"Did Cat... Is she dead?"

Dylan nods.

My chest clenches tight and a sob escapes. Even though Cat caused all this, she was my friend. My best friend. I still don't understand how she could have been so determined to ruin my life. I mourn the person I knew before, not the person she became.

"I'm sorry about your friend."

"Thank you."

"I wanted to go over a few details. We'll have a more formal interview downtown, once you've been released."

He pulls out a pad of paper and pen. He asks me to walk him through what happened from the moment I left his car at the gas station to when he and Matthew arrived at the apartment. I tell him about Cat's theory that we had something to do with Richard's death—that she mistakenly believed we killed him—and that she sought out Carl for that reason.

I tell him everything that happened inside the apartment, how Cat used Rebecca's phone to lure me there. I tell him that Cat wounded herself before going after me.

He doesn't ask many questions. Once we arrive at the moment in the story where he shot Cat, he slides the notepad into his jacket pocket. He pauses, twisting his head to look at the closed door.

"So, Cat did all this because she believed you had something to do with Richard Walsh's death. This would be the case Carl claimed we should have investigated further?"

I nod, can feel my throat burning as I fight to act unfazed.

"And you have no idea why she would think you were responsible?"

I think of Ted. He knows what we did. Would the police reach out to him? Would he be willing to lie about what happened for Matthew? For me?

Cat's final words ring in my ears: *You have to stop lying.*

"Cat has been through a lot since her divorce. I didn't know it at the time, but she was having an affair with Richard. His death left her heartbroken, and she was looking for someone to blame. He was at a party at our house the night he fell."

"And nothing happened at this party?"

You have to stop lying.

"I didn't kill Richard."

It's the only truth I have the strength to speak aloud. And, I realize, I believe it. What happened wasn't my fault.

"You said you spoke with Richard's wife. That you believe he was abusive."

"That's what Blaire told me. But she had nothing to do with his death, if that's what you're suggesting. She was at the party with me after he left."

Dylan nods. I sense he wants to believe me, but I'm not sure he does.

"There will be more questions about this," he says. "For you. And Matthew. And Blaire."

"I'll answer them." Behind him, I see Matthew standing in the doorway. Dylan follows my gaze, standing when he sees there is a visitor.

"Am I interrupting anything?" Matthew asks.

"All finished here." He looks back at me. "Feel better soon."

Before sitting down, Matthew shakes Dylan's hand. He waits for him to leave before he speaks.

"How are you feeling?"

"Like I took a massive hit to the head."

He smiles, but only for a moment. "I don't know what to

say. I still don't understand what Cat had to do with Carl or Richard."

"Cat and Richard were having an affair," I say. "She found out what happened to Richard because she overheard you confessing to Ted—"

"Now isn't the time to talk about this," Matthew says, looking over his shoulder at the closed door. "Police are all over the place."

But in the moment, I don't care about police or repercussions. After all that's happened, after all the lives that have been lost, I deserve answers. Cat's final words ring in my ears: *You have to stop lying.*

"You promised you wouldn't tell anyone what happened. You promised me."

Matthew buckles before my eyes. "I was drunk. Ted was the only person I told, and he's never betrayed my trust. We had no idea Cat heard us."

"She did. And she enlisted Carl to help her get even. When Carl wouldn't do what she wanted, she killed him and framed me. He's the one who planted the bugs inside our apartment. He was hoping one of us would admit what happened."

Matthew's face changes. He's thinking. "Ted found bugs inside his office, too. He thought the police were surveilling us. It must have been Cat."

Cat told me she had ways of keeping tabs on Ted. She claimed to get information through his secretary, but now I wonder if Cat had planted recording devices long ago. She could have given the technology to Carl, which is how she knew to find him at my apartment that day.

Suddenly, I remember. "Rebecca? Is she—"

"She's in surgery. The doctors are hopeful." He looks away, and I pity the pain he's carrying. Mine might be physical, but his is worse. "We tracked Rebecca to the apartment. That's how we found you. Dylan thought she was behind this."

"The tequila. I thought it was from her because Cat planted it alongside her gift."

"What you said about Blaire... was it true?"

"Yes. I went by her house to talk." I stop myself from admitting I almost came clean about Richard's death. "She told me he made her life miserable. She said she's thankful he's gone."

I feel guilty about breaking my promise to Blaire to remain quiet, but I believe she will forgive me. The truth about Richard needed to come out so Cat could see just how twisted her actions were.

Matthew lowers his head and lets out a sob. I know what he's experiencing. That burden we've carried with us the past two years is lifting. What we did still wasn't right, but Richard was far from innocent. The world has been easier on those left in his absence.

Matthew lifts his head and places his hand over mine. "We'll get through this, Lillian. We always do."

He squeezes my hand, but I jerk it away.

"When Cat overheard you talking to Ted that night, she said you told him I hit Richard over the head and got rid of the body. She said you told him everything was my fault." There's controlled anger in my voice. "That's why she was trying to frame me."

"I... I don't remember what I told him. I was drunk, upset."

"But you know that's not the truth. What happened was an accident, but I wasn't the one wrestling with Richard. You were."

"I know—"

"So, why would you put the blame on me? It's bad enough you told Ted in the first place, but you had to protect yourself. You couldn't even tell him the truth!"

"I'm sorry, Lillian. I had to tell someone what happened. I was losing you. Losing everything, it seemed. I wasn't trying to put the blame on you. Honestly."

Even if he wasn't trying, even if that wasn't his plan, he did. He was convincing enough that my own best friend plotted against me, determined to make me pay for something Matthew did.

"You chose to protect yourself over me. How am I supposed to trust you after that?"

"I wasn't... I didn't."

His face is puzzled, perhaps trying to recall that night, wondering if he can even trust his own memories. Maybe Matthew wasn't working with Rebecca or Cat against me, maybe he wasn't spying on me in the apartment, but he still betrayed me, and it's a stain on my heart that won't erase.

There's nothing we can do to change the past. But the future? That's now in my control.

FIFTY-FIVE

LILLIAN

One Year Later

I hear the car pull up outside.

Matthew is in the driver's seat, his suitcase beside him.

"What time will you land?" I ask.

"Around six. I'm grabbing dinner with Ted, then I'll check into the hotel." He looks over my shoulder, watching as Mabel skips outside. "Let's get this over with."

He exits the car, squats down for a hug. Mabel squeezes him tight, standing on her toes to kiss his cheek. It's harder for him to say goodbye now, knowing she'll be so far away.

"I'll miss you," she tells him.

"I'll be back before you know it."

Matthew and Ted eventually worked out an agreement with the board. Ted would head the new Voyage offices in Florida, while Matthew would remain in Anne Isle, flying back and forth when necessary. So far, he heads down south twice a month.

"We'll be here when you get back," I say, wrapping my arms around Mabel.

He looks at the house we once shared together. Matthew doesn't live here anymore. After everything that happened, it became clear we needed to have our own separate spaces. He agreed to allow me to live in the Seaside Cliffs house full-time, while he moved into Ted's apartment across town. We co-parent Mabel with the same ease as before, but our boundaries are more defined.

Across the street, I see Blaire and the boys approaching. When Mabel sees them, she wriggles away from me and runs toward them. "Devon!" she shouts.

"Heading out of town?" Blaire asks Matthew when she gets closer.

"I'll be gone for the next week," he says.

"Have a safe flight," she says.

"Head on to the backyard," I tell her. "I've already pulled out the floats and towels."

"Thanks," she says, ushering the boys inside the house. Mabel follows.

For a moment, Matthew and I lock eyes, but neither one of us says anything. He knows Blaire and I have become close in the past year. The friendship has been good for both of us, but there's still the constant reminder that Richard died only steps from where we presently stand.

"I'll call you when I land," Matthew says. He pulls me in for a quick hug.

"Give Ted my best."

He nods, then gets into the car. I remain outside, watching as his car pulls away. When it's gone, I'm left with the view of the cliffs.

My phone buzzes with a text message. It's from Dylan.

We still on for dinner?

I smile as I type back my reply. Blaire has agreed to watch

Mabel so I can enjoy a much-needed date night. Ever since I returned to my job as a guidance counselor, the only time I have left for myself is on the weekends, which are usually centered around her.

Dylan and I remained in contact after Cat's death, mostly for the case. The police investigated Cat's claims, but came up empty. There was no proof of what she said. There was, however, proof her mental health had deteriorated in the wake of her divorce. She'd become paranoid, was abusing a plethora of pills prescribed for anxiety and depression. With little to go on, there was nothing for the police to pursue.

I certainly didn't give them anything that could incriminate Matthew.

I kept my silence for Mabel more than I did for him. She deserves a father in her life, even if he's flawed.

Cat wasn't the only one with secrets. Turns out Carl was running his own business selling car parts illegally, using Eleventh Street Mechanics as a front. Although it's clear Cat killed him that day in a fit of rage, he'd racked up his own enemies. That's why Alaina was reluctant to help the police; she was unsure what they might find.

Once the case was closed, Alaina ended up leaving Anne Isle. We never spoke again, but I still think about her at times. I think of her baby. I hope that they, like me, have found peace.

Dylan is now part of my life. He must wonder, on some level, if Cat's claims about what happened to Richard are true, but we never talk about it. He's been around me enough in the past year—and Matthew and Mabel and Blaire—to see all the good that has come from Richard's death. Some mysteries are better left unsolved.

I still regret that night and the series of events it put into motion. For two years, I let what happened destroy me. Now, I've learned to replace my grief with appreciation. Blaire and the boys are thriving. I've not only returned to the woman I was before that night, but I've become a better version. Mabel still has two parents who love her very much, and that's enough to make her world complete.

My relationships with everyone around me have been tested. Harriet and I no longer speak. Cat exists only in my memories—even her sins can't erase my friend from long ago. The people I'm around the most—Blaire and Dylan and my colleagues—are genuine, exactly what I need after spending so much of my life trying to keep up with appearances.

At least I'm no longer looking over my shoulder, wondering who I can trust.

Who, really, can live like that?

FIFTY-SIX

MATTHEW

"Can I get you anything to drink?"

The flight attendant smiles, bright white teeth popping against her coral lipstick.

"I'm fine, thank you," I say, settling into my seat.

She nods and walks away, but my eyes follow her. She's attractive. I rarely find myself noticing women anymore. I've spent most of the last year trying to conquer my own demons.

Rebecca and I remained close in the weeks following her release from the hospital, but she ended up accepting a teaching position in a different state. Although I was sad to see her leave, I was happy for her new opportunities. She'd overcome her own trauma in Anne Isle, and it was important for her to start over.

The engine rumbles as the pilot's voice comes over the intercom.

"Anne Isle heading for Orlando," he says, promising it will be an easy flight with clear skies.

Keeping the Voyage headquarters open in Anne Isle was crucial for my personal life, but I'm happy to be afforded this time on my own. Time away from Mabel and Lillian and all the other difficult memories Anne Isle holds for me. What happened with Richard that night will never go away, but I've found healthier ways to cope.

I think what's important, going forward, is to live my life with intention. It's when I'm not mindful of the decisions I'm making that everything seems to go wrong. I've chosen to learn from my mistakes. If it weren't for my careless confession to Ted, Cat never would have gone after Lillian the way she did. I have to refrain from being so impulsive in the future.

The flight attendant brushes by my seat, helping another passenger.

"Excuse me, miss?"

She looks at me.

"I think I will take that drink. Red wine, please."

"Of course," she says, leaving me with another mega-watt smile before sashaying down the aisle. I sink lower into the seat, preparing for what I hope will be a relaxing flight.

One thing I never made clear to Lillian was how much I despised men like Richard Walsh. The way they sail through life with arrogant ease. They have money, even if they don't know how to manage it. Children, too. While Lillian and I struggled month after month to have Mabel, the Walshes had children with ease. Three healthy boys, not that he spent enough time with them. He was too busy at fancy hotels with women that weren't his wife. And of course he was also abusive to Blaire.

Where I had to fight for Lillian, fight for Voyage, fight for Mabel... everything came easy to him, and he squandered it.

In short, men like Richard Walsh are the reason nice guys, like me, continue to come in last. I might have the same feelings about Ted, if he weren't my best friend. There's a vulnerability in him few others have ever seen. A softer side might have existed in Richard too, but now he'll never have the opportunity to develop it.

Perhaps if Richard had made better choices, carried himself

in a more decent way, none of us would have ended up on the edge of that cliff.

I know this: I didn't intend for Richard to die that night. I definitely didn't intend for all the heartache that followed.

But in those moments, when Richard was pummeling his fists into my torso, I did push him.

I pushed him and every other man like him I'd encountered in my miserable life.

I pushed him, with intent, toward the edge of the cliff.

A LETTER FROM MIRANDA

Dear reader,

Thank you for taking the time to read *The Family Home*. If you liked it and want information about upcoming releases, sign up with the following link. Your email address will never be shared and you can unsubscribe at any time.

www.bookouture.com/miranda-smith

When I was younger, I remember a family member suggesting that when couples get divorced, the kids should keep the house while the parents rent apartments. While most families may not have the finances to make this situation work, it's one that sounded appealing.

Fast-forward two decades, and it turns out "nesting" has become a popular co-parenting solution. This scenario became the premise of the book. I was curious to see how a couple would react if the trust they had in one another began to falter, especially if they were hiding their own secrets. This is crime fiction, after all! I know "nesting" is a peaceful and responsible solution for many families. I also believe there's a lot to be said for Cat's philosophy: *Even if you want your ex to be happy, you never want them to be happier than you...* Whatever your take, I hope you enjoyed this story.

If you'd like to discuss any of my books, I'd love to connect! You can find me on Facebook, Twitter and Instagram, or my website. If you enjoyed *The Family Home*, I'd appreciate it if you left a review on Amazon. It only takes a few minutes and does wonders in helping readers discover my books for the first time.

Thank you again for your support!

Sincerely,

Miranda Smith

www.mirandasmithwriter.com

facebook.com/MirandaSmithAuthor

twitter.com/msmithbooks

instagram.com/mirandasmithwriter

ACKNOWLEDGMENTS

Thank you to everyone at Bookouture who helps make each book the best it can be, including Sarah Hardy, Jane Eastgate and Liz Hurst. I'd like to thank my editor, Ruth Tross. If it weren't for you, I wouldn't be an author, let alone releasing my seventh book! Thank you for your expertise and encouragement.

I'd like to thank the book reviewers and bloggers who help promote each release. I'd like to thank the readers who continue to support my books for allowing me to live out my dreams.

Thank you to my family, both near and far. To my parents, thank you for everything. To Chris, thanks for providing love and laughs when I need them most... and for not getting too nervous about my research into divorce and murder. To Harrison, Lucy and Christopher, I love you.

This book is dedicated to my oldest son, an exceptional storyteller. Your creativity amazes me. If I can do this, I can't wait to see what the future holds for you.

CPSIA information can be obtained
at www.ICGtesting.com
Printed in the USA
BVHW041735290922
648315BV00002B/15